THE SABLE DOUGHBOYS

Books by Tom Willard

THE SABLE
DOUGHBOYS

Book Two of the Black Sabre Chronicles

Tom Willard

A TOM DOHERTY ASSOCIATES BOOK
New York

THE SABLE DOUGHBOYS

Copyright © 1997 by Tom Willard

A Forge Book
Published by Tom Doherty Associates, Inc.
175 Fifth Avenue
New York, NY 10010

Forge® is a registered trademark of Tom Doherty Associates, Inc.

Library of Congress Cataloging-in-Publication Data

Willard, Tom
   The sable doughboys / Tom Willard.—1st ed.
     p.   cm.—(Black sabre chronicles ; bk. 2)
   ISBN 0-312-86040-4 (alk. paper)
   1. World War, 1914–1918—Participation, Afro-American—Fiction.
2. United States. Army—Afro-American troops—Fiction.   3. Afro-
American men—Fiction. I. Title. II. Series: Willard, Tom.
Black sabre chronicles ; bk. 2.
PS3573.I4445S23   1997
813'.54—dc20   96-44259
                                                 CIP

First Edition: February 1997

Printed in the United States of America

0 9 8 7 6 5 4 3 2 1

For my father-in-law, Lloyd John Lipp, Minot, North Dakota, who died during the writing of this novel. A wonderful husband, father, grandfather, and friend.

Thanks, Dad, for all you gave us. You will be remembered by your children, your wife, your friends, and forever by your legacy . . . your grandchildren.

Good job!

Fades the light;
And afar
Goeth day, cometh night,
And a star,
Leadeth all, speedeth all,
To their rest.

—From "Taps," author unknown

Show me a hero . . . and I'll show you a tragedy.
—*F. Scott Fitzgerald*

Foreword

★ ★ ★

On Friday, April 6, 1917, President Woodrow Wilson was having lunch with his wife, Edith, and her friend Helen Bones when he was interrupted to sign a document of great importance to the future of the United States.

The document was a joint congressional declaration of war against Germany.

On May 19, 1917, the U.S. War Department created the 17th Provisional Reserved Officer Training Corps (ROTC) for college-grade Negro men to receive military training as officers. The 17th Provisional Training Regiment, organized in June 1917 at Fort Des Moines, Iowa, immediately began receiving recruits, and more than sixteen hundred Negro men from all parts of the United States were accepted.

The 17th became the first training regiment in American history with the specific task of training Negro officers to lead Negro troops into battle. Of the class of sixteen hundred, more than twelve hundred men received commissions ranging from second lieutenant to captain.

During the Great War, 404,348 African-Americans served in the army and navy. More than 200,000 African-American enlisted men and officers served in France.

While the author of this novel has chosen to focus on the 93rd Division, specifically the 372nd Infantry Regiment, it should be noted that there were numerous Negro units, including the 92nd Division, that served with distinction during World War I.

Distinctive combat service of the 92nd and 93rd divisions included their playing major roles in the battles of the Meuse-Argonne, the Champagne offensive, Château-Thierry, the Vosges, Metz, and Alsace-Lorraine.

On November 11, 1918, the day the armistice was signed, African-American troops of the 92nd Division were the soldiers closest to the Rhine, the river separating Germany from France.

The people of France called these African-American soldiers . . . the "Sable Doughboys."

PROLOGUE

Augustus Sharps—1869

The heavy-caliber rifle fire from a buffalo gun broke the silence on the Kansas plains every twenty seconds, the time Trooper Darcy Gibbs, H Troop, 10th Cavalry, figured it took the buffalo hunter in the distance to reload, aim, and fire.

Trooper Gibbs, a buffalo soldier, as the Plains Indians had named the Colored cavalry troops, was on patrol northwest of Fort Wallace, Kansas, with orders to warn settlers and buffalo hunters that the Cheyenne were raiding ranches and work camps along the Smoky River line of the Kansas Pacific Railroad.

Gibbs watched as another buffalo dropped to the frozen plains. "Pretty good shootin', Sarge." Gibbs sat back in his saddle, chewing on a twig, watching Sergeant Moss Liberty study the situation through a telescope.

Liberty sat astride his horse, the reins held tight in his gloved hands. He had sat there for nearly ten minutes, giving careful thought to his next move, if there was to be a move. Liberty was not a man of indecision, but at thirty-five he knew there was a time to exercise patience. There had been a time in his life when he had had to wait to be told what to do. That had been expected of him; required, as a matter of fact.

At that time he had been a slave in Tennessee.

Liberty had escaped from bondage in 1852, making his way north by following the Big Dipper, which the slaves called the Freedom Cup. He had traveled at night, sleeping by day in the trees to prevent discovery until he swam the Ohio River near Owensboro, Kentucky, and came ashore to freedom in Indiana. That was sixteen years ago; ten of those years had been spent in uniform following his enlistment in the 54th Massachusetts Infantry. He had fought at Fort Wagner, South Carolina, where he was wounded in the final charge that had cost the life of his commander, Colonel Robert Gould Shaw. Liberty had learned firsthand that the price of liberty was not cheap.

That was why he had chosen Liberty for his last name.

Moss, his first name, was given to him by his mother because his dark hair was curly and soft like moss growing in a wet, dark place. Now a sergeant of cavalry, he was tall and muscular. A quiet man by nature, in the two years he had served on the plains he had learned to spot trouble and avoid the situations that often drew Colored soldiers into conflict.

He was now confronting one of those difficult situations, one that pulled at his guts as he again extended the telescope and surveyed the hills in the distance.

The plains stretched endlessly toward the west, where the sun was beginning to settle onto the horizon. A light breeze blew easterly, carrying the smell that Liberty knew could come only from a slaughter. And a slaughter was what he had found.

He had been watching what the buffalo hunters called a stand, a large cluster of dead buffalo lying at the edge of the herd—a herd that stretched as far as Liberty could see.

"Must be more than fifty in his stand," Liberty said, looking again through the telescope.

"How many in the party?" asked Gibbs.

"A gunner and a skinner."

"Just one gun?"

Liberty nodded but wasn't impressed; he knew it took no particular talent to build a formidable stand, except for a steady hand on the trigger and a constant supply of bullets. Buffalo would not run or move so long as a shot felled one of their herd; but a *wounded* buffalo would generally start a panic and the herd would bolt. He also knew the buffalo were their own worst enemy because they were predictable. The buffalo always moved into the wind; therefore, the hunter had only to position himself crosswind and begin shooting.

Not that the sight of a large stand bothered him. He knew this area, called the Republican, was prime hunting grounds for the buffalo hunters, who would strip the hides from the animals, then stake the hides for fleshing and drying, marking the snowy landscape with dark splotches, leaving the meat to rot on the prairie, carrion for the vultures and other predators.

Predator. The word seemed to have special meaning as Liberty heard the thunder of a Sharps rifle and saw another buffalo drop nearly one-quarter of a mile from the gunner, who lay a half mile from Liberty on the top of a knoll.

Liberty examined the hunter again, making certain he was seeing the unbelievable truth.

There were some things a man could not walk away from.

Augustus Talbot was eighteen years old, tall and wiry, his skin and eyes the color of charcoal. He wore leather breeches that were coated with dried buffalo blood, and was wrapped in a heavy buffalo robe as he lay atop a hill on the open prairie south of the Republican River, his leg tied to a stake driven into the frozen ground. Smoothly, he inched over the mound of snow that he had built to support the long barrel of his .50-caliber Sharps buffalo gun, took aim, fired the "Big Fifty," as it was called by the buffalo hunters, and watched as another buffalo fell dead.

Charlie Calhoun, a skinner with failing eyesight, knelt behind him, a Colt .45 pistol ready should Augustus violate the single rule that kept him alive and gave him hope: keep the barrel pointed toward the buffalo.

"You're shootin' too slow, boy. We're losin' daylight." Calhoun thumped Augustus in the back with the heel of his boot, then leaned forward, checked the rope attached to Augustus's leg, and gave it a sharp tug. The stake held firm. Calhoun spit a long stream of tobacco juice and wiped his beard with the heavy sleeve of his buffalo robe.

To Augustus's immediate front, low on the side of the hill where he was positioned, twenty-four buffalo lay still, their legs jutting parallel to the ground. Steam rose off some of the bodies in twisting, ghoulish clouds as the crisp cold began to cool the carcasses.

"Come on, boy. Shoot!" Calhoun slapped Augustus in the back of the head just as he pulled the trigger, throwing off the shot. A buffalo screamed, tumbling into the snow, still alive. The herd bolted and, in the moment of madness, turned toward the buffalo hunters.

"Damn your black ass!" Calhoun jumped to his feet, running toward the wagon filled with hides.

Augustus pulled desperately at the rope; the stake held fast as the buffalo herd thundered closer. Again he kicked, pulled, and thrashed, but the stake wouldn't break free. He turned to the herd and saw the lead buffalo closing on him, no more than twenty yards away, followed by thousands more, their great heads plowing in imperfect rhythm.

In that instant Augustus fell calm, as though death would be a blessing. He stared directly into the buffalo's eyes. Suddenly, from the corner of his eye there was a flash of blue. He looked up and saw what he thought could only be a dream: two Colored men dressed in army uniforms were riding toward him, the tallest of the two gripping a long, curved sabre.

The tall soldier leaned over and, as he swept past Augustus, swung the sword, cutting the rope. The second soldier followed close behind but didn't stop, merely reined in sharply next to Augustus and extended his hand.

"Come on, boy," he shouted.

Augustus gripped the hand and swung onto the back of the horse. The soldier spurred the horse toward the wagon, where Augustus saw Calhoun hiding behind a wheel as the buffalo charged closer.

Augustus could see the tall soldier racing toward the wagon, then wheel diagonally when he realized there wasn't enough time to reach the skinner.

At that moment Augustus's eyes met with the eyes of Calhoun, who then disappeared beneath a sea of black fur.

An hour later the earth appeared to have been plowed by some great machine in a long path that continued as though to the edge of the horizon. The wagon lay in splinters among buffalo hides strewn like black boils; the air was still, but the ground continued to tremble though the herd was no longer in sight.

Liberty could only shake his head in amazement while Gibbs and Augustus walked among the ruins.

There was little left. Calhoun's mangled body lay in four separate pieces over a fifty-yard stretch of broken ground.

Augustus looked into Calhoun's dead face, what was left of it, staring emptily toward the sky, his head severed at the throat. He suddenly reached to the ground and retrieved the Sharps rifle. It was covered with mud, and the stock was cracked nearly in half.

"Ain't much good now," Liberty said.

Augustus wiped at the mud, sighted down the barrel, and replied, "The barrel's straight and I can fix the stock."

This brought a laugh from Liberty. "How you going to do that?"

Augustus smiled as he picked up a buffalo robe.

Gibbs approached, carrying a cartridge belt he had taken from Calhoun's body. He handed it to Augustus.

They slept that night in a thicket of trees around a fire pit dug low in the frozen ground to prevent the flames from giving away their position. Over the sunken fire they roasted a piece of buffalo hump, and the buffalo soldiers watched Augustus work on the rifle stock.

He cut strips of buffalo hide and stretched them over the fire until the fat began to bubble; next, he slowly worked the hot fat into the cracks of the stock. He then wound the strips tight around the stock and soaked them with water. Augustus then turned the stock slowly over the fire, patiently drying the strips until the hide formed a rigid cast around the wood.

This mightily impressed Liberty. "Where'd you learn that, boy?"

"From the Kiowa," Augustus replied softly.

"Kiowa!" Liberty exclaimed. "What were you doing with the Kiowa?"

Augustus shrugged. "I was a slave."

Liberty chuckled. "I didn't know the Kiowa bought Colored slaves."

"They didn't buy me. I was captured by a raiding party just after the end of the war."

Augustus's comment spurred Liberty's curiosity. "You want to tell us about how you come to be here on the Republican?"

Augustus nodded slightly, then spoke in a low, deliberate voice. "I come from west Texas. I was captured by the

Kiowa three years ago. The Indians sold me to Charlie Calhoun last year for three horses and a rifle."

Liberty waited, but Augustus said nothing more.

"Is that it?"

"That's all I want to say."

"What about your folks?" asked Gibbs.

"Both my momma and poppa are dead. They died during the war."

"I expect you learned a lot of things living with them Injuns," said Gibbs, who was cutting off another piece of meat.

"I learned many things, Mr. Gibbs."

"Did the Kiowa teach you how to shoot?"

Augustus shook his head. "My massah in Texas taught me how to shoot. He said I had a natural eye with a rifle."

This prodded Liberty further. "Can you ride as good as you can shoot?"

Augustus nodded, then held the stock up for closer examination. He was pleased with what he saw.

The stock would hold firm.

The next morning they rose from the stiff buffalo robes and stretched their muscles. Noting that the fire was out and fresh snow had fallen during the night, Augustus took a robe, cut off a square the size of his hand, turned it fur-up, took kindling, and began scraping his knife against a piece of flint he carried in his leggings. The fur from the robe began to slowly burn, throwing off a stinging odor, but as he added more wood he had a good fire going within minutes.

Liberty and Gibbs glanced at each other. Liberty grinned. "This here Augustus Talbot knows a few tricks, Trooper Gibbs."

"He sure does," Gibbs replied admiringly.

When they finished what was left of the buffalo meat, Liberty said, "We best be moving. We're going to Fort Wallace, Augustus. Come with us; you can make plans from there. If you want to hunt buffalo, the Goddard brothers are hiring shooters out of Hays to fill government contracts on land the Injuns don't own."

Augustus shook his head. "I'd rather starve to death."

The trio reached Wallace, Kansas, the next afternoon. Wallace was a sprawling community of canvas tents, mud huts (called "soddies"), and Conestoga wagons, now trapped along the frozen tracks of the Kansas Pacific Railroad.

It was the first town Augustus had seen since being captured by the Kiowa, and he found Wallace was uglier than a boil on a sow. He had seen many Kiowa villages with greater prestige. Wooden saloons and sporting houses lined the main street, a soggy bog splattered with manure. They rode along, the mud sucking at their animals' hooves.

Liberty turned to Gibbs. "Let's spend a few minutes over with my family before we head out to the fort."

They turned off the main street and rode into a neighborhood of old wagons and worn tents. Augustus saw Colored children playing in the snowy streets, heard the voices of women singing hymns. Smelled chitlings, ham and beans, and roast buffalo hump. It smelled good!

"Must be Sunday," Gibbs said.

"Where are we, Sergeant?" asked Augustus.

"This part of town is called Buffalo Bottoms, on account it's where all the Coloreds live who have families and serve in the army. Colored soldiers are called buffalo soldiers by the Injuns, you know. They says our hair looks like the fur of the buffalo. So they call this Buffalo Bottoms 'cause living here is about as close to being at the bottom a Colored man can get."

"We called something else by the white cavalry. Everything from brunets, moacs, to niggers," snorted Gibbs. "We at least got some pride in being called buffalo soldiers."

"My wife and daughter live right down yonder." Liberty pointed at a tent that was more patchwork than canvas.

In front of the tent steam rose off two large cauldrons of boiling water, carrying from one the heavy smell of lye soap.

"My wife, her momma, and my daughter are laundresses. They take in laundry from the fort. It helps add some money to my pay. Twenty-four dollars a month for a sergeant with a family don't make ends see each other, much less meet." He stopped his horse as a young woman ran from the tent.

"Daddy! Daddy!" Selona Liberty ran and jumped up and threw her arms around him, startling the horse.

"Whoa, girl, you going to scare my hoss to death." He was grinning as he pulled her up onto the saddle and gave her a great hug. "How's my baby?"

"I ain't no baby. I'm almost twelve years old. Almost a woman grown. Besides, you married Momma when she was fifteen."

Augustus looked at her and saw that her face was mature beyond her age.

Liberty started to say something, when the voice of his wife interrupted. "It's about time you come home. Off gallivanting like some crazy man."

At only twenty-nine, Della Liberty looked worn to the bone; the skin appeared loose on her cheeks and thin arms. The post doctor called her illness "the consumption."

An older woman, probably the grandmother, thought Augustus, stood at the flap of the tent, a corncob pipe clamped tightly in her toothless mouth. She reminded him of a horse that had been rode hard and put away wet too many times.

Gibbs leaned over and whispered to Augustus, "That old woman's named Miss Marie. She's meaner than a two-legged dog and watches over the girl like a hawk."

Moss lowered Selona gently to the mud street and swung his leg over the saddle. He removed his kepi hat, placing it over his heart, and walked smartly to his wife. He held her close, but pulled her to him slowly. Carefully.

Augustus stared at Selona; her right eyebrow raised.

"Where you from?"

"Texas."

"Don't they have soap and water in Texas? You're so dirty, I can smell you from here."

He had never spoken to anything so beautiful and been embarrassed so deeply at the same time. "Smell washes off. Manners are something that must be learned with time," Augustus retorted.

Her eyes widened. "You the one that needs manners, boy."

"I'm not a boy. I'm a man."

Selona harrumphed, then turned and hurried into the tent. The old woman followed, puffing her corncob pipe and cackling with laughter like an old hen.

Augustus sat there, realizing he had said both the right and wrong things in the same breath.

Moss hugged Della and remounted, telling her, "I'll be back tonight."

Sergeant Major Roscoe Brassard sat at his desk, his face smoothly shaven except for the thick mustache that flowed from beneath his broad nose to join his sideburns, when the door to the regimental headquarters orderly room flew open, admitting a blast of cold air followed by Liberty and what Brassard could only describe as the filthiest human being he had ever seen in his life.

The young man was wearing a heavy buffalo robe; his face was coated with a sheen of buffalo fat, blood, and dirt. Brassard rose slowly, noting that despite his dirt, the boy had a certain bearing.

"Boy, when's the last time you had a bath?" Brassard asked.

"Don't call me boy. My name is Augustus Talbot."

Brassard swallowed a grin. "Very well, Augustus Talbot. When's the last time you had a bath?"

"About three years ago."

Brassard's eyebrows rose as he looked at Liberty. "What's going on here, Sergeant?"

Liberty bit into a plug of chewing tobacco. "We found this here boy—this here Augustus Talbot—yesterday afternoon up on the Republican."

"Buffalo hunter?" asked Brassard, not taking his eyes off Augustus as he slowly moved around the desk.

"Yessuh. And one helluva buffalo hunter. This man can shoot better than any man I ever seen. Except he didn't have no choice in the matter."

"What's that supposed to mean?"

"He was captured three years ago—"

Augustus cut him off. "I can speak for myself, Sergeant." He stared into Brassard's eyes. "I was captured by the Kiowa three years ago. The Kiowa sold me to a buffalo hunter last year."

"Sold! You was a buffalo hunter's slave!" Brassard's voice nearly shook the building.

"Yes, sir. Born a slave. Set free and captured by the Kiowa. Probably would have died a slave had it not been for your men."

"Your slave name was Talbot?"

"Yes, sir."

"Most Colored men are picking a new name since freedom."

Augustus shrugged. "I've had too much on my mind the past three years to think about a new name, Sergeant Major."

"Can you read and write?"

"Some. My massah was a rancher, but he was also the

local preacher before he went off to the war. He taught me to read and write."

"Can you cipher?"

Augustus said, "My massah's wife had to teach me ciphering after the massah went off to war."

"Why's that?"

"Her health was too poorly for her to take care of business. I did it for her."

"What about the overseer? He could have done the business."

Augustus shook his head. "There wasn't an overseer. Massah didn't have the money to hire one."

"What about your family? You got any kinfolk left alive?"

Augustus's eyes hooded with sadness. "No, sir. My momma and poppa died during the war."

Brassard sat back down, planting his boots on top of the desk. "I expect you must have a powerful hatred for Injuns."

"More than you can know." Augustus's eyes were like banked coals.

Brassard could feel the deep hatred in the young man. He understood that kind of hatred: hatred that could destroy or, if channeled properly, could be of great use. "You got any plans?"

Augustus replied, "I'd like to borrow some soap and take a bath."

Brassard laughed. "You surely need a bath. You smell like death warmed over." He motioned to Liberty. "Get this buffalo hunter a hot tub, some soap, and some clean clothes."

"Yessuh." Liberty spat into the spitoon. "Come on, Augustus. Let's get that buffalo stink off you."

Augustus Talbot stood six feet tall; he was scrawny from malnutrition but strong and sinewy. The hot bath was the most wonderful experience he had known in three years. Once he'd lowered himself into the tub, he scrubbed for nearly an hour. Liberty brought him some fresh clothes, laughing in a secretive way as he placed a pair of black boots atop the blue trousers and tunic.

Once dressed, Augustus headed out to the parade grounds. Mounted troops came and went through the main gate; the air was filled with the sounds of the military. His pace quickened as he saw Brassard walk out of the orderly room. They shook hands.

"You hungry?" Brassard asked.

"I could eat a horse."

Brassard led Augustus to the mess hall. When Augustus stepped through the door, he heard the crisp bark from a soldier, "Atten-hut!"

From their tables, the troopers rose sharply, standing at attention as Brassard led Augustus to a table. Brassard studied the men for a moment, then nodded and said smartly, "As you were."

The men sat down and returned to eating; then a soldier brought two plates of food for Brassard and Augustus, who began eating like a wolf. Brassard ate slowly, watching Augustus, saying nothing until three plates of food had vanished.

"You thought about what you're going to do, Augustus?"

Augustus sipped hot coffee, shaking his head. "I suppose I'll have to find a job."

"Not many jobs in these parts for a Colored man, unless you want to go back to hunting buffalo."

Augustus exhaled heavily. "No, sir. I'd rather starve."

Brassard came to the point. "You don't have to starve. I know where you can get fed, clothed, and give yourself a chance to get your feet on the ground."

Augustus chuckled, as though he already knew what Brassard's next words would be. "You mean the army?"

Brassard replied, "I mean the Tenth Cavalry. It's a chance

to do something important. Important for you . . . and our
people."

"Why important? And why would I want to risk my life
as a soldier?"

Brassard went into his recruiting pitch. "This nation just
finished a bloody civil war to set slaves free. A lot of good
men died, mostly white men. Now we're a country again,
and if the Colored man is going to stand shoulder to shoulder with the white man, we're going to have to pitch in and
do our share. Until the Colored men and women of this
country help carry the burden we'll always be considered
slaves." He paused for effect. "Besides, it'll give you a
chance to settle your account with the Kiowa, and we need
young men like you. Hell, boy, you just spent three years
with the Kiowa and on the plains. I expect you got a lotta
Injun in you now."

"I learned how they fight. How they think."

"That's what I mean. You'd make a perfect scout for the
regiment."

"A scout?"

"Among other duties. But most of all you know Injuns."

"What other duties?"

"Do you know who does most of the paperwork in this
regiment?"

"I couldn't say."

"The white officers, and a few noncommissioned officers
like myself who can read and write. There ain't many of us,
either. You could be very valuable to the Tenth."

Augustus had been watching the troopers in the mess
hall. They appeared confident, self-reliant, and carried
themselves with an obvious pride.

"I don't know anything about being a soldier."

Brassard grinned. "I do. You'll train right here, under my
supervision."

"You can do that?"

"Damn right, I can do that. I told Colonel Grierson about

you while you were cleaning up. He ordered me to enlist you into this regiment by reveille tomorrow morning, or he'd have my stripes."

"What about my rifle?"

"The Sharps?"

Augustus nodded. "I'd like to keep it."

Brassard thought for a moment, then said, "Troopers in the Tenth carry the Spencer rifle. But I reckon we can make a special exception. But you'll have to carry the regulation Spencer as well."

Augustus wolfed down more food, then said, "That'll give me more to shoot with, Sergeant Major."

"But you'll have to supply your own cartridges. The army don't issue Sharps cartridges. You can buy them in town."

That sounded fair to Augustus. "I'll buy my own cartridges."

Brassard took an enlistment form and asked, "Do you know how to sign your name?"

"I know."

Brassard pushed the form across the table and handed him a pencil. "Sign your name, Augustus Talbot, and you'll be a member of the Tenth Cavalry."

Augustus signed, but not the name Brassard was expecting.

"You signed this form with the name Augustus Sharps. Is that for the rifle?"

Augustus thought about the other freemen cutting their ties with the past, and said, "The Sharps has a good sound. A good feel. Most men know the Sharps is a serious rifle. A name should be the same. Sharps is a name that stands for pride."

Selona Sharps—1876

At Fort Davis, Texas—the night her second child arrived—Selona Sharps jerked awake to a brilliant flash
of light; when she tried to rise from the straw-filled mattress
in her adobe house, she could move only her eyes, and she
could see the cloud of light begin to drift toward her from
near the hearth.

She was not confused; the recurring nightmare had
haunted her since the night she was attacked by evil men in
1874 while her father was posted at Fort Sills in the Indian
Territory.

A man suddenly appeared from the cloud, his features
growing more distinct with each advancing step.

When he pressed the point of the blade against her tem-
ple she tried to rise, but to no avail. Then there was the sting
of the knife slicing through her flesh, cutting evenly above
her ear, around the circumference of her head. Smoothly.
Well practiced.

Selona screamed as she felt his fingers slip into the inci-
sion above her ears. Then there was a sucking sound, like

a foot pulling from deep mud. Her head felt as though it would be pulled from her shoulders, when suddenly the man straightened up above her.

In his hand he dangled her bloody scalp.

His piercing laughter rose higher until it turned into a shriek, then a howling, like the wind . . . howling . . . howling . . .

Selona thrashed violently to the floor and tore herself from the nightmare that had tormented her for two years. She was soaked with sweat, and the sound of thunder crashed through her head. She instinctively reached for her hair, and when she felt her smooth scalp, and saw there was no blood on her hands, the shock began to wear off and she could distinguish between the howling in her nightmare and that of the wind.

She trembled as she adjusted the hairpiece made for her from the fur of a buffalo hide and opened the door to find Vina Gibbs standing veiled in lantern light. Vina, a short, stocky woman with powerful arms and short, wiry hair, was married to Private Darcy Gibbs, the best friend to her husband, Corporal Augustus Sharps.

Selona had been disfigured by the scalping and it was Augustus who had come up with the idea to use a piece of buffalo robe to fashion her a hairpiece. Several months later, in the fall of 1874, after her father was killed at the battle of Anadarko Agency, Augustus and Selona had been married.

"Selona? Are you all right? I could hear you screaming from the other end of the row."

The Fort Davis Suds Row was nestled at the base of Sleeping Lion Mountain, near the fort hospital. In 1876, the army had decided that the traveling troupes of washwomen had caused too many problems, and in order to work on a military post the laundresses had to be married to a soldier.

Selona rubbed her face roughly, trying to push away the remnants of the nightmare, and motioned Vina inside.

Vina handed her the lantern, and in the swinging light Selona could see that her friend carried a bundle pressed against her breast. The bundle moved, then it squalled.

"What do you have there, Vina?"

"Trouble." The woman paused, taking in Selona's disheveled appearance. "You had that nightmare again?"

"Never mind. What trouble?"

Vina thrust the child into her arms. "This baby boy was born this afternoon to one of the young Mexican girls at Adams's hog ranch. One of our Colored troopers is the father. Don't know which. Guess she didn't neither. Old man Adams brought the baby to the fort. He said, 'Coloreds are the father . . . Coloreds can look after him.' One of the troopers brought him to me."

The "hog ranch" was one of the saloons where the troopers of the 10th Cavalry could buy female company and cheap whiskey for a few dollars.

Selona slowly unfolded the bundle and stared at the dark-skinned newborn baby. He was so beautiful.

"Why did you bring this baby here?"

Vina's face tightened. "The Mexican girl died just after sunset. That child's hungry, and you're the only woman I know that's got momma's milk."

Selona looked to the straw bed where three-month-old Adrian lay beneath a shawl. Then she suddenly realized . . .

"You mean to say you want me to feed this child?"

Vina smiled softly. "You're the only one I know." She had the look of someone waiting for a blessing. "This baby ain't been fed since it drew first breath."

Adrian suddenly chimed in with his own urgent wail of hunger, the two babies forming a chorus that Selona might have thought comical were it not so tragic.

Then she motioned for Vina to take the newborn while she opened the top of her nightshirt. Vina helped her, guiding the newborn to her left nipple while Selona guided Adrian to the right.

She sat on the edge of the bed in the flickering lantern light, feeding the two babies and wondering what would become of them.

"What am I going to tell Augustus?"

Vina's eyes glistened. "Tell him the Good Lord called on you with another child lost in the wilderness."

She never had the nightmare again.

Bonita, Arizona—1917

The Sharps ranch was east of Bonita, a small Arizona mining town eighty miles northeast of Tucson, in the Pinaleno Mountains. Selona was given the rugged land, once sprawling with miners, as a gift for shooting a bank robber who had stolen the townspeople's money. Now she sat on the front porch, reading a newspaper whose banner headline read: WAR!

"Why do we want to go to war with those Germans?" Selona asked. Then she looked past Augustus at the two rising columns of dust approaching from the west.

She had no doubt what the dust columns meant.

She looked at Augustus, who now wore an artificial left leg after being shotgunned by Ku Klux Klansmen in Murfreesboro, Tennessee, in 1898, when he and their two sons, Adrian and David, had ridden with Buffalo Bill Cody's Congress of Rough Riders.

Augustus was whittling, his artificial leg propped up on the railing. He glanced up at the approaching riders and smiled knowingly, then went back to his whittling. The artificial leg, which he had purchased years before from a Chicago prosthetics clinic, allowed him to walk, even ride, but there was a problem: Each time he purchased a new pair of boots, he had to make some adjustments on the feet. A whittle here, a whittle there, until the boots fit perfectly.

Selona said, "You buy another new pair of boots and you won't have a foot left. If that was a real foot you'd have already whittled off your big toe."

"Hush, now, Selona," Augustus said softly, slipping the boot easily over the artificial foot. "Why don't you fix me and the boys something to eat?"

She stormed into the house as Adrian and David rode up.

"You've heard?" David asked.

Augustus nodded. "A patrol from the Tenth Cavalry passed through this morning. Sounds like there's going to be a ruckus."

The two men were now in their early forties. Adrian was tall like his father, his skin a rich charcoal, and a widower. He had served in the 1st Volunteer Cavalry—the Rough Riders—with Colonel Theodore Roosevelt, one of three Colored men to do so.

David, the child brought to Selona from Adams's hog ranch at Fort Davis, Texas, was cinnamon in color, much shorter than Adrian, boasting the pork chop sideburns and flowing mustache of the cavalryman. Which he had been, having served with the 9th Cavalry during the war with Spain.

"What's your plans?" asked Augustus.

"We're going to Fort Huachuca this afternoon," Adrian replied. "We're going to enlist. I expect the army will be needing some Colored troops."

Augustus grew serious. "I expect the army *will* be needing some Colored officers."

"Officers!" they chimed.

Augustus stood and walked off the porch toward the stable. The boys followed, leading their horses behind them.

In the stable Augustus saddled his horse and mounted. The three rode east into the desert.

Augustus told them, "Captain Lewis Morey was leading the patrol. He said the army is going to recruit noncommissioned officers from the Colored regiments to become officers. Right off he's recommending First Sergeant Houston and Corporal Queen of K troop."

Adrian and David both knew the men. They had distinguished themselves nearly a year before during a punitive expedition into Carrizal, Mexico, when fifty troopers of the 10th had engaged more than five hundred Mexican cavalrymen. The 10th had been soundly defeated, and the engagement considered a disaster, but the courage of the 10th in the face of such overwhelming odds was a source of regimental pride.

"What about Theresa?" Augustus asked.

David shrugged. He had been married for nearly ten years and had two children. Adrian had married a year later, but his wife had died during childbirth and he hadn't remarried.

"She'll be fine. She understands."

"Your momma will want her and the children to stay with us," Augustus said.

David nodded. "I expect she will."

Augustus paused at the edge of a deep canyon. He stared out over the wide expanse. "Your momma thinks you boys are too old to be going off to war."

"General Pershing wasn't too old to fight in Mexico last year," Adrian said quickly.

Augustus nodded toward the canyon. "Maybe you best find out for yourself."

Augustus's right hand came up in a sharp salute and he spurred his horse over the edge. Down he rode, driving the horse furiously until he reached the bottom. He then spurred the horse to a gallop, charging the unseen enemy he had attacked so many times before. When the dust had settled, he motioned to his sons, who sat mounted on the rim above.

Adrian saluted smartly, then drove his horse over the edge, the reins tight as he pushed the stallion downward while holding the mount's strength in check. When he reached the bottom he made the same charge as his father, then wheeled and made another attack, then reined in beside Augustus.

On the rim, David did the same, galloping down the steep ledge, following the trail cut by his father over the years. The trail the sons had ridden many times in their lives.

Augustus studied their faces for a long moment, as though he were looking at them for the last time. Then he spurred his horse and raced toward the mouth of the canyon, followed by Adrian and David.

"Fort Des Moines, Iowa!" exclaimed Selona. "Why is there a fort in Iowa? There's never been Injuns or comancheros or Mexican bandits in Iowa. Probably aren't any Germans, either."

"It's where the Colored officers' candidate school is located, Momma," Adrian replied.

Two months had passed since Adrian and David had ridden to Fort Huachuca and spoken with the fort commander. He accepted their application for enlistment and forwarded his letter to the War Department recommending the OCS appointment of Adrian and David Sharps.

"Probably do to you what they did to Lieutenant Flipper," Selona said acidly. "Colored officers don't do well in the army."

"Colonel Charles Young has done well for himself," David snapped back.

Charles Young, the third Negro to graduate from West

Point, had served in the late 1800s with the 9th Cavalry, and was the first Negro officer to serve with a white cavalry regiment—the 7th Cavalry, Custer's old regiment. He was promoted to major during the Spanish-American War, serving with the 9th Ohio Infantry, and the first Negro in the American military to be promoted to colonel. The newspapers had recently reported that he was riding on horseback from Ohio to Washington, D.C., to prove he was still physically fit to serve in Europe.

Selona ignored him. "Besides, I don't know why you would want to risk your life fighting white people in France who've never done anything to you. Why don't you fight for the Coloreds in America who are being murdered by white Americans!"

"Don't be unpatriotic, Selona," said Augustus in a stern tone.

"Unpatriotic! I'll talk to you about patriotism. Was it patriotic for you to risk your life for more than thirty years in the army and have some white man in Tennessee blow your leg off because you tried to stop white men from lynching a young Colored man? Now you're talking about my babies going to the other side of the world and fighting for white people's freedom when their own people don't have freedom in this country! Damn you, and damn your patriotism!"

Selona ran from the house, slamming the door behind her.

Augustus rose slowly, as though the words were more painful than the phantom pain in his amputated leg. "I best go after her."

They stood beside a tall cactus near Darcy Gibbs's grave in the hot afternoon sun, listening to the wind whip along the ground. His breath was labored by the old agony in his leg; her breath was angered by the agony in her heart.

"You could have stood by me, Augustus," she said softly.

He shook his head. "You were wrong, Selona. I won't abide you when I know you're wrong."

"Wrong? What's wrong with a mother wanting her children to be safe?"

"They're men, Selona. They're not children. They have to make a man's way—and a man's decisions."

She stared off into the distance. "But France! God Almighty, that's so far from home." Then she stopped suddenly. "If they're killed they won't even be brought home. They'll be buried in some foreign place where nobody knows them."

He touched her arm gently. "They won't die. They survived Cuba. They'll survive France."

"So many young men are dying in that war. I read that over a million men died at that battle called the Somme. A million men, Augustus. We ain't never lost a million soldiers in all the wars this country ever fought. That was in just one battle."

Augustus knew, and privately also feared, the incredible casualties of the war. "Sure must have been a ruckus."

She shook her head. "No. A slaughter. That's why I'm scared. Who do you think will be the first Americans they'll put in those trenches? Not the white regiments! They'll put the Coloreds up there first. Our sons!"

He said something he had said many times. "When the bugle calls, a soldier must answer."

She shook her head in anger. "You and that damned bugle. That bugle has killed a lot of good young men."

He turned and walked toward the house. Inside he found Adrian and David sitting in the kitchen. He looked at them both affectionately; then to David he said, "I have something I want to do. But I don't want you to be offended."

David stood and put his arms around his father. "I think I know. I won't be offended."

Augustus walked into the sitting room and reached over the mantel, removing his cavalry sabre from the wooden pegs. He looked at Adrian, then held the sabre out in his upturned palms.

Adrian looked at David, who nodded with a smile toward the sabre.

"Adrian, I carried this in battle for over thirty years. I think it's only fit that the oldest son should carry this as a reminder of what our family has done for this country. I expect you'll do the same with your son one day if he has to go to war."

Adrian took the sabre and hugged his father. David joined the embrace as Selona walked through the door.

She had tears in her eyes as she put her arms around the three men in her life and whispered, "You have a long journey. I best fix you some food to take on your trip."

Then she did what she had done most all her life, knowing she was just one woman in a world where her voice was always consumed by the tempest of war: She went to the kitchen and had her cry in private.

PART 1

THE APPOINTMENTS

1

✷ ✷ ✷

The morning found the bayou country of northwest Florida wrapped in a veil of low, clinging fog, painting the land an eerie purple. Through the mist, railroad tracks could be dimly seen rising above the swamp on a wide berm threading through the bayou like a snake. Minutes after the sun touched the dew-slick tracks, the rails burned copperish for a moment, then brightened to a soft silver.

Below, in the black muck, a lone alligator plied smoothly along the surface, his cruel snout thrust menacingly above the water, flagging his position while pushing forward a steady wake of rippling tide. To the creatures of the swamp, this signaled that the gator was awake, hungry, and on the prowl.

Near shore, the warning was respected in the tall reeds, where frogs plunged for the bottom and cranes lifted hurriedly into the air.

Then there was silence.

When the alligator had its fill, the swamp might have returned to normalcy had another presence not found its way into the bayou, breaking the serenity with a punctuality the animals had grown to accept as part of the morning ritual, like the rising sun.

A slow but accelerating vibration rumbled along the tracks; then the smoking engine boomed into the bayou, moving with funereal purpose from the darkness of the east. Behind the diesel trailed an endless caravan of open flatbeds stacked with lumber, their integrity uniform except for a single boxcar captured at the center of the shaking procession bound for New Orleans.

The train appeared as it always had: a dark and intrusive, noisy, shaking apparition pumping an ugly black cloud into the pristine sky.

To the alligator, whose empty eyes focused on the open door of the boxcar, instincts came alive at the possibility of fresh opportunity.

A young woman stood defiantly in the door of the boxcar. Her coal-black hair was whipped back by the wind, revealing a grime-coated cinammon face.

Hannah Simmons saw no options and found no time to curse her dilemma, for another danger pressed from the dusty darkness three feet away. She gripped the knife in her long slender fingers.

"Stay away from me, Billy. I'm warning you. Just leave me alone. Sit down and leave me alone!"

"You nigger bitch!" The man stepped from the shadows and nearly stumbled into her blade.

His name was Billy Turner and he too held a knife in one hand; his free hand pressed the dirty sleeve of his dungaree shirt to his cheek. Beneath the cuff trailed a thin streak of blood that the wind shaped into a wet pool beneath the dripping lobe of his ear.

"Don't come any closer, Billy. I'm warning you." Her voice left no doubt that there would be a price to pay: She had cut him. Now Billy rolled the knife confidently through his fingers.

"I'm going to cut off your ears," he said. "Then I'm going to feed you to the gators."

Hannah leaned back, glancing down the length of the tracks. There was nothing but the lurching framework of the flatbeds and jostling stacks of lumber; nothing that might offer a safer way out of the situation.

How did this happen? Her mind rocked with the question but this was not the moment to reflect on the past. It was the present that mattered. Not the moment to wonder why she had boarded a train in Tallahassee with a stranger, a man who taught her two things: one, that he was from South Carolina; the other, learned shortly after dawn, that when he was drunk, he was mean.

She had learned that when the sun had drifted into the boxcar where she slept, using her rucksack for a pillow. When dreams of where she was headed had been suddenly interrupted by the nightmare of the present—him looming over her, swaying drunk, his words slurred but his intentions made clear by the knife he held in his hand.

She pulled her own knife from her back pocket and slashed the man across the cheek and raced for the door, where she waited for the right moment to jump.

Could she jump?

She had learned early in life that choices don't always provide a better answer; that choices merely provide a means of measuring the loss against the gain.

It was the result that mattered, and she knew what the result would be if she stayed aboard the train.

Then Billy made the decision for her, and regardless of the outcome there was only one choice.

When Billy stepped closer she kicked him sharply in his crotch.

The moment Billy screamed and doubled to his knees, Hannah stepped free from the boxcar. She glided into the muggy air and floated toward earth.

She felt the breeze in her hair and from behind she heard

Billy's trailing string of obscenities. Then she drew her knees up and exploded into the cool, green water of the bayou.

She relaxed and allowed herself to sink, shedding the heat and filth of the boxcar; then, she reached upward, pulling hand over hand toward the surface, where the light grew brighter, the temperature warmer, until, like a child breaking the embryonic seal of the womb, she reached through to the surface.

She was basking in her triumph, pleased there was no injury, when she spotted the alligator and swam to the shore, threading her way through the reeds and paddies, through sea oats and cattails, where she found a small beach beneath the trestle. She stripped herself naked, first washing her shirt, then her overalls.

She climbed to the top of the trestle, where she beat her clothes across the tracks to dislodge the dirt from the fiber. The tracks were still hot from the friction of wheels against steel, so to hurry the drying process she stretched her clothes across the hot tracks and went back to the beach.

She washed her body with handfuls of sea oats she pulled from the marsh, and was pleased when their rough texture scrubbed away the grime and gave her face a stinging glow.

She found a tree branch and used her knife to cut the twigs along the branch's axis to form a row of teeth, then brushed her hair in smooth, easy strokes, taking care not to break the makeshift brush, nor cut her tingling scalp, which she had washed with mud from the swamp.

While drying her hair against the warm sea air coming in from the south, she began to realize where she was and recall where she was going. From the slow, steady breeze, which she calculated was drifting in from the Gulf of Mexico, she was reminded that she was in control again, and remembered jumping from the train, and though she was stranded in the middle of a wilderness, she was not lost. She knew where she was, knew that one part of her journey had ended and a fresh part, the most exhilarating, was about to begin.

She stepped naked onto the tracks and stared for a long moment to the south.

Hannah saw the blue, cloudless sky and, in the distance, appearing like nothing more than a slit, lay a thin white fringe barely visible on the horizon where the sky met the green swamp.

Too excited to wait for her clothes to dry and enjoying her naked freedom in the isolation of the swamp, she tied the laces of her scuffed brogans together and threw them over her shoulder; she put the knife in the back pocket of her overalls and draped them and her shirt neatly over her arm.

She walked barefoot and naked toward the west, one of hundreds of thousands of Negroes working their way north toward the opportunity that had been created since the beginning of the Great War in Europe in 1914.

Her destination was East St. Louis, Illinois, a city on the banks of the Mississippi, where she had heard there were jobs in the factories, meat-packing plants, foundries, and loading docks.

She didn't know what she would do to survive. She did know one thing: At the age of twenty-five, she would never again chop cotton!

2

Adrian and David Sharps thought their opportunity for serving in the Great War had vanished at Fort Huachuca, Arizona, where they had ridden from the Sharps ranch on April 7, 1917, to join the regular army.

That disappointment was shared by their father; however, to their mother the news brought sheer delight.

"Them Germans ain't going to kill my boys," she cackled.

Selona still rose early each morning, cooked breakfast for Augustus, hitched her horse and buggy, then made the short ride into Bonita to tend to her thriving laundry and restaurant business.

Arriving at the restaurant on Main Street, she found her sons sitting at a table, brooding over their rejection.

"Good morning, Momma," David said.

"Good morning, boys," she said, her voice almost musical.

Adrian nodded to her, then looked away, as though not

wanting to see her eyes. He knew they would be filled with joy while his ached with anger.

She saw they didn't want to talk, but Selona Sharps was not a woman to be dissuaded for lack of conversation.

"I know you boys are disappointed, but life has its disappointments and we all know that. What you got to do now is get on with your business."

Adrian grumped, "What business do we have? Washing dirty drawers and serving food to strangers while our country is fighting a war in Europe."

Selona's eyes suddenly turned fiery. "This family's done enough for this country. We don't need to do no more except to raise our children and look after one another. Let the world look after itself."

Adrian and David stood quickly, and without a word left, not wanting to hear again the sermon they had heard all their lives. They walked into the dusty street, oblivious to the heat and the sputtering of an approaching motorcar.

"Good morning, men," a voice called.

Adrian and David smiled for the first time since being rejected at Fort Huachuca nearly a month before.

"Good morning, Senator," said Adrian. David reached out his hand and said, "Welcome home."

Senator Ernst Bruner was now retired from Congress and had recently returned from Washington. He was tall, with gray hair that still had a few sprigs of the natural blondness inherited from his German ancestry. His blue eyes quickly detected that the sons of his old friend Augustus Sharps were unhappy.

"Is there a problem?" he asked.

Adrian was admiring the Ford motorcar, walking slowly around the vehicle while talking. "David and I tried to join up over at Fort Huachuca, but the army said we're too old."

Bruner thought for a moment, then said to Adrian,

"When you served with me in the Rough Riders, I was older than you are now. Good God, Colonel Roosevelt and Colonel Leonard Wood were older than us all. It doesn't make sense that the army wouldn't take men like you."

David shrugged. "That's what we were told, Senator."

Bruner's eyes narrowed. "Climb in, gentlemen. I think it's time I paid my respects to your father."

The motorcar sputtered off, leaving a rooster tail of dust in its wake.

Augustus was in the stable and had removed the McClellan saddle from his horse when he heard the motorcar approach. He removed his Sharps rifle from the carbine boot and stepped into the brightness of the morning sun to see the vehicle screech to a stop in front of his house.

He recognized the driver, and walked hurriedly to Bruner. The senator stared for a long moment into Augustus's eyes, then looked admiringly at the rifle. For an instant, his mind tumbled back in time to 1874 and the small farm he and his family worked near the Red River of the Indian Territory. His mother and father had been brutally murdered by comancheros, Ernst and his two sisters taken prisoner. All three might have wound up in the horror of slavery in Mexico had it not been for the courage of a young private in the 10th Cavalry named Augustus Sharps.

"Are you still carrying that old buffalo gun, Augustus?" Bruner teased.

"Yes, sir. Me and this old Sharps have history together." Augustus motioned toward the house. "The coffee's still hot."

Bruner nodded. "Sounds good."

The men sat around the table and talked about old times, from Augustus and Selona's first arrival in Bonita when the 10th was transferred to nearby Fort Grant during the Geronimo war, to the lynch mob that greeted Augustus and the Colored families upon their arrival. They relived the time when Ernst, who was the sheriff, broke up the mob and of the time when Selona saved the townspeople's money by shooting a bank robber in the middle of Main Street.

"What a shot that was," Bruner said. "I'm laying there with a bullet in my leg and the robber riding off. Then I see Selona haul a rifle from the boot of a nearby horse, take aim, and shoot that varmint out of the saddle!"

The men roared at that moment in 1885, an event that endeared the Sharpses to the community of Bonita.

"We were a lot younger then, Augustus," Bruner said reflectively.

Sharps nodded in agreement, then looked at his sons. "Age seems to be important these days, Senator."

Bruner came to the point of the reunion. "Your sons told me about being rejected by the army. But I think there's a solution to that."

Adrian and David straightened.

"What?" asked Adrian.

"A presidential appointment."

"I don't understand," said Adrian.

Bruner spoke confidently. "What if President Wilson were to receive a letter from a former U.S. senator asking that he use his powers of office to appoint two fine men, both veterans of foreign war, to the new Colored officer training center that will be organized next month?"

Sharps was surprised by this. "What Colored officers training center?"

"Just this week the War Department established a plan to organize the Seventeenth Provisional Training Center, a plan that will provide Colored officers to the Colored regiments being organized for service in France."

Sharps breathed a long sigh. "I never heard of such a plan."

"The plan is fresh off the drawing board. I understand there will be more than a thousand recruits selected for

training from all over the country. The recruits must be educated—college, preferably—and of good character and
physical health."

Adrian shook his head. "We didn't go to college."

"The experience you have from the war in Cuba is of
greater value than reading a book."

"Do you think it's possible?" asked Augustus.

Bruner stood and drained his coffee. He turned to the
door, saying, "Come with me, gentlemen. We need to send
a telegram to the president of the United States."

3

The acrid stench of the offal stung Hannah Simmons's nostrils, and though she had learned in the past three weeks how to endure the smell, she had yet to get used to the taste it left in her mouth, almost as tormenting as the brutal heat in the meatpacking warehouse where she worked.

She stood at the third station of the cattle-processing line and looked down the long distance to the first station, where the cattle were suddenly killed from the impact of a twenty-pound sledge hammer swung by the muscular Joseph Harwood. His nickname was "Dalmatian," for he had pink eyes and a pinkish complexion with spatters of dark skin.

At station two stood the four skinners, who stripped the hide from the cow with such speed that the workers at Hannah's third, gutters station would barely have the carcass gutted before another arrived for processing.

Hannah and her partner, Elisa Foster, a twenty-year-old from Macon, Georgia, jumped to one side of the incoming steer. Hannah ran a long knife from the point of the sternum to the base of the tail; Elisa then shoved a bone-saw into the slit at the sternum and started sawing the rib cage.

Before the teeth of the saw touched bone, Hannah's hands would be deep into the cavity, slicing at the trachea. Once severed, the heart and lungs spilled out. The last step was to toss the offal into a hole in the floor, where the innards fell into a wagon that waited below.

Once finished, the steer, on a long trolley cable, was winched to the next station, where hooves, head, and neck would be removed. This was the easiest job on the line, so leisurely the white butchers found time to talk as they worked.

At least she wasn't chopping cotton, she thought as she heard the foreman call, "Be here tomorrow morning at six if you want to work."

Hannah had hired on for two dollars an hour, an unheard-of sum in such bad times. But the contracts were flowing in, as was the cheap, Colored labor, taking jobs from white men, and creating an atmosphere of racial tension.

The Coloreds saw the whites as their own worst enemy: The whites demanded four dollars an hour while the Coloreds were glad to get two.

Although two dollars an hour was the promised pay, the Coloreds actually received one dollar an hour. Every other dollar went to the foreman and the "prospector," the lackey who strolled the Colored tent-camps looking for workers. There was only one rule: Show up every day and pay the Man at the end of the week. Any absence during the week and there was no Saturday payday.

Nearly half her wages went to paying rent on the tent Hannah shared with two female workers in Jody Town, one of the many tent cities that had sprung up around East St. Louis in the past two years. The other half paid for food and the few luxuries she could afford.

On her first payday she went to a store and bought an inexpensive dress, hat, and shoes, which she wore every Sunday to the Jody Town Holiness Church, where she would place a silver dollar in the offering tray at the end of services.

The moment Hannah felt his rough hands touch her, then smelled his foul breath and heard his throaty voice, she knew she was in trouble.

"Come here, girl. Let's sit and talk a spell." The man was huge and had an iron grip on her shoulders, stepping backward into the shadows of the tent, dragging her into the darkness.

"No, please. Don't hurt me, mister. I'm just trying to get back to my tent. My momma's sick and I got to bring her medicine."

She could feel his firebrand eyes on her. Then he grunted and began ripping at her dress. Suddenly, she was on the ground, and when she tried to scream, his rough palm clamped over her mouth, sending the terrible scream back into her lungs.

She wore no panties, for that was a luxury she could not afford, so his access to her was made easier. She felt him roll between her legs, then felt him fumbling to unbutton himself.

Where is my knife! she thought, then remembered she never carried the knife to meeting on Sunday.

She swung wildly, but his arms were so muscular, and her own arms and hands ached as she slapped his skull, forearms, and shoulders.

She felt herself go limp; then, the great weight seemed to rise, as though God had reached down and pulled him off her body.

She opened her eyes and saw another man had her attacker by the throat. The second man drove his knee into the groin of the first. Then there was only the methodical grunt of two beasts warring in the quiet night.

Seconds passed; too terrified to run, she watched, and

saw that one was starting to weaken. Slowly, he slumped to the ground but the other man did not release his grip. After several minutes she knew her attacker was dead.

She saw one of the men rise, then half stumble toward her. He stopped, and reached into the shadows and took her wrists and began pulling her into the light, where her eyes widened as she saw the pinkish-brown skin on the powerful arms of Joseph Harwood.

Then she slumped into unconsciousness.

Hannah awoke to whispers coming from the cot in the corner of the tent, where Joseph and Alice Harwood sat talking. Hannah felt a cold cloth on her forehead, then winced as she touched the bump above her eye.

Alice came and sat on the bed, replacing the cloth with a fresh compress. She had kind eyes framed by long hair. "How are you feeling?"

Hannah could barely move but she managed to say, "I'm fine."

Joseph stood behind Alice. He was twenty-four and they had been married for a year. She was pregnant with their first child.

Hannah asked, "That man. Is he dead?"

Joseph nodded. "He's dead."

"Oh, God. What are we going to do? We'll be lynched."

He shook his head. "The Man don't care about a drunk Colored found dead in Jody Town. You ought to know that."

"Are you sure he was Colored?"

Joseph chuckled. "I know the difference between Colored and white."

The tedium of the next few weeks was broken only by the new friendships she had found. Hannah had few friends and her tentmates were not among them. Elisa and another young Colored woman, Sally Bates, from Charleston, South Carolina, worked their nights at one of the local saloons surrounding the tent city. They sold their bodies for bottles of whiskey, which they in turn sold out of their tents to Colored laborers.

She was on her way home from work when, passing the Harwood tent, she heard a loud scream. She dashed through the tent flap to find Joseph hugging his wife.

"Has the baby started to come?"

Joseph shook his head. He held out a piece of folded paper. "This came today. It's almost as good as a baby."

Hannah took the letter and unfolded it. She stared at it for several seconds. It was the first letter she had ever seen.

She handed the paper back to Joseph. "I can't read," she said softly.

Alice looked at her husband, then said proudly, "Joseph can read. He has two years of college."

Hannah had heard that there were Colored men who had gone to college, even a few women, but she had never met one.

"I'll read what's important in the letter, Hannah," Joseph said. " 'The War Department has reviewed your application and wishes to congratulate you on being accepted into the 17th Provisional Reserved Officers Training Corp. Presentation of this letter to whatever public conveyance is required provides authorization for travel at government expense.' "

Hannah looked completely lost. "What does it mean?"

Alice looked at Joseph and said proudly, "It means my man is going to be an officer in the United States Army."

4

June came but still there was no word on Adrian and David's application. Augustus saddled his horse and rode into town to check the mail, a task usually handled by Selona, since she was in town each day of the week.

Augustus tied off his horse at a hitching rail and went into the telegraph office, which doubled as a post office.

"Good morning, Sergeant Major," called the telegrapher, Ansel Barkunin, a Russian immigrant who had once been a miner.

"Good morning," Augustus replied. "Has my wife picked up the mail today?"

"That she has, Sergeant Major."

"Has there been any mail for my two sons—from the government?"

Barkunin nodded. "Certainly was. Let's see, two days ago. Your boys never get mail so I gave it to your missus since she sees them every day."

Selona had said nothing. "Do you recollect where the letters came from?"

"I do. It's not every day we get mail in here from Washington, D.C."

Selona was serving the noon meal when Augustus stormed through the restaurant's front door. All mouths stopped chewing and talking; all eyes were on the big man filling the doorframe.

Selona quickly turned and walked into the kitchen with Augustus hot on her heels.

"Did Adrian and David get a letter from the War Department?" Augustus's voice boomed.

She said nothing, her back still turned.

"I asked you, did those men receive a letter from the War Department?"

Selona stepped to a cupboard and brought down a large jar and removed the cover. Her hand trembled as she reached inside and withdrew two letters. Without facing him, she handed over the letters.

Augustus took them, saw the seal, then his eyes widened as he realized what she had done. "Selona, you've opened these letters."

She turned, her face streaked with tears. "Yes, I opened them. I wish I had burned them."

His chest heaved, then he gritted his teeth and asked, "What do they say?"

Her words were frozen in her throat.

Augustus turned and left the restaurant, walking quickly next door to the laundry, where he knew he would find Adrian and David working over huge vats of boiling lye soap.

"Boys, I think there is some word of your application."

He held out the letters. Both men dried their hands on their shirts, all the while staring at the letters.

"They've been opened," said David.

Augustus nodded. "Yes. But don't be angry."

Adrian took his envelope and removed the letter; David

did the same. Both walked away a few paces as though not wanting to share the moment with anyone.

Augustus watched their faces begin to crack into beaming grins.

"I've been accepted," said Adrian.

"So have I," David said, then shouted, "We're going to be officers!"

Vina Mae Gibbs stood watching her daughter kneading dough in the kitchen of the Gibbs house—built for her by Selona in 1899—which sat only a stone's throw from Selona's own home. Theresa Sharps had been twenty-two when she and Vina had come back to Arizona, and had been married and divorced. In 1907 she married David Sharps and gave him two sons, Jonathan and Benjamin, named after two officers her father had served with in the 10th Cavalry.

In 1885, during the brief war with Geronimo, Vina's husband, Sergeant Darcy Gibbs, was killed by the Apaches, and Vina had taken her children to live in New York City. That, she admitted later, was the worst mistake she ever made. Augustus Sharps arrived in New York in 1899, while performing with Buffalo Bill Cody's Wild West Show, and told her children and grandchildren about all the contributions made to the west by Colored soldiers. Augustus's stories made her want to return to Arizona, although Theresa was the only one of her children who wanted to accompany her.

Selona paid for the trip, built Vina a house, and she was again a woman of the west.

Now she watched Theresa and listened as David, who had assumed his father's mantle as family historian, told his sons about how the west was won.

Sitting nearby was Selona, Augustus, and Adrian, gathering together for a farewell dinner on the eve of Adrian and David's departure for officers training.

"Most folks think it was gold that brought settlers to the west, but that isn't true. First there were the fur trappers, discovering the land and making friendships with the Indians. Then the government sent surveyors, who mapped out the west, giving the government an idea: to build a great nation.

"Problem was, there wasn't many people to fill all that open space, and how do the people get to where the land is waiting? That's when the government decided to build a railroad, and go over to Europe and tell poor farmers there was free land for the taking in the American west.

"That caused another problem: What about the Indians?

"That's how Colored soldiers came to the west. Your granddaddies were two of the first Colored soldiers on the frontier. Your grandmothers were two of the first Colored women on the frontier.

"The farther west the railroad went, the more hostile the Indians became, and more forts were built until soldiers were everywhere. Finally, the Indians were killed or driven onto reservations, and the immigrants from Europe owned most of the land."

Selona sat shaking her head, then looked at Augustus and said, "I swear, Augustus, he's worse about remindering than you are."

"Nothing wrong with that." Augustus eyed David warily. "Only trouble is, he makes us sound like a bunch of thieves and the Injuns a bunch of victims."

Selona nodded to that notion. "I guess that's the truth."

Augustus's eyes narrowed. "What are you talking about?"

"We stole their land and killed most of them off and put the rest on reservations. Just like he said."

"It wasn't that cruel."

"I reckon it *was* cruel. Now our sons are going to Germany to fight for white folks' freedom and they don't even have freedom in this country." She adjusted her hairpiece, knowing the battle was now joined.

Adrian chuckled. David grinned. Theresa and Vina started laughing in the kitchen while the grandchildren sat watching wide-eyed as Selona used her husband as a whetstone to sharpen her tongue.

Augustus stood slowly, then walked to the hearth. Over the mantle, on two wooden pegs driven into the wall, hung the sabre that had been issued to Sergeant Darcy Gibbs in 1866 when he had joined the 10th Cavalry at Fort Leavenworth, Kansas.

He reached up and affectionately touched the hilt of the sabre, then ran his fingers along the scabbard. Then he turned and glared at Selona.

"We were soldiers," he said, his words coming deliberately. "We were soldiers protecting a nation. Protecting a way of life. That's why Adrian and David are going to the army. Why, them Germans even planned to get the Mexicans to join them and start a ruckus right here in the southwest so we couldn't fight in Europe."

British intelligence had intercepted a plan in which the German government would finance and supply the Mexican government in exchange for military action against the United States. The Germans promised that in return, Mexico would receive Texas, New Mexico, Arizona, and southern California once the United States had been defeated. The Mexicans wanted no part of the German proposal—called the Zimmerman Plan—but the die had been cast for war with Germany.

Selona laughed. "Texas! Who would want Texas? And New Mexico ain't much better."

"What about Arizona? What about our land?"

"What about Arizona? The Mexicans backed down. What we need is for Mr. Wilson to tell the French government we ain't going to war with the Germans."

Augustus stared incredulously at Selona. "We would look foolish in the eyes of the world."

"I don't mind looking foolish." She touched her hairpiece. "I've looked foolish most all my life. It's better for my babies to look foolish than to go and get killed on the other side of the world."

She sat back, waiting, knowing what she would hear from her husband.

"Woman, you must be crazy! You know when the bugle—"

Selona jumped straight out of her chair and wagged a finger at him. "There you go with that bugle. I knew I was going to hear about that bugle before the night was over."

Augustus bit his tongue, knowing he'd walked into her trap.

"You and that bugle has got a whole lot of young men killed in the last fifty years. Now that bugle's going to sound again and kill a whole lot more. Only now it's going to be for the freedom of people who don't even live on this side of the world."

Augustus said nothing as he walked out of the house.

Adrian was the first to break the silence. "You had no right to talk to him like that, Momma." He stood and left the house.

David stood, looked sternly at his mother, then walked out without a word.

Vina and Theresa came into the sitting room and sat with Selona, in silence at first. Then Vina began talking.

"Augustus Sharps is the finest thing that's ever happened to you, Selona. What I heard you say to him made me ashamed for you."

"I'm not ashamed," Selona snapped. "I'm scared."

Theresa said, "I'm scared too, Miss Selona. But my man wants to be an officer. Just a few weeks ago he was told he couldn't even be a soldier in this country's army. We've sat and talked about this a great deal since he made his application, and I know how important it is to him. He knows how important that is to our people, and I don't just mean Coloreds. I mean all Americans."

Selona set her jaw in defiance. "America don't care about the Coloreds. Only Coloreds care about Coloreds."

"You may be right. But men like my father and your father, your husband, and your sons have done so much to show the white people of this country what Coloreds can do. A whole lot of white boys are going to die in that war, Miss Selona. A lot more than Coloreds."

"Why do my sons have to go? They went to that war in Cuba. Once is enough."

Theresa said, "I asked Adrian about that. He said, 'I've been in combat. I know how a young man must act to become a fighting soldier. They will need someone to help steady them until they know they can steady themselves. I know more will come back alive if I'm there.' "

Selona harrumphed. "He sure thinks highly of himself."

"No, Miss Selona. I think it's you who thinks too highly of herself. You act like you're the only one that stands to lose her sons."

Theresa stood and left the house and walked to a tall cottonwood, where she knew David would be talking with his father and brother.

As she approached, Augustus apologized to her. "I'm sorry, Theresa. Selona's been acting strangely ever since this war started."

"I understand how she feels. I stand to lose something important, too." Theresa looked at Augustus. "You don't know what it's like to have your loved ones off fighting a war. You and my daddy was always off fighting, and I remember as a little girl how Momma and Miss Selona used to die a little every time a dispatch rider came into the fort with a report from a campaign. I remember my momma crying when my poppa was killed by the Apaches. You know, she cried every night when we lived in New York City. She never got over losing my poppa. At least in Cuba, you had Adrian and David close by and could see each other once in a while. My momma and Selona did nothing but wait— and that's the hardest part about war."

Theresa turned and walked quickly back to the house.

Augustus turned to David and said, "It looks like you and I married fine women."

Later that night, Theresa was standing in front of her father's grave when David walked into the cemetery. Above the gate, gleaming in the moonlight, two cavalry sabres had been welded at the center, and hung suspended from an archway.

David stood beside Theresa and looked at the headstone. "What I remember most about him was his laughter."

Theresa smiled. "He sure did love to laugh."

David told her, "Pop said he was laughing when that Apache bullet hit him in the chest."

She nestled against his body. Then they walked through the gate and into the house.

The next morning all the families rose early, had breakfast at Selona's, and then began the painful—and uncomfortable—task of readying for the journey.

Augustus had decided he would not accompany his sons to the train depot in Willcox, Arizona.

After breakfast, their horses saddled, the sons of Sergeant Major Augustus and Selona Sharps mounted. Adrian had his father's sabre tied to the saddle. Theresa reached up and pulled David's face to hers, and kissed him gently on the cheek.

Vina suddenly said, "Wait. There's something I have to do." She hurried to her house, leaving everyone dumbfounded. She returned a few minutes later and walked to David's horse. There was nothing but silence as she said, "Darcy would want you to take this with you. For him."

David reached down and took the cavalry sabre of Sergeant Darcy Gibbs.

Augustus said nothing as he walked in silence to the stable.

Without a word, the two men wheeled their horses and trotted off; momentarily, they were at a gallop, standing in the iron stirrups, and even from that distance, all could see the sabres were drawn, extended forward in a classic cavalry charge.

Then they were gone from sight, leaving only a trail of dust to mark their passage.

An hour later, Selona left the crying Theresa at Vina's house and went home. Augustus was not there, so she went to the stable.

As she started to open the door she suddenly stopped, hearing Augustus's voice: a soft voice, unlike his normal, deep baritone. Carefully, she eased the door open, and through the crack she saw her man on his knees, his hands joined, tears streaking down his face. She carefully closed the door, and with tear-filled eyes ran to the house.

Inside, she fell on her bed and wept, and realized it was the first time she had ever seen Augustus pray as she had prayed for him so many times before.

5

When Adrian and David boarded the Colored-only passenger car in Willcox, Arizona, they were the only passengers. During the journey that took them to Bent Fork, Colorado, then Denver, and east toward Kansas City, the Colored population increased, especially in Kansas, where so many descendants of the buffalo soldiers lived. All along the line of the Kansas Pacific Railroad, which followed the Old Smoky River, the train stopped at depots where the 10th Cavalry had been posted for nearly a decade: Fort Wallace, Fort Dodge, Fort Riley.

On the fourth day of the journey they arrived in Kansas City, where they boarded another train that would take them to Iowa. This time there were five Colored-only passenger cars, and that was not enough to accommodate the more than sixteen hundred men traveling to the 17th Provisional Training Center at Des Moines.

Adrian and David had both worn their cavalry hats and drew the stares of many of the officer candidates. The two realized something immediately: The Sharps brothers were nearly twenty years older than the average candidate.

And there was something else both men found intriguing: The Colored men in the passenger cars whiled away the time during the journey reading newspapers, books, writing letters, and engaging in rather complicated political discussion.

Adrian recalled the Rough Riders, where there were so many educated Easterners, compared with the mostly illiterate Westerners.

David recalled the 9th Cavalry, where only a handful could read and write.

Now they sat among men younger than them. Men better educated, and for the first time in their lives, each felt somewhat intimidated.

The man and woman sitting across from Adrian and David were a handsome couple, although the man had a peculiar appearance.

Joseph Harwood leaned over and put out his hand. "Are you gentlemen going to Fort Des Moines?"

Adrian shook hands, saying, "Yes, we are. How about you?"

Harwood grinned. "I certainly am." Then he introduced Alice and said, "May I ask where you gentlemen went to college?"

Adrian shrugged. "San Juan Hill."

Harwood looked dumbfounded. David explained, "We have never received formal education, other than primary and secondary schooling. We were both in the war with Spain. Adrian served with Teddy Roosevelt's Rough Riders. I served with the Ninth Cavalry. As a matter of fact, our father is a retired regimental sergeant major of the Tenth Cavalry. So we grew up in army forts from Texas to Arizona. You might say we've been in the army most of our lives."

Harwood was astonished. "The Rough Riders! You were a Rough Rider? I didn't know they had Colored men in the Rough Riders."

Adrian nodded. "There were several Coloreds in the regiment, most of us experienced at scouting and tracking."

"What about San Juan Hill?" Alice asked. "What was it like to charge up that hill?"

Adrian laughed. "The only one riding a horse up that hill was Colonel Teddy." Adrian paused momentarily, then remembered something from that day. "The colonel had three pairs of his spectacles shot off his face, had a bullet wound in his elbow, but he kept waving us forward with his pistol. The pistol belonged to a young naval officer killed in the sinking of the *Maine*. Colonel Teddy received the pistol from the officer's father with the understanding that the weapon would be used against the Spanish."

Harwood thought this incredible; his wife found it fascinating. "You are from the west? The real west, with cowboys and Indians?"

"Yes, ma'am. We're from Arizona," Adrian replied. "But most of the Indians are gone now. There hasn't been a ruckus in Arizona since my father helped capture Geronimo."

"Geronimo!" Harwood breathed. "Your father fought against Geronimo?"

"He certainly did. He was wounded by an Apache warrior. Him and the Tenth even fought in Texas against another Apache named Victorio."

Harwood could only stare in astonishment. By now the noise and conversation in the passenger car had ended; an air of calm hung over it as all the young men listened to Adrian and David Sharps.

"Come on, now. Tell us more," Harwood said.

The brothers began to feel embarrassed; never in their lives had they spoken so much about themselves. "Did any of you ever see Buffalo Bill's Wild West Show?" asked Adrian.

There was a resounding "Yes!" as he continued. "My father was the standard bearer for the Tenth Cavalry in the
Congress of Rough Riders. Shortly afterwards, we joined
the Congress as standard bearers and riders. We were the
only Colored father-and-son performers in the history of the
show."

"What's Buffalo Bill Cody like?" one young man asked.

David answered, "He's a real gentleman. He and my father met in Kansas after my father had been a captive of the
Kiowa. He was a captive for two years, then was sold to a
buffalo hunter. He was rescued by the Tenth Cavalry, then
joined the army. His slave name had been Talbot, but he
changed the name to Sharps, for the buffalo gun he carried.
Why, he even outshot Buffalo Bill back in 1869. That's how
they first met. Colonel Custer called for a shooting match
between the Seventh and the Tenth, and my father shot for
the Tenth. He thought he was going to be shooting against
Wild Bill Hickok, but Custer brought in Buffalo Bill."

"How far did they shoot from?" Harwood asked.

"Started at six hundred yards, then worked back to one
thousand yards."

"One thousand yards!" Harwood shook his head. "I
can't even *see* one thousand yards."

"What about your mother?" asked Alice.

The brothers chuckled. "She and our father married after
her father was killed by the Kiowa in Oklahoma. She was
a laundress for the army."

"She sounds like a remarkable woman," said Alice.

David grinned and continued. "She was raised in an army
tent, and was scalped by drunken Texas Rangers when she
was seventeen. She even shot a bank robber off his horse in
Arizona, and started her own restaurant and laundry service. Yes, ma'am, she is quite remarkable."

"You said your mother was scalped?" Alice said with a
gulp.

"Scalped clean to the bone. She wouldn't show her face

around people until my father made her a hairpiece from a buffalo robe. Even then she wouldn't come out in public, so her grandmother set the tent on fire, burned it to the ground and brought my mother outside. She's never shown embarrassment since that day."

The conversation continued, with the younger men enthralled by the tales told by these two men wearing weathered cavalry hats.

Harwood noticed the Sharps brothers' valises. "May I ask what those are?"

Adrian and David removed their sabers from the tie on the valise handles. "This belonged to my father," said Adrian. He held up the sabre for the others to see.

David held up his sabre to Alice. "This belonged to my wife's father. He served with my father and was killed in an attack by Geronimo in 1885."

Harwood slowly pulled the blade from the scabbard; his eyes roamed over every inch of the weapon. "What will it be like, Adrian?"

"The training?"

Harwood shook his head. "The fighting."

Adrian looked thoughtfully at Alice, who appeared not to want to hear the answer. "In Cuba there was mostly confusion, before and during the battle. But you'll get used to that by the time training is complete."

"I want to be a good officer," Harwood said, as he handed back the sabre.

"You will," said Adrian.

6

The first time he saw Fort Des Moines, Adrian Sharps was reminded of the training center for the 1st Volunteer Cavalry when it gathered in San Antonio in 1898.

In Des Moines, trains filled with young officer candidates arrived throughout the day and night. The initial quarters for the men were hot, stifling tents.

The first of the many long lines Adrian and David would stand in for hours covered administrative details, with each man's papers and orders verified for authenticity. Then came the line for medical examinations, followed by the last, that for issuing uniforms and equipment.

The fact that the United States had not been properly prepared to go to war could not have been more clear than in the issue of uniforms and underwear.

A white corporal quickly assessed Adrian's size, then plopped a pile of uniforms onto his outstretched arms.

"Here you go, Pop."

Adrian pressed the material against his face. The material was a heavy wool.

"These are winter uniforms, Corporal."

The man shrugged. "That's all we got. Now move on down the line."

At the next station Adrian received socks and underwear, all heavy wool.

At their assigned billet stood a sergeant of infantry who began their military training by demonstrating the proper way for each man to store his equipment in the wall locker and properly dress in his uniform.

The dressing was simple enough, as socks and drawers were pulled on, then the trousers and blouses, and finally the hobnailed boots and the scourge of the doughboy soldier, the puttees.

Sergeant Stephan Kozak had served with General John J. "Blackjack" Pershing, in 1916 the commander of the American expeditionary force into Mexico pursuing the notorious bandit Pancho Villa. After nine frustrating months, and having never layed eyes on Villa, the expedition returned to the United States. Kozak was assigned to the 25th Infantry at Houston, Texas. He had experience with Colored soldiers and little respect for their abilities, especially when it came to leadership.

He was a tall, skinny southerner with harsh blue eyes, hay-colored hair, a bushy mustache, and a perpetual sneer, as if he had spent a lifetime taking orders from lesser men. Kozak took particular delight in making the training as torturous as possible.

Kozak demonstrated putting on the puttee by winding the cloth around his leg from the top of his ankle to just beneath the knee. This prevented the baggy trousers from tangling on barbed wire and thick brush.

"You wrap it too loose, the puttee will come undone," he said. "You wrap it too tight and it will cut off the blood flow in your legs. So do it right."

He had the men put that final touch to their uniforms and marched them in loose formation to the mess hall. "Chow" consisted of dried beef, hardtack, molasses, and coffee.

Adrian looked at the plate in front of him, and David noticed a slight fracture in his brother's normally unruffled demeanor.

"Not as good as Momma's cooking, but we've had worse."

Harwood sat beside them and shook his head. "I doubt anything could be worse than this. Now I see why it's called 'mess.'"

"Ten-hut!" someone shouted, and the candidates dropped their forks and stood quickly, their eyes frozen to the front.

Major Daniel Graves stood at the door of the mess hall, flanked by a sergeant-major and a sergeant. Graves was short, and wore riding breeches and tall boots; his campaign hat drooped over his forehead. Steel-blue eyes were hooded in dark recesses.

He slowly walked along the aisle, studying the candidates, stopping once to touch his riding crop against a soldier's tunic. "Button it, soldier."

At the table where the Sharps brothers stood, Graves looked at David in a peculiar way.

"You're a little old to be in the army, aren't you, soldier?"

David smiled. "I'm the same age as you when you had your first command with the Ninth Cavalry at Las Guasimas, El Caney, and San Juan Hill."

The officer stared hard at David, but while he couldn't quite recall the face, he did recall his first command after graduating from West Point in '95.

"You were my company commander in the Ninth. I'm David Sharps."

A smile slowly threaded across Graves's mouth. "My God. Trooper Sharps!"

The major extended his hand. For most of the young Colored officer candidates, it was the first time they had ever seen a white man offer his hand to a Colored man.

"How is your father, the sergeant major?"

"He's retired now, sir. He and my mother have a small ranch near Fort Grant. But I think he'd rather be getting into this ruckus."

Graves nodded. "I'm sure he would. Please give him my regards the next time you write."

"I will."

"Sir, may I present to you my brother, Candidate Adrian Sharps? He served with Colonel Roosevelt's First Volunteer Cavalry in Cuba."

Graves shook hands with Adrian. "That was some day at San Juan, wasn't it, Candidate Sharps?"

"Yes, sir. Quite a day. If it hadn't been for the Ninth and Tenth tearing through all that barbed wire and knocking out all those Spanish positions, we would have been slaughtered."

The major looked pleased as he nodded. "Not too many people are aware of that fact, Candidate Sharps."

He moved on, then turned to the sergeant major. "Make certain these two men are appointed platoon leaders."

The house where Alice Harwood boarded was drab and dreary, certainly not an ideal place to bring her child into the world. But it would have to do, she thought, as she walked downstairs for the noon meal.

Coretta Dobkins was not a woman to run lean when it came to the meals she prepared for her boarders. A former slave, she knew hunger, especially as a child in Louisiana during the Civil War. She had only one rule: Eat as much as you want—but don't waste. The tenants soon learned she practiced what she preached. She saved leftovers in the evening.

Coretta had opened her boardinghouse a year before to accommodate young women working in the packing plants that had cropped up in the Des Moines area since the be-

ginning of the war in Europe. She was sixty-eight, short, rotund, with broad facial features, and enjoyed good health
with the exception of an occasional attack of gout. She
doted on her tenants, all of whom were women, and provided a sitting room where they could entertain friends.

Her baby had dropped and Alice moved slowly and carefully, as though carrying a tray laden with priceless crystal.
Coretta didn't mind her boarding house being a way station
for a woman in need, but having a newborn in residence
could tax the patience of the other tenants. So, she had
agreed to accept Alice as a tenant with the provision that
once her baby was born and Alice on her feet, she would
find other accommodations.

Coretta watched Alice slowly seat herself, then leaned
over and whispered, "That baby's going to be here by sun-
down."

Alice stiffened at the thought. Joseph was at the fort and
would not be allowed off the grounds until Sunday. She
didn't know if the baby would wait that long.

"We're going to try and wait for his daddy."

Coretta's eyes widened. "*His* daddy? What makes you
think it's going to be a boy?"

Alice smiled. "He kicks like a mule . . . just like his
daddy."

The women at the table laughed and Alice felt better for
the moment.

"Well, if *he* does come today, I'll fetch Dr. Champeau.
He's not much more than a horse doctor, but he does know
how to deliver a baby in a proper fashion."

What worried Alice was finding another place to live.
Coretta's boardinghouse was by far the most comfortable
she had seen of dozens of such houses that had sprung up
near the fort, all filled with wives and children of the Colored officer candidates.

There would be no chance of families living together
until the candidates had received a commission and post-

ing. This philosophy followed the military adage that "If the army had wanted a soldier to have a family, the soldier would have been issued one."

Alice finished eating, then started up the stairs. She had taken only a few steps when there was a sharp sting in her womb, then a rushing of water that flowed down her leg. She doubled and nearly fell, but was caught by Coretta, who followed behind like a mother hen.

"Get Dr. Champeau," Coretta said firmly to one of the women.

Coretta led Alice to her room and sat her on the bed and began to undress her.

"Can you call my husband?"

"Don't you worry," Coretta said. "I'll let him know. But let's get this baby into the world first. Your man won't be able to leave the fort, so you might as well leave off from worrying him."

Alice lay quiet, the pain moving sharply through her body. She whimpered with the first, but by the time the third had passed she had begun to prepare herself mentally for the ordeal.

Wave upon wave followed as the day drifted by. By nightfall, the doctor still had not arrived, and the moans had turned into shrill screams.

"That's right, baby, you go on ahead and scream," Coretta said. "If there's a time a woman has the right to scream, it's birthing a child."

A slight breeze drifted in from the north, carrying Alice's agony into the thick summer night.

Then, near midnight, the cry of a newborn baby echoed along the narrow street.

7

The end of the first week of training brought the much awaited Sunday pass, and the candidates, who had first entered the main gate of Fort Des Moines as civilians, now would pass through as soldiers.

For Joseph Harwood the first pass of his army enlistment meant more than a respite from training; it meant visiting his wife and newborn child.

Sweat streamed down Joseph's face as Adrian helped him close his collar button. Adrian stepped back and said, "Candidate Harwood, you look splendid."

"One last item and you might look like an officer and a gentleman," added David, who stepped forward with Joseph's highly polished Sam Browne belt. Harwood slipped his arm through the diagonal shoulder strap as David buckled the belt around his waist.

Harwood took his round campaign hat, straightened the braid above the brim, poked four fingers into the top, giving it a military look, placed it on his head, adjusted the rear leather strap so it fit tightly, and saluted the Sharps brothers. "Gentlemen, I'm ready to visit my family."

Adrian quickly glanced at David and saw the look of pain on his face.

The word "family" stung David's heart for a moment as he thought about Theresa and the children, but he quickly put them out of his mind. He had made his choice, and their absence from his life at the moment was a sad part of that choice.

Harwood also saw David's expression and said, "Come, my friends, let's enjoy this day together."

Adrian and David both shook their heads. "No, Joseph. You'll want to be alone with your family."

"Nonsense," Harwood countered. "If we're to be brothers in arms, we can be brothers in sharing our joys."

With Harwood tugging at their arms, they started for the barracks door.

At the motor pool, they loaded into a heavy transport truck and were shuttled into Des Moines over dirt farm roads filled with deep grooves from heavy travel. The soldiers didn't seem to mind the discomfort, for at least it meant that for a few hours they could feel the freedom away from the regimen of military life. Adrian and David had always been amazed at how hard men worked to become soldiers, yet there wasn't a single soldier known who didn't live and breathe for the moment when he would be freed from the constant discipline of the profession of arms.

Harwood couldn't think of anything pleasant at the moment. Instead, his mind zoomed to the thought that had plagued him since learning of Alice's pregnancy.

What would his son look like? Harwood's pink, splotchy skin had been the topic of many discussions with Alice. She told him it made no difference, but he knew better. Growing up, his mottled skin color had made him the subject of ridicule from both Colored and white. His size and strength had become his suit of armor against cruel and insensitive treatment from Colored people, who would only laugh behind his back. But whites would laugh openly at him, pointing their fingers, staring with amusement, knowing he would not strike out against them.

He would know soon if that same curse had fallen upon his child.

Coretta Dobkins opened the door, releasing the smell of sweet potato pie, baked ham, hot biscuits, and roasting corn, a tantalizing reminder to the Sharps brothers of their mother's cooking.

"Come in, gentlemen." Coretta motioned them inside.

The three stepped into the foyer and were greeted by a loud, demanding cry from the second floor.

Harwood's eyes widened, and before he could introduce himself to Coretta, he rushed past her, bounded up the stairs, and disappeared.

Coretta said, "I expect he's the new father."

Adrian grinned. "I expect you're right."

Harwood followed the cry to a room where three women stood at an open door. He pushed his big frame past the women without apology and found himself standing in front of a bed where Alice lay holding the baby to her breast.

She looked radiant, he thought as he approached speechlessly and kissed her on the forehead.

For Alice, it was the first time she had seen her husband in his uniform, and she swelled with pride. In such a short time she had become a soldier's wife, and the mother of a soldier's son.

Harwood knelt and stared at mother and child; Alice extended the child to him. "Would you like to hold your son?"

"No. I better not. I might hurt him."

"Go ahead." She laughed. "He only bites when I'm feeding him."

Almost painfully, Harwood took the bundle.

"He sure is light."

"That won't last. The way he eats, he'll soon be as big as you."

Harwood stood as the baby squirmed.

"I know what you're wondering," Alice said. "Look for yourself."

He opened the blanket and saw his son's face, then slowly peeled away the swaddling until the child was fully exposed.

He sighed, grinning wildly as a tension-relieving shudder coursed through him.

"My boy is perfect," he said to Alice. "Perfect."

8

While the foundation for the preacher's trade lies within the covers of the Bible, the soldier's foundation lies within the *Manual of Arms*. The manual dictates how the soldier will talk, eat, sleep, dress, and walk, including how to march in formation, the process by which a soldier learns discipline and untrained men are forged into a cohesive military unit. In Fort Des Moines, the individuals responsible for that formidable task were the noncommissioned officers assigned to the training platoons: men who were tough veterans of many years of service. And all of them were white.

Until now there had been only preliminary physical training and close order drill, but at the beginning of the second week, the easy work came to an abrupt halt.

At 1300 Kozak came into the tent of Adrian's platoon in A Company and ordered, "Fall out with your field packs and rifles."

Minutes later the men were assembled and, under the sergeants' orders, were marched to the edge of the fort.

Kozak pointed to a tall pile of rocks. "All right, you fu-

ture officers. Let's start separating the boys from the girls."
He paused, then said with delight, "Fill your packs with
these here rocks. We're going for a stroll in the countryside."

Packs were filled and hoisted onto each man's back,
where the straps cut into shoulders and the lumpy packs
scraped against spines. Kozak mounted a horse and motioned the platoon forward, and beneath a blistering Iowa
sun the candidates moved out in two long lines.

The men marched in silent route step along a dirt road that
seemed to have no end. Sweat ran down their faces, stinging their eyes, while the sun baked their lips. But none com-
plained, even when they stepped into manure droppings
from Kozak's horse.

When the platoon reached a small stream, the surly
sergeant ordered the men to halt.

"You get twenty minutes of rest, then we return to the
fort. Do not remove your packs. Anyone that removes his
pack will not receive a weekend pass. Is that understood?"

A low mumble rose from the two columns, then the men
spread out and found shelter from the sun beneath trees lining the creek.

Adrian slumped beside Harwood, who took out his canteen and took a long pull on it. "Don't drink too much. Your
stomach will cramp up," Adrian said.

Harwood poured water over his head, then leaned back
and loosened the straps on his pack.

"My shoulders feel like they're dislocated."

Adrian loosened his pack straps and felt the numbness in
his feet and legs. He stood and called to the candidates,
"Men, if your feet are numb, loosen your puttees and the
laces in your boots, but don't take off your boots. Your feet
will swell and you won't be able to get them back on."

The twenty minutes passed quickly. Kozak remounted his

horse and shouted to the candidates, "I'm riding back to the fort. Remember, any one of you who falls out of this march will be disqualified from further training. The same goes for any one of you who empties the rocks from his pack. I'll see you at the rock pile, and your packs better be filled."

The sergeant spurred his horse and rode off in a cloud of dust. The men stared after him for a long moment, as though not certain of what to do. Adrian could see a few at the point of quitting as he walked among them, saying, "On your feet, men. Tighten the straps on your packs and sling your rifles. You want to be officers, but first you have to be infantry soldiers. An infantryman marches . . . or he dies. It's as simple as that. You won't be able to quit in France, and I won't let you quit in Iowa. So get on your feet!"

The men struggled up, and Adrian and Harwood checked each man's pack.

"Take a good drink of water," Adrian shouted, "then empty the remaining water into your campaign hats. The less weight you carry, the farther you can march. You can go without water until we reach the fort."

The men followed the order. Adrian kept his canteen full in case of an emergency.

When the men were ready, Adrian motioned them to follow. The two columns moved out in route step. Two hours later the column continued to trudge mechanically along the dirt road, the men exhausted and near collapse.

Harwood turned and looked back on the men, then stepped beside Adrian. "They're exhausted; should we take a break?"

Adrian shook his head. "If we stop, some won't be able to get started again and they'll wash out. That's what Kozak wants. I intend to deny him that if I have to carry these men to the fort on my back."

"You may have to. Look at Wilson."

Carl Wilson, a former law student from Howard University and the smallest man in the platoon, walked stooped forward, with an occasional stumble that nearly caused him to trip the man in front of him.

Adrian stepped to the center of the road, looking into each man's face as he passed. Most were handling the fatigue and would finish the march, but he doubted Wilson would make it another mile.

Adrian fell in beside Wilson and removed his canteen without breaking his pace. "Take a drink, then slip off your pack and give it to me," he said.

Wilson took a drink but refused to take off his pack. "I can carry my weight, Candidate Sharps."

Adrian chuckled. "You want to carry mine for me?"

Wilson laughed weakly. "I'm not going to fail. I'm not going to let Kozak win. You know he doesn't like Coloreds, and that's fine by me. But I'm not going to quit. Not while I can still breathe."

At that moment Wilson stumbled and went crashing to the dirt road. Adrian pulled off the man's pack while motioning for Harwood. "Give me your rifle, Candidate Wilson."

Adrian took the wooden rifle and ran it through the pack straps, then nodded at Harwood, who picked up the barrel end of the rifle as Adrian picked up the butt. Together the two men hoisted the pack and walked in unison in single file, with Adrian at the lead.

They were surrounded by silence, except for the occasional grunt or groan, and the slap of the heavy boots tramping along the dirt road.

An hour later Wilson recovered his pack and fell back in the column, and appeared repaired enough in strength to finish the march under his own power.

The column reached the rock pile, where Sergeant Kozak waited with Major Graves.

Kozak's face was clouded with anger as he saw the men approaching.

Adrian saluted Major Graves. "First platoon, A Company, all present, sir."

9

As the sun rose over the Arizona desert near the ranch, Augustus and Selona took their morning ride. In the distance lay Mount Graham, wreathed in clouds, where Selona's friend Marcia O'Kelly had died in an avalanche while taking Adrian and David on a hike over the mountain in 1885.

Augustus watched her stare long at the mountain and knew what she was thinking. "They'll be all right."

She dabbed at her eyes. "I don't know. You and the boys have had so many close calls with death, it seems only natural that one day the account's going to come due on one of you."

He did not answer and patted his horse on the neck. A thin sheen of dust sprayed from the horses' hooves as they rode side by side.

Selona looked at his saddle, the McClellan he had used for so many years. Then she realized for the first time that something important was missing.

"You look naked without that old, dented sabre strapped onto that saddle."

Augustus looked straight ahead, nudged his horse forward. "I'll be getting it back one day."

The two rode west, then disappeared into a deep ravine as the sun continued its easy glide across the desert.

Later that afternoon, Selona sat on the front porch of her house with Theresa, who was reading the latest edition of the *Pittsburgh Courier,* a national Colored publication.

What she read infuriated her. "It says here that Colored soldiers are being lynched and burned all over America."

"Why does that surprise you?" asked Selona. "Colored soldiers have been targets for white meanness ever since they put on the uniform. White folks don't want to see disciplined Colored men in uniform. It scares them."

"It frightens me," Theresa said as she put down the newspaper and pulled a letter from the pocket of her dress.

Selona eyed Theresa cautiously, remembering that she had brought the letter that afternoon from the post office.

"What does David have to say?"

Theresa looked at the unopened letter. "I'll read it tonight. Before I go to bed."

There was mischief in Selona's eyes. "Can I read it, then? I'm his mother."

Theresa smiled. "I think it's best I read it first."

She took the letter and walked off toward the stand of cottonwoods. Selona watched her read the letter several times before returning to the porch. Theresa took a single page of the letter, folded it, and tucked it into her pocket. On the porch, she gave the letter to Selona.

Selona noticed the last page was missing. "What about the last page?"

"There's some things said private between a man and his woman that even his momma don't have the right to read."

Selona cackled as Theresa walked back to the cottonwoods, taking out the page and reading it again.

*   *   *

That evening Selona and Augustus were sitting on the front porch watching the sun set when Theresa approached, sat down in a rocker beside them, and, with a voice filled with apprehension, said, "I'm going to Fort Des Moines. I might not see him except on Sunday, but at least I'll have that."

Selona laughed. "I've been expecting as much. I followed his father all over God's creation. Why should you be any different than I was?"

"Then you understand?"

"I expect telling me or your mother that you're going . . . is the most understood thing in the world to us. When do you plan on leaving?"

"Tomorrow, if Augustus will drive me to the train in Willcox."

Augustus said, "A woman ought to be with her man. We can leave at daylight."

"I'll need to borrow a little money from you, for train fare, if that's all right."

"Whatever you need," Selona replied.

Theresa leaned over and kissed Selona lightly on the forehead and walked to her mother's house.

Selona said nothing, wiped at a single tear, and in her heart cursed a world gone crazy, a world that was spreading her family from Arizona to Iowa, and would soon spread it across the world.

"At least they'll be together for a bit," she said softly. "That's more than most get to enjoy in these times."

She sat unmoving until well after midnight, her thoughts traveling from Kansas to Texas to Arizona.

Augustus rose before sunrise to the aroma of Selona's cooking drifting into the bedroom. He hopped on his one good leg for the chair where he always propped his artificial leg, when he stumbled and crashed to the floor. He sat up bewildered, then saw the heavy leather trunk Selona had bought when she joined him with Buffalo Bill Cody's Wild West Show in 1899.

Without putting on the leg, he hopped to the kitchen and stood in the door frame. He couldn't believe what he was seeing.

"What are you doing, woman? You've got enough food there to feed a regiment."

Selona paused, wiped at her forehead, then said firmly, "Not a regiment, just family."

She stood at the stove, preparing chicken the way she had learned from her grandmother—floured, then fried lightly in butter, then baked to a golden brown in her Dutch oven. On the table was a huge plate piled with baked chicken; nearby sat another plate with a mountain of thick buttermilk biscuits.

Augustus realized she must have been up all night cooking.

"Why so much food?" he asked, slipping his suspenders over his shoulders.

"We'll need a lot of food for the trip."

"We?"

She lay down her fork and looked at him. "I'm going with them."

"Them?"

"Theresa and the children. We talked again and we think the children should go with her. That means she'll need help on the trip."

"The hell you say."

"The hell I do say." She turned over a chicken breast in the sizzling pan, then removed the skillet from the stove.

"You can't go to Iowa."

"You'll think different when you see me climb into that buggy with my family."

Augustus was stunned. "What about me?"

She looked at him with mischief in her eyes. "What about you, Augustus?"

It took him a moment, then he caught her meaning. "You want me to go with you!"

She stepped close and put her arms around his waist. "It'll give us time together, honey. Time we might never have again with our children. Besides, you been wanting to go to Kentucky and look at them blueblood hosses you been talking about for twenty years." She paused, then asked curiously, "Is Kentucky near Iowa?"

He mentally measured the distance. "I'd say about four hundred miles."

"There. You see, Kentucky's just a short ride for an old hoss cavalryman like you."

The thought was absurd, of course. "I'm too old to ride a horse to Kentucky."

"Then take the train, or walk, but I'm going to Iowa."

"Where will you live?"

"In a house, of course. I'm sure if there's Coloreds in Fort Des Moines, there'll be houses for Coloreds. If not, I'll get me a tent, the way I lived until we got married." She smiled as she reflected. "You remember that old tent we lived in after we got married. Lord, the times we had in that tent."

Augustus grinned. "Those were some times. But we was young then."

She laughed a girlish laugh. "Maybe we'll be young again."

Augustus turned and started to leave.

"Where are you going?"

He shrugged in defeat. "To get my leg. Then I'll get my Sharps and McClellan."

"Why you want that old rifle and saddle?"

"If we're going to an army fort, I might be able to show those young boys how to shoot. And if I'm going to ride a horse to Kentucky, I want my tired old bones in a saddle that ain't no stranger to my fanny."

Selona raced into his arms with such excitement, Augustus's leg gave way, sending them both crashing to the floor. They lay there giggling, then Selona kissed him on the cheek. "You are a surprising man, Sergeant Major Augustus Sharps."

He grinned. "I wonder who I got that from."

The caravan of two buckboards loaded with trunks, valises—and enough food to feed the five members of the Sharps family for a week—pulled away from the ranch at midday.

Vina Gibbs remained behind to look after the ranch and assume Selona's responsibilities at the laundry and restaurant.

In Bonita, Selona went to the bank and withdrew enough funds for train fare and expenses for the entire family; she also received a letter of introduction from the bank president and a bank draft for funds that would be needed for living expenses once they reached Fort Des Moines.

The caravan arrived at Willcox, the closest train depot, just after midnight, where the Sharpses shared a single room in a hotel.

The next morning, the family boarded the Colored-only passenger car and began the long journey to Iowa.

It was July 1, 1917, and while the sky was clear, the mood ebullient, they did not know that they were moving toward a tempest boiling on the banks of the Mississippi River.

10

"There is no freedom for Colored people in East St. Louis this Independence Day," warned Reverend Ezekiel Johns, the pastor of the Jody Town Holiness Church. He was a small man with a thin mustache and sad eyes, and now his voice was low, not high-pitched and filled with its normal fervor. "There is only fear and hatred."

Hannah Simmons sat in the front pew, watching the small man wipe at the sweat streaming from his forehead. Behind her, a dozen members sat huddled in terror.

"We all have to leave, and we must leave now," Johns said. "Pack what belongings you can carry and get across the Mississippi. That's our only hope."

A large woman holding a baby stood up in the back pew, her voice trembling as she asked, "Why are the white folks doing this to us Coloreds, Reverend Johns?"

Johns shook his head sadly. "Because they don't want us here. You folks are willing to work for cheaper wages than white folks. I can't make it no plainer than that."

A younger man stood and shouted angrily, "A two-year-old baby was shot and thrown into the doorway of a burning building. What kind of people would do something like that?"

"Four Colored men were hanged from the Mississippi River bridge last night," said another voice.

"They gonna kill us all!" one woman shouted hysterically.

"They done killed more than forty Coloreds," said another.

Johns raised his hands to calm the congregation. "You all know what the white folks said, that a Colored man attacked a white woman in an elevator a few days ago. The sheriff said last night a Colored man shot at his deputies. But we all know that ain't the truth. There's only one truth: We got to get out of this town."

Hannah had joined the other members of the congregation in the only haven of safety they knew. The streets were filled with gangs of white men burning, beating, lynching Colored people wherever they could be found.

Johns leaned over the pulpit and pleaded, "Please, go. All of you get out of this town."

Before there was another word, an angry shout was heard from beyond the door.

"Get rid of the niggers! Then our women will be safe."

Johns's eyes widened as he heard the sound of pounding on the door. He hurried down the aisle and pulled back a drape at a window. The glow of torches lit up the outside night. "Good Lord. They've come to burn the church."

Hannah watched the thin man straighten his frock coat and turn, a look of sadness on his small face as he said softly, "Go out through the back window. I'll try to talk to them."

The congregation hurried to the rear of the church and began climbing through the window. Hannah was at the end of the line, and when she eased through the window, she looked back for one last glance at the preacher.

Johns smiled lightly, then cracked the door and walked outside to face the angry crowd.

Hannah watched the rest of the congregation hurry off into the darkness, but she slipped along the side of the building to an alley across the street. She hid behind a group of garbage cans where she could see Johns trying to talk to the crowd.

The furious voices of the angry white men drowned out his words, but she knew what was happening when the pastor suddenly bolted from the steps and began running.

The night filled with more shouts; she saw white men running, carrying torches, cursing, a mob that moved fast along the street in pursuit of Johns.

She heard a shot ring out, watched as Johns stumbled, veering slightly and heading straight for the alley. He fell at the alley entrance. Reverend Johns's eyes joined Hannah's, and she saw the man's terror.

She started toward him, but Johns shook his head. "Get back, child. Hide from them! They'll kill you, too!"

He struggled to his feet, dashed away, somehow finding the strength to run to the other side of the street with the mob in pursuit.

Hannah could only watch helplessly as the mob suddenly blocked the entrance to the alley.

Reverend Johns disappeared from sight, as her vision was blocked by men who were now filling the entrance to the alley.

She smelled the whiskey, heard the cursing, watched a white man come into the alley, unzip his fly, and relieve himself.

She saw the rope fly up and over a street pole, and could not stop the scream that burst from her throat.

The white man turned, saw her, and approached. "Well, now, girl. What you doing back here? Come and join the party."

Hannah heard Johns scream in pain, followed by harsh shouts and laughter as the man stalked her.

Her hand went to her pocket and she whipped out her knife. The moment he stepped within range she lunged, driving the knife into his stomach. Through the glow of the torch light she saw the man's face twist with agony and surprise; then he turned and, without a word, stumbled toward the street.

Hannah followed close behind, using the man's body as a shield, until she reached the street.

The band of white men were facing the lamppost, their backs to Hannah, when she reached the street.

She paused only once, when she saw Reverend Johns suddenly appear half naked above the men, the rope around his neck, rising upward slowly.

Johns's body kicked, twisted, jerked violently for several moments in the throes of death, then grew still above the laughing shouts.

Then, the white man stumbled and fell to the street, holding the hilt of the knife.

One of the men in the crowd saw him, then saw Hannah, and shouted, "Get her!"

Hannah ran with all her strength, not once looking back.

Mohammad Mostafavi had come to America from Egypt at the turn of the century in search of the dream of prosperity and freedom. He had arrived in New York aboard a freighter from Alexandria, where his wife and three children had died from cholera in 1899. He made his way west to St. Louis, and for many years worked on the barges plying the murky waters of the Mississippi until he saved enough money to buy his own lighter, a small barge used to transport goods from one side of the river to the other.

Mostafavi, in his fifties, heavyset with powerful arms, had prospered, remarried, and had two more children.

This was July 4, 1917, but he knew the red glow on the black eastern horizon was not from the annual Independence Day fireworks display.

Mostafavi tamped out his pipe as his first mate, Jack Collins, a thin, ferret-faced man, boarded with the manifest of the goods to be delivered in St. Louis.

"The cargo's loaded, Cap'n." Collins handed the manifest to Mostafavi, who glanced quickly to the hold of his boat. Loading had taken most of the day, not the usual two hours, since his Colored stevedores did not show up and Collins had had to scour the bars along the waterfront to find laborers not too drunk or running with the mobs.

"Good. Start the engines. I want to get out of this hateful place before someone burns my barge."

Collins looked at the Colt pistol Mostafavi had tucked into his belt, protection should the mobsters mistake his dark skin for that of a Colored.

Collins went aft and slipped the mooring line from the piling while Mostafavi went forward to do the same at the bow. The lines hit the water and Mostafavi was about to take the helm when he heard someone running along the pier. Through the darkness he could make out a lone figure running toward the boat.

Then there were shouts, and the flames from torches dancing through the night, carried by others running after the lone figure, who was drawing closer to the barge.

There was a gunshot, then another, and the figure stumbled but didn't fall, continued forward, fighting for balance.

The boat slid away from the pier and was nearly five feet from the pilings when the figure jumped, sailed through the air, and landed among the heavy bales of cotton being transported to St. Louis.

Mostafavi pulled his pistol and eased into the open hold, cocking the weapon as he kept the bales between himself and the intruder.

The shouting mob streamed to the edge of the pier; some of the men carried rifles, others handguns.

"Throw the nigger over!" a voice shouted.

"Stop or we'll shoot!" another demanded.

"That nigger killed a white man!" Another shout, filled with hatred.

Mostafavi crept along, moving from one bale to another. Shots were fired.

The lighter was backing away from the pier. Collins would turn her to head for the western shore. But before the turn could be made, Mostafavi looked back and saw Collins jump overboard and the barge begin to run back toward shore.

"Damn!" Mostafavi cursed, then started moving faster toward the helm. At one point he could see the scrawny Collins in the water, swimming desperately for the Illinois side.

Finally, with bullets raking the bales and the tiny shack constructed to protect the helm against foul weather, Mostafavi gripped the tiller and turned parallel to the bank. He glanced back to see the attackers running along the pier toward shore.

He grinned, and when the angry gang reached shore, he turned back toward the Illinois side of the river.

By the time they realized they had been outfoxed, Mostafavi and his lighter were out of rifle and pistol range.

He maintained course for ten minutes, then tied the tiller with a rope that held the lighter on course for the western shore, drew his pistol, and started again toward the bow.

With each step forward he could hear the breathing of the intruder.

Mostafavi cocked his pistol and said calmly, "Come out now. I won't harm you."

The figure stood, terror written on her face.

"Who are you?"

A trembling voice replied, "Hannah Simmons." She

stood, holding her hand to her left shoulder. In the moonlight, Mostafavi could see blood seeping through her fingers.

"Come here," he ordered.

She started forward, paused, looked at the pistol Mostafavi held, then begged, "Please don't shoot me."

Mostafavi lowered the pistol and smiled gently, saying, "I won't shoot you."

PART 2
THE GATHERING

11

✴ ✴ ✴

On July 10, Augustus Sharps stepped down from the Colored-only passenger car at the depot in Des Moines, carrying his Sharps rifle and McClellan saddle. He wore his cavalry hat, highly polished riding boots, and khaki riding breeches. On his blue coat the gold stripes and rockers of a sergeant major shone like a beacon.

"I don't know why you want to wear that old coat," Selona snapped, climbing down to the platform. Theresa and the children followed, carrying their luggage.

"Hush now. This is an army town. I'll fit right in."

She looked around. "I expect you best go find us a buggy and ask about how we get to the Colored part of town."

Augustus nodded and looked around. He saw a livery across the street and shoved his Sharps in the boot of the saddle, threw the McClellan over his shoulder, and started away from the depot.

At the livery he rented a buggy and two horses, and upon returning Selona asked, "What you need two hosses for? This buggy don't need but one."

"I might want to ride out to the fort. The man at the livery gave me directions. It's just a few miles out of town."

"How much did you pay for that hoss?"

"I didn't buy it. I rented it for a few days."

"First we got to find a place to live. Any idea where we might find us a house?" she asked.

Augustus was saddling the roan gelding, and paused to take a piece of paper from his pocket. "The man told me they have something called the Urban League."

"What's that?"

"It's an outfit that helps Coloreds get settled."

"I never heard of such a thing."

"We're not in the west anymore, Selona. There's lots of things we don't know about."

He hoisted the trunk into the rear of the buggy, helped Selona and Theresa board, then called to the children, "Let's go, boys."

Jonathan and Benjamin climbed into the back, and Selona took the reins and skipped them lightly off the horse's back. Augustus climbed onto his horse and rode at the front. He had ridden no more than a block when he realized that for the first time in his life, he was riding a horse in a modern city. Automobiles were everywhere, but the horses were accustomed to the contraptions and ignored them.

The streets were cobblestone and the *crack* of the horse's hooves reminded him of the sounds he heard while riding the hard ground of Arizona. Here, the clop of hooves on stone was pleasant compared with the overpowering noise in every direction. Horns blared, tires squealed, engines roared. This, he thought, would take some getting used to.

The office of the Urban League had been established to assist the needs of the many Coloreds working in the meat-packing plants that had cropped up in Des Moines since the beginning of the war in Europe. The director was a young man who eagerly helped the Sharpses find a four-bedroom furnished house they could rent on a monthly basis in the part of town that was exclusively Colored.

"Ain't much of a house," said Selona, who stared distastefully at the wood-frame structure.

"It'll do, Selona," said Augustus, hoisting the trunk from the buggy.

Augustus and the boys were carrying in the trunk when he heard Selona call his name. He followed her voice to the upstairs, where she stood at an open door.

"What in the world is this?" she asked.

He peered in and saw what looked like a small wooden seat with a hole in the center of the lid. He had seen one in Washington years ago.

"It's the toilet." He reached up and pulled a chain. The sound of water flushing brought a puzzled look to Selona's face.

"In the house?"

"Appears to be."

"How does it work?"

"You do your business, then pull the chain." He pointed to a tank overhead. "Water flushes everything into the ground beneath the house, into what's called a cistern."

"It don't seem civilized, a toilet inside the house."

He left and for the next fifteen minutes heard the monotonous flushing of the toilet and the loud giggle that followed each flush of water.

Selona and Theresa spent the rest of the morning setting up housekeeping while Augustus returned the buggy to the livery. When all was completed, Augustus took his Sharps and shoved it into the carbine boot of his saddle and mounted.

It was time to visit the fort and see his sons.

The ride to Fort Des Moines brought back a rush of memories. Augustus thought of his years of service on the plains of Kansas as a young trooper in the 1860s; he remembered being held captive by the Kiowa, freed by Trooper Darcy Gibbs and Sergeant Moss Liberty, Selona's father. He thought of Sergeant Major Roscoe Brassard, Lieutenant Colonel Jonathan Bernard O'Kelly, and his regimental commander, Colonel Benjamin Grierson, the finest soldier and man he had ever known.

The sentry at the main gate gaped in astonishment as Augustus rode up, as though something out of the past had come riding into the present, which was precisely the case.

Adrian Sharps was conducting close-order drill with his platoon when he saw his father walking his horse toward the reviewing platform, where Major Graves stood watching.

The moment Graves saw Augustus, he spoke quickly to a sergeant and walked with a swagger toward the buffalo soldier.

Augustus saluted and they shook hands. "My God, Sergeant Major Sharps. Don't tell me you've come to enlist."

They both laughed, then Augustus looked across the parade ground and saw David leading his platoon in close-order drill. He stood staring for a long moment, his eyes moving from Adrian to David.

"Come on, Sergeant Major. Let's have a drink. We'll join your sons on the rifle range in an hour."

In his office, Graves raised his glass. "To the cavalry."

Augustus downed the whiskey, then looked around the office. "Not much of a fort, is it, sir?"

Graves shook his head. "Not what we're used to, by God. But it'll have to do. We're trying to raise a million-man army and there isn't much time for luxuries."

"A million men. That don't seem possible."

"It's a fact. But the problem is equipment. Hell, these men don't even have weapons, except on the rifle range. They have to march carrying wooden rifles."

"I didn't realize equipment was in short supply."

"It is for a million soldiers."

"What about the Colored regiments?"

"The army is raising two Colored divisions, the Ninety-second and the Ninety-third. Most will come from National Guard units, except for one regiment of draftees. That's the 371st, at Camp Jackson, in South Carolina. And the Ninth, Tenth, Twenty-Fourth, and Twenty-Fifth regiments will be in the Ninety-second division. Even at that the units won't be joined into a division until they reach France. The plan is to organize the units here in the United States at separate forts, then ship them to France, where they'll receive their final training."

"Doesn't sound like a very good plan," Augustus said. "Fighting men need to feel a part of their unit if they're going to perform well in combat."

"I agree, but the powers that be see things differently."

There was a pause before Augustus said, "The powers that be don't want to see thousands of Colored troops formed in stateside divisions."

Graves poured them another drink. "I'd say you're right, Sergeant Major. The world has changed since the war with Spain. I doubt it'll ever be the same once this war is over."

Augustus downed the whiskey; it eased the ache in his leg, caused by the ride to the fort.

"Come on. Let's go to the rifle range," Graves said.

On the rifle range noncommissioned officers walked among the candidates, barking commands to load, aim, and fire. For most of the candidates it was their first experience at firing a rifle.

Augustus and Graves arrived to the sound of Kozak giving A company its orientation on the Springfield rifle. In his hand, Augustus carried his Sharps rifle.

"This is a Springfield rifle. We call it the .03, since it was designed in 1903 by the Springfield Arms Company. It's important that you understand that this is not called a gun, it's called a rifle or a weapon. It's also important for you to know that a soldier's weapon is as much a part of the soldier as his uniform. A rifle is a personal tool to a soldier, and like a soldier, each rifle has its own personality. Each rifle has its own feel, like that of a woman, or a handshake. Each sight will be slightly different. The weight will be different. You will begin your instruction by learning how to sight-in the rifle, keeping in mind that each time you fire on the line you will have to resight the rifle you are using for the day's training." Kozak pointed at a wooden rack where rifles were stacked. "Form a line and draw a weapon and report to the firing line."

Kozak approached Augustus and Graves. He looked disgusted. "I doubt any of them can hit their butts with both hands."

Augustus grinned, then said softly, "I'd wager you're wrong, Sergeant." He was watching Adrian and David walk to the firing line.

Kozak looked at Augustus. Graves said, "Sergeant Kozak, this is Sergeant Major Sharps."

Kozak nodded, then walked back to the firing line.

"The men really do need a personal weapon, Major."

Graves nodded in agreement. "If we had them, Sergeant Major, they'd be issued. The truth of the matter is, this country is not prepared to train for war, much less fight a war."

Augustus watched as Adrian and David knelt on the firing line while Kozak and other NCOs instructed each man in the loading and sighting of his weapon. He would fire three shots, adjust the sight, and fire until the sighting was fairly accurate.

Augustus was pleased as he watched Adrian and David compensate for the poor sight by using windage and elevation after firing their first round, the way he had taught them as youngsters. If the bullet struck high or low from the target, the elevation adjustment of the sighting was made up or down to the target. A shot to the right called for a windage adjustment, sighting to the right or left of the target.

Augustus asked Graves, "Mind if I join my boys?"

Graves smiled and motioned him forward.

Adrian had just fired his third round and knew where to aim for the fourth shot when he felt movement at his side. He didn't have to look to know it was his father, who knelt beside him, his Sharps cradled lightly in his arms.

The target was a hundred yards away, a silhouette of a man from the waist up. Each time a shot was fired, a spotter in the trench below would flag the target to show where the bullet struck. The targets were at gradients of one hundred yards, and while some had come close at one hundred yards, all shots beyond that were total misses.

Adrian took aim, squeezed the trigger, and felt the butt kick against his shoulder.

The spotter flagged the target at the right shoulder of the silhouette.

"Not bad. But you only grazed him," Augustus said softly.

Adrian looked up and grinned at his father. "Can you do better?"

Augustus opened the breech and inserted a cartridge into the Sharps. "Let's see."

Behind him, Augustus heard a man snicker, saying to the major, "Look at that old fool. Him and that rifle are as old as God."

Graves ignored the comment of Sergeant Kozak.

Augustus took aim and squeezed the trigger. The roar of the "Big Fifty" buffalo gun shook the firing line.

Graves nodded toward the target. The spotter flagged the silhouette at the center of the chest.

Augustus turned and looked severely at Kozak, and said

to him, "Fools don't get old, but graveyards are filled with a lot of dead young wise men."

Then he shoved the cocking lever down, sending the spent cartridge cartwheeling into the air. He loaded the Sharps and stood with it against his shoulder. Six hundred yards downrange was a single silhouette.

He adjusted his rear sight, took aim, and squeezed the trigger.

He could only imagine the surprise on the face of the spotter when he heard the boom, then saw the bullet cut the silhouette at solid dead center.

12

On a Sunday afternoon in the third week of July, Selona was surrounded by her family and new friends, and she thought the day offered more than she ever could have hoped for.

"You don't have to worry about a place to stay," she told Alice the first day they met. "We've got plenty of room. I been through lots of wars with babies, and I know how to go about that chore with a child in one hand and a pistol in the other."

Selona was standing at the kitchen table, holding the baby. She had mixed warm butter with sugar, spread the mixture at the center of a clean cloth, made one diagonal fold, then twisted the apex, concocting a sugar teat. She slipped the oozing end, no thicker than her pinky finger, into the baby's mouth and watched him suckle with sheer delight.

Through the kitchen window she could see the men sitting in the backyard at a table filled with food. Theresa and David were standing away from the group, talking beneath a tree, while Jonathan and Benjamin swung from a rope tied to a thick limb.

Augustus propped his leg on a chair and leaned back, clasping his hands behind his neck as he listened to Adrian and Harwood talk. The conversation centered on the war, the national topic of discussion.

" 'Lafayette, we are here.' " Adrian uttered the words that had flashed across America upon the arrival in France on July 4, 1917, of General John J. Pershing, commander of the American Expeditionary Force. "What a sight that must have been."

"Do you know how General Pershing got the name 'Blackjack'?" asked Augustus.

Harwood shook his head. "No, sir, I don't."

Augustus smiled reflectively, remembering a young 10th Cavalry officer during the war with the Apaches. "General Pershing commanded Colored troops in the Tenth Cavalry in the war with Geronimo. So he was later called 'Blackjack.' "

"There'll be a lot of Colored soldiers in this war, Sergeant Major," Harwood said.

"I expect. Everything from National Guard to volunteers, and those drafted in the Selective Service. Yes, sir. A whole lot of young Coloreds are going to be in uniform before this ruckus is over."

"Word around Fort Des Moines is that the First Division is going to be there by October," Adrian said. "We don't graduate until October. The war'll probably be over before we get there."

"I don't think so, son," said Augustus. "This war's been going on for years, and it won't end overnight because American troops have joined in the fight. I'd expect they'll leave you a fair share of the fighting."

Harwood laughed sarcastically. "We'll probably be sent to pioneer battalions."

Augustus had never heard of them. "What are they?"

"Mostly laborers in uniform: stevedores unloading ships on the docks, Coloreds working on the roads and driving trucks with the supplies, but not in the real fighting."

The sergeant major shook his head. "Don't you believe that, Joseph. You'll be officers in a fighting unit, you'll see." He thought about that for a moment. "Imagine, Colored soldiers fighting on the other side of the world. That'll be a first in American history."

Adrian wasn't certain if it was the way Augustus spoke or the distant look in his eyes, but he recognized a special sadness in his father that could not be veiled. "You wish you were going with us, don't you, Pop?"

Augustus slapped his artificial leg. "That I do, son. But there ain't no room for an old, broken-down horse soldier the likes of me. This is a young man's war. But it would be a sight. I swear, it would be a sight."

Selona arrived at that moment carrying more food, followed by Alice and Theresa. Augustus reached for a piece of sliced ham, but received only a slap on the hand.

"Not until after the blessing," she warned.

The blessing was said; then, beneath a soft summer sky, the misery suffered by the world that was pulling families apart all over the country was forgotten for a few hours.

There was no more talk of war. Not at Selona Sharps's table.

Late that night, Selona found Augustus sitting beneath a tall tree. He had carried a lantern outside and sat on the ground beneath a carpet of stars. She knew that he had been moody since his visit to the fort that first day of their arrival in Des Moines.

She walked up to him silently and saw him fold a paper, quickly tuck it in his pocket, and remove his spectacles.

"You've been reading that old letter from Lieutenant Colonel O'Kelly again, haven't you?"

Augustus reached up his hand. "Come here, old girl; give me a hand up."

She helped him to his feet and watched as he slipped his spectacles into another pocket. "I was just funning with a notion."

"What notion is that?" she asked, already certain of the answer.

"It's not too far to North Dakota, you know. I'd like to see the man at least once more."

"North Dakota! You don't even know if he's alive. Or if he still lives there."

"He's alive." Augustus slowly pulled the letter from his pocket. The paper was worn and the words nearly faded, but he had memorized them years ago and could recite easily the entire letter he had received from Lieutenant Colonel Jonathan O'Kelly.

"You could send a telegram," she said.

"I already did." Augustus grinned as he took another folded paper from his pocket. "I received this at the telegraph office this morning. He sounds poorly."

Selona took the paper and held it to the lantern as she read:

PLEASE COME. IN BAD HEALTH, BUT WOULD BE DELIGHTED
TO SEE YOU, SERGEANT MAJOR. RESPECTFULLY, J. O'KELLY.

"You've set your mind to this, haven't you?" she asked.

He nodded. "I'd like to see him . . . one more time."

She took his hand, felt the coolness of his skin, and gently kissed his knuckle. "You go on to North Dakota. He's a good man and a good friend. Old friends need to see each other one more time. Just do me one favor."

"What's that?"

"Leave that old buffalo gun at home. There ain't no more buffalo and it might make folks nervous to see a big Colored man walking around carrying a rifle."

Augustus was still chuckling when Selona went into the house.

13

Hannah Simmons sat on the west bank of the Mississippi River, staring idly across the span of muddy water to the lights of East St. Louis. Her left arm was in a sling. The wound in her shoulder had begun to itch that morning, a good sign of healing, according to Mohammad Mostafavi.

The riots in East St. Louis had ended, but the reign of terror continued, driving Coloreds farther north toward Chicago and the major packing houses. But not Hannah. She had determined her next move, and Chicago would not be her destination.

Mostafavi wiped at his sweaty brow with an oily cloth and sat beside Hannah, following her line of sight to the distant pier where she had narrowly escaped certain death. She had been wracked with nightmares; the faces of the men chasing her were vivid and the sounds of their angry voices filled her mind. But one bright side emerged from the incident: She had become a part of the Mostafavi family. Mohammad's wife had been very attentive to Hannah in the days following her injury but now the time had come to move on.

"You should stay here with us, little one," Mostafavi said, watching the lights of East St. Louis dance on the murky surface of the river.

Hannah shook her head. "I can't stay here, Mohammad. Every time I look across that river, my skin crawls."

He nodded. He understood fear. "When will you go?"

She remembered Alice Harwood. "I have friends in Des Moines."

"When will you go?"

"In the morning."

Mostafavi wiped again at his face. "Then there are preparations to be made."

She shrugged. "None needed. I'll hop a freight train like I always did."

He shook his head vigorously. "No, that is too dangerous. You will ride in the railway passenger car."

"I don't have enough money to throw away on a train ticket."

Mostafavi handed her an envelope. "This is for you."

Hannah opened the envelope and withdrew a twenty-dollar bill. She started to protest, but his huge hands closed around her fingers. "We wish to help you. When you get settled you can pay me back."

Hannah's eyes glistened. She could not recall the last time she had wept.

14

Augustus boarded the Colored-only passenger car and settled into his seat. As the train pulled out of the depot, he sat reading the latest edition of the *Pittsburgh Courier,* the edition filled with the riots in East St. Louis. While local authorities estimated no more than a dozen Colored deaths, the *Courier* reported that seven thousand Coloreds had streamed across the two bridges to St. Louis, and hundreds had been lynched or otherwise murdered.

Other articles reported the changing social aspects of America as the nation gradually built its war machine. Many of those changes involved Coloreds.

But the story that astonished him most was of the actions taken against the "hog ranches" outside of the training centers where Colored soldiers were stationed. The reason behind this was, ostensibly, to prevent the spread of venereal disease.

Augustus chuckled. After thirty years in the army, he knew that soldiers would find female companionship, government interference or not.

He recalled that he had never personally visited a hog ranch while in the army or as a civilian. Except once, and that time not to see a woman, but to see a man who took great pleasure in tormenting the buffalo soldiers at Fort Davis, Texas.

A man named John Armitage, a captain of the Texas Rangers. In the early hours of an August morning in 1882, the sound of horses awoke Augustus and Selona. He pulled on his trousers and stepped outside to talk with two troopers, who had brought an extra horse. They spoke briefly, then Augustus hurried inside and started to dress.

Selona sat up in bed. "What's wrong?"

"Trouble at the Adams hog ranch."

The troopers rode at a gallop with Augustus in the lead, making good time in the darkness.

The Adams hog ranch was one of several ranches servicing the Colored troopers at Fort Davis. The women there were Mexican and Indian girls recruited by the owner, Frank Adams, with the promise of making good money and maybe finding a husband.

Augustus tied off his horse and walked into a wall of stink—cheap whiskey and homemade tequila—permeating the front room. Four troopers sat quietly at a table playing cards with two Texas Rangers. The two Rangers sat behind a large pile of money.

At the bar, Armitage leaned over his glass of whiskey. His face broke into an evil grin as Augustus stepped up to the bar.

"I don't drink with niggers," Armitage said softly.

"You don't have to," replied Augustus. He nodded to Frank Adams, a burly man with a flowing beard. Adams's eyes were wide with apprehension as he stood frozen behind the bar.

"Whiskey," said Augustus.

Adams's hand shook as he poured Augustus a drink. Armitage's arm flashed across the counter, raking the glass and bottle onto the floor.

Augustus stared calmly at Armitage, then there was a roar of laughter from one of the Rangers at the table.

"You going to bet, boy? Or you going to fold?" he asked one of the troopers.

The trooper, young and scared, his voice cracking, said, "I can't bet my hoss and saddle. They belong to the cavalry."

Augustus recognized the ploy. It was a favorite used against the young Colored soldiers. The troopers would be invited to play cards by the Rangers, who would cheat them out of their money, then try to strip them of their horse and saddle.

Augustus turned to Armitage. "The boy's horse doesn't belong to him, Captain. Why don't you get your men and get out of here? We don't want no more trouble."

"Don't talk to me—talk to your boy. All he's gotta do is call the wager."

"He can't call the wager and you know it. He'll be court-martialed if he loses his horse in a poker game."

"That's his problem, now ain't it, Sergeant?" Armitage picked up his glass. As he started to drink, Augustus's big hand closed around Armitage's and guided the glass to his own lips. Slowly, forcefully, Augustus tilted the shot glass and drank Armitage's tequila.

Armitage's free hand went for a pistol but Augustus slammed the hand holding the glass onto the bar. The glass shattered, slicing the Ranger's hand open along the palm.

Armitage howled, staring in disbelief at his own blood. He made a move for his sidearm; at the same time the two Rangers stood up from the table and reached for theirs. Suddenly, the windows exploded; from outside two Springfield rifles appeared, trained on the card-playing Rangers.

Augustus kneed Armitage in the stomach, then slammed the butt of his pistol against his ear. There was another howl.

Augustus pointed his pistol at one of the Rangers. "You boys drop your weapons through the window. Nice and easy. We don't want any more trouble."

The Rangers did as they were told and huddled against the adobe wall.

Augustus motioned to the troopers at the table. "You men get on back to Fort Davis. Report to your company commander after roll call. You understand?"

The troopers nodded, then slowly eased away from the table and out the door.

Augustus looked at Adams. "Any more of our men in here?"

Adams shook his head. Augustus reached into his pocket and drew out a dime. He tossed the coin on the counter and, walking through the door, called over his shoulder to Adams, "Buy the captain a fresh drink."

A thin smile formed on Augustus's lips as he recalled the incident. A long time ago, he thought, watching the countryside roll past as the train rumbled west.

15

Selona typically made her decisions without consulting anyone. She had learned young that if a Colored woman waited for permission to do what she wanted, she would still be waiting when lowered into the grave.

"A boardinghouse!" Theresa and Alice were stunned. "You don't know anything about running a boarding-house."

They were sitting on the front porch watching the boys chase fireflies around the front yard.

"I know how to cook. I know how to make beds. I know how to wash and iron. All I need is a bigger house," Selona said. "There's hundreds of Coloreds looking for a decent place to live."

"We'll only be here until October, when Adrian and David graduate. Then there's no telling what will happen," Theresa insisted.

"We'll decide when that time comes. Until then we can own a business and make a little piece of money. Once the word gets around about my cooking, we'll have a full house.

Besides, I'm tired of just sitting around. So the first thing is to find a bigger house."

"What will Augustus say?" asked Alice.

Selona shrugged. "I doubt he'll say anything. Especially if I'm already in business when he gets back."

"You sly old fox," Theresa said. "You had this planned all along. That's why you didn't object to Augustus going up to North Dakota. You wanted a week or so to put your scheme to work."

"Scheme?" Selona tried to look insulted, but it didn't work.

"Scheme." Theresa laughed. "So I guess we better get started finding you a bigger house."

"I've already found a bigger house."

"Where?" asked Alice.

Selona said nothing. She merely smiled and rocked slowly as the boys romped about the front yard.

Hannah Simmons arrived in Des Moines with the name of her friend, and after getting directions from several strangers, found her way to the Colored community on the edge of Des Moines.

Then she set about finding Alice Harwood.

For three hours she knocked on doors and stopped strangers, but no one knew Joseph and Alice Harwood. Hannah was growing concerned when she saw a heavyset woman sitting on the front porch of a boardinghouse.

"Excuse me, ma'am. Could you help me?"

Coretta Dobkins stood and walked to the front steps. "How can I help?"

"I'm looking for a friend. Her name is Alice Harwood. Her husband, Joseph, is a soldier in the army. Do you know her?"

Coretta smiled. "I certainly do. She had her baby boy born right upstairs in this house."

A wave of relief flooded Hannah. "Thank God. Is she home?"

Coretta shook her head. "She had to move. I don't allow for babies in my establishment."

"Do you know where she went?"

Coretta came down the steps and pointed to the south. "Three blocks down that street, two blocks to the right. The house is number sixty-four."

Minutes later Hannah found the house. She couldn't read, but she knew the numbers six and four. She heard the sound of a baby crying.

Alice was on the porch nursing young Joseph when Hannah approached. "I declare," Alice said. "Hannah Simmons. I didn't think I'd ever see you again."

Hannah stepped onto the porch and into the embrace of Alice. "I didn't know if I'd find you."

Hannah looked at the tiny child suckling at Alice's breast. "He's beautiful. What's his name?"

"Joseph Taylor Harwood, Junior. His daddy calls him Little Joe."

Hannah heard another woman's voice call from inside the house; then the woman stepped onto the porch. Hannah's eyes widened as she gazed at the strangest-looking woman she had ever seen. A woman who wore what appeared to be a scrap of fur tied onto her head with a scarf.

"Selona, this is my friend Hannah Simmons. She's come here from East St. Louis."

"East St. Louis! Isn't that where there was riots against Coloreds?"

"Yes, ma'am. I barely got out alive." Hannah slipped her arm out of the sling and pulled at the collar of her shirt, revealing an ugly scar near her shoulder. "I was shot by one of the rioters."

"Good Lord," Selona exclaimed. "Child, you're still not healed up good. Come inside where it's comfortable."

The three women went inside and sat on a sofa. Selona went into the kitchen and Hannah looked wide-eyed at Alice. "What happened to her hair?"

Alice chuckled. "She was scalped by Texas Rangers in the Indian Territory back in 1874."

Hannah's eyes widened. "Scalped?"

Alice motioned with her hand for Hannah to speak more softly.

"What's that on her head?"

"It's made from buffalo fur. Her husband made it for her after the incident."

Incredible, thought Hannah. "What's she doing here in Des Moines?"

"She rented this place and turned it into a boarding-house. Her two sons are at the fort with Joseph. One of the sons is married, and his wife and two children are also stay-ing here."

"Is Selona married?"

"Yes. Her husband is one of the old cavalry soldiers who fought against the Indians."

"Where is he?"

"He left a few days ago to go up to North Dakota to visit an old army friend. He'll be back next week."

Hannah's eyes drifted about the room and settled on a rifle hanging on the wall. "What's that?"

Alice giggled. "That's an old buffalo hunter's gun. It's called a Sharps. When the sergeant major joined the army, he changed his slave name to Sharps, after that rifle."

Selona returned with a tray of coffee and sandwiches. Hannah devoured a sandwich with three bites.

"When's the last time you ate?" asked Selona.

"Two days ago," replied Hannah.

"Them little old sandwiches won't fill you." Selona went back to the kitchen and returned with a plate heaped with sliced ham, baked sweet potatoes, and what appeared to be a stew wrapped in thin white bread.

Hannah took her fork and dug into the white bread. "What is this?"

"It's called a burrito. The bread is called a tortilla. Instead of using beef I use rabbit meat for the stew."

"Selona is a wonderful cook," said Alice.

"What are your plans, Hannah?" asked Selona.

"I'm going to look for a job."

"Do you have any money?"

"A little."

"What about your possessions?"

Hannah sighed. "I got out of East St. Louis with nothing but the clothes on my back. I don't have anything to my name except what I'm wearing."

Selona stood quickly. "We'll see to that first off. I'm going to fix you a hot bath. After your trip you need some freshening."

The bath was prepared. Selona brought Hannah one of her dresses. "You take your time," said Selona. "Just take your time."

Selona came into the sitting room to the sound of heavy boots on the front steps. The door swung open and there stood Adrian and Joseph.

Adrian took off his campaign hat and hugged his mother. Joseph did the same with Alice, then took the baby into his arms.

"What are you two doing away from the fort?" Selona asked.

"We were detailed to pick up equipment at the depot. We're on the way back but thought we'd stop by and visit," Adrian said.

Alice and her husband went out onto the porch and sat in a swing, leaving Adrian alone as Selona went to the kitchen to prepare a meal for the two men.

Adrian went upstairs to the toilet. He reached for the door handle just as the knob turned, then stepped back, startled by the sudden presence of a young woman wrapped in a blanket. A young woman with the deepest, most beautiful eyes he had seen in his life.

16

On the third day of his journey, Augustus arrived in Grand Forks, North Dakota. Not since serving at Fort Wallace, Kansas, had he seen such flat terrain. The land seemed to roll endlessly to the west, unbroken by hills or mountains.

He stepped off the train and went to the ticket office, where he found a man sitting at a telegraph key, busily sending a message. The man looked at Augustus. "Can I help you?"

"I'm looking for the residence of Lieutenant Colonel Jonathan O'Kelly. Do you know him?"

"What you want with Colonel O'Kelly, boy?"

Augustus bristled but held his temper in check. "He's my friend. We served together in the army."

The man went to the door and pointed toward the main street of town. "He's staying at Doc Tollefson's. Two blocks west, then one block north. It's a white house with a picket fence. Doc's sign is out front. You can't miss it."

Augustus nodded politely, then left, and walked the short distance with his stomach tied in a knot.

He knocked at the door and was greeted by a short, rotund man with a balding head and deep blue eyes.

"I'm Sergeant Major Augustus Sharps," he told the man. "I served with Colonel O'Kelly in the army."

"I'm Dr. Tollefson. I've been expecting you, Sergeant Major. Colonel O'Kelly told me you were coming. Please come in."

Tollefson started for the back of his house, passing through the front parlor, which served as his office. Augustus followed.

The doctor opened the door to a bedroom, and what greeted Augustus there nearly drained him of his strength.

"I had to amputate one of his legs," Tollefson said flatly. "Gangrene. His circulation had become so poor that gangrene set into his right leg last week, so I moved him from his house to this room. His leg had festered so badly I had to take it two days ago."

Lieutenant Colonel Jonathan Bernard O'Kelly lay propped on pillows in a large featherbed. His long hair, turned white, lay matted against his forehead; his once flowing mustache drooped raggedly over cracked and swollen lips. His cerulean eyes were barely visible behind slitted lids.

Augustus paled at the sight of his old comrade-in-arms.

This was not the man whom he had known since 1866; not the man who led a cavalry charge at Anadarko in the Indian Territory; not the man who fought Victorio and Geronimo in New Mexico and Arizona.

Augustus straightened to attention and saluted. "Good afternoon, Colonel." His voice nearly cracked as he said, "Sergeant Major Augustus Sharps reporting as directed, sir."

O'Kelly's eyes fluttered, then opened to form two slits above his long nose. His lips moved slightly as he tried to smile, and his right index finger tapped the bed lightly. Augustus sat on the edge of the bed and lowered his ear to O'Kelly's mouth and listened to the voice, which was less than a whisper.

"For God's sake, get me out of this place. I don't want to die in this bed. I want to die on the prairie. Like a soldier."

"Yes, sir. I'll do that right away, sir." Augustus took O'Kelly's hand and squeezed the white fingers gently.

Augustus asked Tollefson, "Where's the livery?"

"The livery! What for?"

"The colonel wants to go for a buggy ride in the country."

"You can't take him for a ride in a buggy. It'll—" Tollefson's mouth froze without another word.

"Kill him?" Augustus said. "If he dies, he'll die like a man. Like a soldier. Not rotting away in this stinking room with nothing to look at but the ceiling. Now . . . where's the livery?"

"Across from the train depot," Tollefson said with defeat.

"What about a general store?"

"What do you want a general store for, Sergeant Major?"

"I'll be needing some supplies."

"What kind of supplies?"

Augustus looked across the room to where O'Kelly lay in his sweat-rumpled bed.

"Supplies for two old soldiers to go on their last scout together."

The doctor doesn't understand, thought Augustus. But how could he? Tollefson had never stood in iron stirrups with a sabre in one hand, a pistol in the other, leather reins clenched between his teeth, aboard a horse that was charging toward the enemy.

Sergeant Major Augustus Sharps and Lieutenant Colonel Jonathan Bernard O'Kelly had made that charge more times than they could remember.

*   *   *

In less than an hour Augustus had rented a buckboard, bought the supplies he needed, and was ready to return to Tollefson's house. Then he remembered something important, and from the storekeeper received the information he needed.

He stopped at a small building near the depot and spent ten minutes giving the owner explicit directions, then returned to Tollefson's, where the doctor had O'Kelly prepared for the journey.

"This is crazy," argued Tollefson, as he helped Augustus load the colonel into the buckboard.

Augustus remembered what Selona once told him when he had called one of her ideas crazy. "Nothing wrong with being a little crazy; it keeps the mind from going insane."

When the buckboard pulled away from Tollefson's house, Jonathan O'Kelly lay in the back on a pallet of blankets, the bandaged stump of his leg propped above head level. Beside him were the supplies, including a bottle of laudanum given Augustus by Tollefson.

Augustus had decided to travel until it was near dusk, then make a camp, but having never been this far north, did not realize that the sun set much later in the day in summer than in the southern latitudes.

By six o'clock O'Kelly was showing signs of fatigue, so Augustus pulled into a small coulee intersected by a shallow stream. He made a lean-to and piled leaves into it to make a cushion, then added blankets and gently laid his former commander on the makeshift bed. After Augustus had finished making a fire and setting up camp, the sun had begun to drift down the western horizon. The thin signature of the first evening stars began to appear.

Then, as old soldiers do, the tales of the past began to fill the firelit night.

"I remember the first time I saw your wife, Marcia. Good

God Almighty, she was madder than a wet hen," said Augustus.

O'Kelly laughed, remembering the day in 1880 when his second wife had arrived at Fort Davis, Texas, from her home in Dayton, Ohio.

Marcia O'Kelly felt both anger and sympathy streak through her, as though two lightning bolts had entangled and found the same ground at precisely the same moment and place.

It was noon in Del Rio, Texas, a hot, sweltering border town between El Paso and Brownsville on the Rio Grande, far from Marcia's home in Dayton, Ohio, which she had left only three weeks before, sailing from New York to Brownsville to the west Texas frontier to join Lieutenant Jonathan Bernard O'Kelly, her husband of two months.

In Ohio for one of the rare trips he had made back east, Jonathan had met Marcia, a teacher, and after a whirlwind romance of merely a week, they were married. Lieutenant O'Kelly had to return to Fort Davis ahead of Marcia, who had to get her affairs in order for going to what her family considered "the edge of the world."

The journey by ship had been exciting and enjoyable, but at Brownsville she'd had to start the last leg of the trip to Fort Davis by stagecoach.

Now she sat on a wooden porch, caught in the whirling devil-tails skipping from the dusty street, the stench of a dog urinating on a nearby hitching post, and the storm of angry shouts that had erupted moments before in front of the stage depot.

"I don't give a good goddamn what some Yankee colonel has to say," shouted Three-fingers Johnny Braxton, the stage driver. "There ain't no nigger-Injun riding in my stagecoach."

Braxton was short, leather brown from the sun, and quick to use his long flowing beard to wipe at sweat flowing into his angry eyes. From what depot manager Frank McKay could see, Braxton wasn't backing off, despite the order sent him by Colonel Benjamin Grierson, who had returned as commander of the 10th Cavalry, now headquartered at Fort Davis and responsible for maintaining the safety of west Texas against Indian raids, forages by Mexican bandits from across the Rio Grande, and white hooligans rampaging from El Paso to Brownsville.

"It just ain't proper," shouted Braxton. "My God, what would the passengers say?"

"Why don't you ask us?" Marcia stood quickly, her eyes flaming. She adjusted the bonnet covering her long dark hair and for the first time in three weeks wished she had stayed in Dayton. In her hand she carried a parasol as though it were a sabre.

Braxton spat a stream of tobacco juice and hitched up his pants. "Sit down, lady. I ain't talking to you."

McKay held up his hand. "Yes, ma'am. Please stay out of this. This is a stagecoach matter."

Marcia walked quickly over to a young woman sitting in a nearby chair. The young woman who was the focus of discussion.

The moment Marcia had seen her she was immediately intrigued, for she had never seen such a magnificent face: brown but not ebony, features narrow and delicate, black-diamond eyes that stared straight ahead as though oblivious to the fury raging about her.

McKay, a short, balding man with pale blue eyes that seemed to have turned darker from frustration, flashed the letter again to Braxton. "This here girl is Juanita Calderon. She's John Horse's niece from over at Piedras Negras, and her fare is paid through to Fort Davis by the army. You best listen to what I'm saying. Good God, man, do you want all them Seminole-niggers coming over here and burning this whole damn town down! This girl's practically royalty in her family."

Juanita Calderon's facial expression changed only momentarily as a thin smile drifted across her mouth; then she again became stoic. She's certainly special, thought Marcia, who again studied the young woman. She wore a calico dress, a flaming-red bandanna around her forehead, and high leather moccasins, and her long black braided hair hung to her waist.

Marcia knew nothing of the Seminole-Negroes, except what she had heard along the stage trail. The children of runaway slaves and Seminole tribesmen, thousands had been shipped from the Florida Everglades to the Indian Territory before the Civil War, where they had become prime targets for Arkansas slave traders. Under the leadership of John Horse, a former slave who had married a Seminole woman, and Wild Cat, a nephew of Osceola, hundreds had crossed Texas to Mexico, where they provided border security for the Mexican government in exchange for diplomatic immunity from slavery. After the Civil War, dozens had joined the American army in west Texas and became known along the border as Seminole-Negro scouts. The scouts were ferocious fighters but known best for their tracking ability.

"This girl's going to Fort Davis to marry one of them young Colored soldiers," McKay said. "And she's going to ride on this stagecoach if I have to drive the team myself."

Braxton spit again. "She can ride in the boot, or you can damn well drive the team."

"That's inhuman," Marcia said, stepping into the street while opening her parasol with such fury that Braxton stepped back and suddenly looked defensive. "This woman can't ride in the boot. She'll choke to death from the dust."

"That's my final word on it." Braxton snapped a quirt against his leg and walked to the stagecoach, angrily kicking at the dog and the dust-devils.

Without a word, Juanita stepped from the porch carrying her valise and walked to the rear of the stagecoach.
Looking as though she had somehow anticipated such a situation, she pulled her bandanna down, covering her mouth
and nose, and climbed onto the baggage compartment.

Marcia, defeated by now, started to close the parasol, then paused, stepped to the rear of the stagecoach,
and handed it to Juanita, saying softly, "I wish I could do
more."

Juanita took the parasol slowly, and Marcia thought she
saw her dark eyes smiling over the bandanna.

Then Marcia realized the eyes weren't smiling, they were
shining with tears.

After a brutal three-day journey of more than two hundred miles, the stagecoach boiled into Fort Davis followed
by a cloud of white alkaline dust that settled over the coach,
driver, and horses as Three-fingers Johnny Braxton jerked
the team to a halt in front of the sutler's.

Lieutenant Jonathan O'Kelly waded through the cloud
and pulled open the door to find his wife sitting in an inch
of thick dust, her face and clothes white as silver, as was her
dark hair. The only other color was the fire in her eyes.

O'Kelly helped her down. She moved slowly, the pain
from the torturous ride evident on her twisted face. He
started to put his arms around her, but she walked past him
and went to the rear of the coach.

Juanita Calderon was tied to the boot, the parasol nothing more than tattered cloth and the frame twisted wires.
Marcia untied the woman, then gently guided her to the
ground. "Don't just stand there, Jon. Help this poor
woman."

O'Kelly was stunned and seemed to move automatically
as he took Juanita's hand and guided her to a chair on the
porch of the sutler's.

Private Winston Jackson was tall and slim with narrow
features. Holding a fistful of flowers as he stood on the

porch, his eyes bulging, he, like O'Kelly, wasn't sure what
to do.

Lieutenant O'Kelly's quick glare seemed to pull Jackson
from the trance and he disappeared inside the sutler's, returning moments later with a ladle of water. Juanita sipped
slowly as the coach lurched and stormed off to the stables
for a fresh team of horses.

Selona had been walking to the sutler's when she saw the
coach arrive. Seeing Jackson tending the young woman,
she knew she was the Seminole-Negro sent for by Colonel
Grierson. The colonel often arranged marriages among the
Coloreds and the Seminole-Negroes, using this as a means
to enlist the brothers of the brides into the cavalry as scouts.
That, and the offer of land on the American side of the Rio
Grande.

"Here, missy. I'll tend to her," a voice called gently to
Marcia.

Marcia turned and saw Selona, and her eyes went immediately to her head, for Selona had removed her calico
rag, revealing the buffalo fur hairpiece. In all her life Marcia had never seen anything quite so extraordinary. She
stood dumbfounded as Selona dipped the cloth in the water
and gently wiped at the dust crusted around Juanita's eyelids, then her cheeks, all the while talking in a soothing
voice.

"Got to find out what kind of pretty girl we got under
all this Texas dust," she whispered. "I know there's got to
be something pretty waiting for my eyes to behold." She
looked at Jackson, then said, "I know you going to be pretty
enough for Trooper Jackson no matter how you look, because he ain't much to look at himself."

This brought a slight smile to Juanita's face, then her eyes
went to Winston Jackson.

Then, for the first time in the three days since the stagecoach left Del Rio, Marcia heard Juanita speak: "He is a
fine-looking man. We will have fine-looking children."

Trooper Winston Jackson stepped forward and gave her the flowers. She accepted them with a smile.

"Come with me," said Selona. "We got your quarters all ready for you over on Suds Row. The chaplain's waiting to get you two hitched nice and proper."

Lieutenant Colonel Jonathan O'Kelly's eyes shone with a brightness as he remembered that day. "God, I thought that woman was going to eat me blood raw when she stepped off that stagecoach."

Augustus laughed, and he wasn't certain if it was his presence, the memories, being out of that dreary room at Tollefson's, or the colonel rejuvenated by the open air of a country he had helped settle, but something began to breathe life into the man.

"We did have some great campaigns, didn't we, Augustus?"

Augustus looked quickly at O'Kelly. In the more than fifty years he had known this man, O'Kelly had never called him by his first name.

"Yes, Jonathan, we surely did." And he realized that was the first time he had ever called a commanding officer by his first name. A barrier had fallen as easily as it had been constructed. There was no separation now on this piece of barren ground as there had been on so many others they had shared while soldiering.

"What campaign do you remember best?" asked O'Kelly.

That was easy for Augustus to answer. "The Victorio wars in west Texas. Good Lord! We chased him for weeks and never caught sight of him. But we did give his warriors a licking and kept them from raiding north Texas and New Mexico."

O'Kelly coughed as he tried to laugh. "That was at Rattlesnake Springs. We chased him into Mexico, and the Mexicans killed him and what was left of his band. But the Tenth Cavalry never received proper recognition."

"No, sir," Augustus said. "But that didn't bother us none. We was proud of how fine a job we did of protecting the folks along the border.

"Those were some mighty fine times, Colonel. In my mind, the best of times."

Then there was the slight look of disappointment in O'Kelly's eyes. "I just wish we had had more luck against Victorio."

Augustus shook his head. "Weren't no luck to it, sir. He just out-soldiered the hell out of the Tenth Cavalry."

O'Kelly nodded. Augustus could see the true respect the colonel still held for the wily Mescalero war chief.

"I guess you're right," O'Kelly whispered, and then after a long, reflective pause, said, "Now your sons are going to France."

Augustus nodded as he threw a few sticks of wood onto the fire.

"Seems my family is bound to fight for this country, Colonel. Like yours."

O'Kelly turned to the sound of an owl hooting in the distance. "It seems that way, Augustus."

Augustus watched O'Kelly's eyes close, then he pulled the blanket beneath his chin. As his former commander fell to sleep, Augustus whispered, "It seems that way, Jonathan."

The next morning O'Kelly raised from his bed and saw Augustus leaning over the fire with a frying pan.

"I don't know what smells better, Augustus. The air or the eggs you're cooking."

Augustus laughed. "Must be the air. Selona says I can't cook worth a lick."

The brightness in O'Kelly's eyes seemed to fade for a moment, as though he were trying to remember something important from the past. At length, he said, "Your wife was always a kind and decent woman. I remember the first time we met. It was at Fort Wallace. She was just a child."

"Yes, sir. Even then she had a sharp tongue."

A look of sadness fell over O'Kelly's face. "Did you know she was mistreated by my first wife?"

Augustus, scrambling up the eggs, nodded slowly. "Yes, sir. I knew. She told me about that after we were married."

O'Kelly pulled himself upright and leaned on one elbow. "For God's sake, man, you must have despised me."

Augustus shook his head as he stirred the eggs. "No, Jonathan. It wasn't you that harmed Selona. That was done by a woman driven insane by whiskey. You couldn't have known."

Augustus heard a long, easy sigh, then Jonathan's voice as he said, "Thank you, Augustus."

Augustus sat the skillet on the ground and crawled over to O'Kelly.

The colonel's eyes were wide but peaceful, staring into the sky, as though concentrating on the sun.

Augustus gently closed the man's eyelids. O'Kelly's face had the calm and peace of sleep, not death.

Augustus stood and, under the blue sky of the upper plains, raised his hand in a salute to his dead commander. "Good day, sir."

"Kindness always returns itself," Selona would always say. "Just like the meanness you give comes back even meaner."

That afternoon, Augustus had been thinking about those wise words when he stopped at the small building across from the train depot.

As he climbed down from the buckboard he saw Tollefson approaching. The doctor stopped and looked into the well of the wagon. "I told you he would die, Sergeant Major." There was no chastisement in his voice.

Augustus nodded. "Yes, sir. That you did. But he died under the clean blue sky recollecting days of youth and glory. He didn't die in a dark room that smelled of the grave. He got to do what most soldiers never get to do."

Tollefson looked puzzled. "What was that?"

"Lieutenant Colonel Jonathan O'Kelly got to pick the day and place when he heard the bugle blow for the last time."

Augustus walked into the building, beneath the sign over the door that read: MORTICIAN & STONECUTTER.

Scores of citizens attended the funeral the following day. Augustus and Dr. Tollefson had sent telegrams to O'Kelly's children.

The mortician has made O'Kelly look younger, thought Augustus. The long hair was washed and neatly combed, the mustache trimmed to the traditional cut of a cavalry officer.

The coffin was lowered into the rich black earth of the Red River Valley of North Dakota. Standing on the grave, like a sentinel, was the headstone cut on the day O'Kelly and Augustus had taken their last ride together.

The stonecutter had kept his promise. When he had asked Augustus what was to be carved on the headstone, Augustus had given him a piece of paper, on which he had written:

JONATHAN BERNARD O'KELLY
1842–1917
United States Military Academy, Class of 1866
Lieutenant Colonel of United States Cavalry
Father, Husband, Friend, and . . .
Soldier to the Nation

Augustus walked alone from the cemetery. He did not linger long where soldiers had been laid to rest. Perhaps it was superstition, perhaps habit. The moments to reflect on death and those who had died would come on a later day.

17

When Selona Sharps set her mind to a particular task, only God Almighty could dissuade her, and there had been times when even He seemed to defer.

So it was with the notion she had regarding Hannah Simmons.

"You got to have you a piece of land," she said one night while sitting on the front porch.

"Piece of land? What do I want with a piece of land? The only land I ever lived on was surrounded by cotton, and I watched my poppa work himself into his grave."

Selona wouldn't hear this. "First you get yourself a husband, then you get yourself a piece of land, and then you have some children."

Hannah's jaw dropped. "A husband? I don't need no man. They ain't nothing but troublesome."

Selona smiled softly. "I remember the first time I saw Augustus. He was covered with dried buffalo guts—he had been kept as a slave by a buffalo hunter. My daddy rescued him and talked him into joining the army. I knew the first moment I met him he was going to be my husband."

The sound of a horse approaching stopped the conversation. Selona peered toward the end of the street. Without a word she went into the house and returned carrying the big Sharps rifle. She opened the breech and rammed a cartridge into the chamber without taking her eyes off the blackness at the end of the distant darkness.

Hannah sat terrified.

The steady hoof beats continued, then slowed as a buggy came into sight. Selona lowered the rifle and smiled.

Augustus stepped onto the porch, looking tired. "You ain't going to shoot me, are you, Selona?"

She propped the rifle against the porch rail and walked into his arms.

"Why didn't you telegram? I thought you would be gone for another week."

Augustus shook his head. "Colonel O'Kelly died the day after I got there."

There was a look of pain on her face. "I'm sorry, Augustus. He was a good and decent man."

Hannah stood; Augustus studied her for a moment, then nodded politely. "I'm Sergeant Major Augustus Sharps."

"I know. Selona has told me and I feel like I know you."

The three went inside.

As he stepped through the door, Augustus said to Selona, "I see you've done started yourself another business. You're becoming a regular John D. Rockefeller."

"What business is he in?" she asked.

Augustus's laughter was swallowed by the big house as the front door closed.

18

By the eighth week of training, weekend passes for the candidates began at noon on Saturday. That following Saturday afternoon the family gathered for their weekly picnic in the backyard. Selona had taken in five boarders since opening her business, and since they had practically become family, they were invited to join.

Adrian quickly spotted Hannah. He had not spoken to her since that first day, but she had occupied his thoughts.

"Good afternoon, Hannah." Adrian fumbled with his hat as he approached.

She smiled. "I'm glad you could come, Adrian. Miss Selona wasn't sure if you could leave the fort."

Before he could reply, he heard his mother say to the gathering, "Come on, everybody. Let's eat."

During dinner Augustus shared with Adrian and David the journey to visit O'Kelly. Both of his sons were visibly moved; they had known the man since childhood.

After dinner, the women began clearing the table, when

Selona spoke with Adrian. "I need some cloth for making new curtains for the front room."

Adrian looked at her with surprise, then looked around, hoping no one had heard. "Momma, I'm a man. A soldier. I don't know anything about buying cloth for curtains."

She grumped. "You know how to drive a buggy, don't you?"

"Of course."

"Then you take Hannah and go on into Mr. Humphrey's store and buy me the material. I'll tell Hannah what I need."

Selona walked off and talked briefly with Hannah. Augustus had been watching and came over to Adrian and said, "Do you remember when you were young and your momma taught you how to make a rabbit snare?"

Adrian nodded. "Yes, sir."

Augustus grinned. "I think she's setting a new kind of snare. And you look like the rabbit."

Adrian watched as Hannah went to the buggy. Selona came to him, gave him a five-dollar bill, and said, "Don't take too long. It'll be dark soon."

They had driven into town without saying a word, both staring straight ahead as though the other didn't exist. She was pretty enough, thought Adrian, and his mother's intentions were clear.

Adrian eased back on the reins in front of Humphrey's dry goods store and helped Hannah down, surprised at how light she seemed.

Charles Humphrey was standing behind the counter sorting denim overalls when they came in. He was tall and thin, with wire-framed spectacles that perched on the end of his long, sharp nose.

Adrian tipped his hat. "My name is Sharps. Adrian Sharps. My mother is Selona Sharps. She sent me to pick out some cloth for curtains."

Humphrey stared at Adrian a second, his eyes filled with confusion. "But your mother has already picked out the cloth. She did so yesterday, and said she'd be by today to pick it up. It's done paid for." He rummaged under the counter and brought out a thick package.

Adrian felt the heat rise on his neck; Hannah merely looked down and smiled.

He took the package and went to the buggy, where he helped Hannah onto the seat and climbed aboard. The buggy had not traveled more than ten feet when Adrian began laughing, followed by Hannah.

At the front of his store stood Charles Humphrey, who had no idea of what was so funny. But he did notice Hannah slide a little closer to Adrian.

The two were still laughing when the buggy rounded a corner as the sun was fading into the western horizon.

The laughter ceased abruptly when they saw a man standing in the street, behind him several others. All were white and all appeared drunk. Noise from a nearby saloon filled the heavy air. Adrian eased the horse to a stop as a fat man in overalls gripped the animal's bit. He wore a pistol in his belt and reeked of whiskey.

"Get down, nigger, unless you want us to drag you off that buggy."

Hannah's hand snatched Adrian's sleeve. "Dear God. What are we going to do?"

Adrian eased down from the buggy and looked calmly at Hannah. He whispered, "You be ready to move." He casually handed her the reins, then stood still as the men began to approach. He waited until they were past the head of the horse and his hand flashed and slapped against the horse's rump as he yelled, *"He-e-e-e-y-a-ahhh!"*

Hannah felt the horse bolt forward; she snapped the reins and the buggy plowed through the street with a fury.

She looked back to see Adrian disappear beneath a sea of fists and boots.

*   *   *

Hannah reined in the horse with such fury in front of Selona's house she was nearly thrown to the ground. She jumped down and ran screaming up on the porch as the door swung open.

Augustus knew something was wrong the moment he heard the buggy storming down the street. "Where's Adrian?"

She struggled to breathe and could only point. "Men . . . in front of a saloon. They stopped us and he got down. Then . . . he hit the horse and ran at the men so I could get away."

Selona screamed with terror. Augustus gripped her arms. "I'll find him."

David and Harwood were on the porch when Augustus went inside. The two followed him to the mantel, where he took down his Sharps. He then went to a closet and fetched his pistol and cartridge belt for his rifle. As he was strapping on the iron and leather, he said to David, "Get my horse saddled."

David ran to the back, where a small stable housed Augustus's horse. He was cinching down the saddle when his father boiled in, followed by Harwood.

"We're going with you, Pop," David said angrily.

"Damn right," said Harwood.

Augustus shook his head. "No. You stay here. Your momma and the rest might need protecting. I'll get him and bring him back. You have to look after the rest of the family."

David started to protest but met the hard stare of his father. Augustus swung into the saddle and spurred the horse, and before a word could be said was racing into the street.

Adrian sat in a chair, his hands tied behind his back, his feet tied together. His face was swollen, his lips cracked and bloodied.

The man called George held a long knife and teased it against Adrian's cheeks, then slid the blade down his throat to his coat, cutting the brass buttons off his tunic one by one.

This brought a particular delight to the men in the saloon, who Adrian figured numbered six or seven. The bartender nervously wiped at a glass, wearing the look of a man caught up in something beyond his control.

"He ain't got no more buttons to cut off, George," a voice called out. "Maybe you ought to cut off something else."

George grinned and lowered the knife to Adrian's crotch. Adrian's chest heaved and he tried to struggle but any movement aggravated the white-hot pain in his rib cage.

His mind drifted to Arizona and the cool sunrises and the long rides into the desert. He was sitting astride a horse as a youngster, his mother riding alongside, his father and brother also mounted. There would be an eagle that would make them pause and look to the sky, then they would gallop toward the eagle, the hooves pounding . . . pounding . . .

His eyes opened and he saw the knife near his crotch, could see the men laughing, see their mouths moving . . . but he couldn't hear a sound.

Except the sound of the hooves pounding—on the street outside the saloon!

The horse exploded through the thin plank door as though it were paper. The men saw only a blurry image of the rider gripping the reins in his teeth, standing in the iron stirrups, a pistol in his left hand, in his right the most God-awful huge rifle any had seen in their lives.

George reached for his pistol, then Augustus fired at his feet. The .50-caliber bullet tore a large hole in the floor and George froze in his boots.

Augustus threw one leg over the saddle horn and slowly slid down, keeping his weapons trained on the hooligans.

With a jerk of his head, Augustus told George, "Cut my boy loose. But first, drop your pistol."

George eased his pistol from his belt and let it drop from his hand.

"Cut him loose," Augustus snapped.

George cut the ropes, then moved to the bar as Augustus said, "Can you climb into the saddle?"

Adrian nodded, then rose from the chair. With great pain he stuck his foot into the stirrup and pulled himself onto the horse.

Augustus took the reins and led the horse toward the door, all the while keeping his eyes on the men. Just before going through the splintered door, he said, "If my family has any more trouble from you men, I'll kill every one of you. Is that understood?"

Each man nodded, standing still as Augustus led the horse into the street.

Selona stood waiting at the front gate and heard the horse approaching. She had heard her man ride at the gallop for nearly fifty years and knew the sound made by a horse ridden by him.

"David! Joseph! He's back!" she shouted.

David and Harwood reached the gate as the horse slid to a halt. Augustus shouted, "Get him to the surgeon at the fort. I'll stay here in case we were followed."

Augustus lowered Adrian's limp body to his brother. "Now, go on. All three of you get to the fort."

David started to speak but was cut off by his mother. "You heard your father. You and Joseph take Adrian to the fort."

Adrian was loaded into the front seat of the buggy and David snapped the reins; within moments they were out of sight.

Augustus took his Sharps from the saddle boot and stepped onto the porch. He touched Selona's face lightly, saying, "He'll be all right. He's been hurt worse falling from his horse."

She said nothing as she followed him into the house.

19

Adrian sat on his cot in the field hospital, the bile rising into his throat as he watched Surgeon Carrington gently unwrap the cloth used to support his injured rib cage.

"This may hurt," said Carrington, who removed the last few layers and probed Adrian's ribs with his fingers.

"Your ribs aren't broken, but they are badly bruised. You'll be on your feet soon."

"Why not right now?" a baritone voice called from the entrance to the field hospital.

Adrian and Carrington both looked to the door, where they saw Augustus and Selona approaching, followed by Hannah and Major Graves.

"Hello, Momma," said Adrian. He nodded at Hannah, then covered his chest with his blanket.

Selona stepped to the cot and whipped back the blanket. There was a momentary fracture in her demeanor when she saw his swollen ribs, then she recovered and leaned and kissed his forehead. "Hello, son."

Adrian took her hand and kissed her gently on the knuckles. He looked embarrassed, then said to Hannah, "Hello, it's good to see you again." He looked at Augustus and forced a smile. "Thanks for helping me last night, Pop."

Augustus nodded, then said, "How are you feeling?"

Adrian shrugged. "I'm sore, but I'm alive."

Major Graves looked at Carrington. "Is there any reason Candidate Sharps couldn't convalesce the rest of the week at his family's home in town?"

The doctor's eyebrows rose. "That would be highly irregular, Major."

"So is having your ribs busted," Selona snapped.

"Suppose I were to issue a seven-day furlough?" asked Graves.

"That would free up the cot," said Carrington.

"Consider it done." Graves looked at Augustus. "Stop by headquarters on the way out of the fort. I'll have the papers ready."

Carrington spent the next few minutes rebandaging Adrian's ribs, then told two orderlies to bring a stretcher.

Selona said, "That won't be necessary, Mr. Surgeon. Come on, son. I have a buggy outside. We'll take you home."

When Augustus and Selona helped him to his feet, Adrian grimaced when he felt the sharp pain in his chest. Then the three walked into the sunlight, a weakened man supported by strong shoulders.

That night Hannah unwrapped Adrian's chest and eased him into a tub of hot water dosed with Epsom salts. When she saw the pained look on his face, he suddenly seemed childlike, not the big, strapping man who had protected her from the hooligans. With gentle fingers she began massaging his shoulders.

In the swing on the front porch, Augustus and Selona could hear Adrian's groans and his gasping for air from the therapy. Alice sat on the steps nursing the baby; Theresa sat reading to the boys.

At last the groaning ended. Selona rose from the swing and went inside, followed by the other women and children. She climbed the stairs and knocked lightly on Hannah's door, then entered.

Adrian lay on the bed asleep; Hannah sat on the floor, holding his hand.

"You best get some rest, Hannah. Tomorrow will be the worst of the treatment," Selona said.

Hannah stood. "But where will I sleep?"

Selona gave her a mysterious smile. "In your bed, child. In your bed." She closed the door and walked to her room.

The next morning Selona awoke and started a fire in the stove, kneaded dough for biscuits, sliced fatback, and gathered eggs from the henhouse in the backyard. When the fire was hot she put a kettle of water onto the stove, then climbed the stairs to Hannah's bedroom and knocked lightly on the door. Hannah answered, wearing a look of sleepiness mixed with embarrassment.

Selona lowered her head. "I ain't trying to pry, but you never had a man sleep in your bed before, have you?"

Hannah shook her head.

Selona looked past her to the still-sleeping Adrian. "We best get him up and get started."

Selona woke Adrian, who sat up quickly, then grimaced as his feet hit the floor. "Hannah, get the bathtub ready. There's hot water on the stove. I'll have his father help him into the tub."

Hannah and Augustus came into the room and helped Adrian to the bathtub in the toilet. Selona filled the tub with water, then Hannah brought the boiling water from the stove. The two women left while Augustus slowly lowered

Adrian into the steaming water. "This is going to hurt a bit," his father whispered.

Adrian's face tightened with pain for several moments, then began to relax.

When he was finished with the hot bath, his mother and father guided him to the bedroom, where Selona began the massage. She worked his shoulder and chest muscles carefully, then his stomach and back muscles, and was able to ignore his groans of pain until she could see he had had enough.

"You have to start walking, son," she said. "You have to walk down the stairs, then back up on your own."

Adrian shook his head. "I can't do that, Momma. I just can't."

"Then you can't be an officer in the army," said Augustus.

"What are you saying, Pop?"

"Major Graves told me you've got to make that final march next week or you'll be disqualified from the training course."

Adrian shook his head in disbelief.

"Now, do you want to be an officer?" his father asked.

Adrian nodded, gritting his teeth as he stood. "I'm going to complete that march if I have to crawl on my hands and knees."

Augustus beamed with pride as Adrian started for the stairs, stumbled slightly, then was caught by Hannah, who gently reached up and cupped his face in her hands and kissed him.

20

✫ ✫ ✫

On Sunday afternoon, David Sharps watched two mallards swim lazily on a sparkling pond south of the fort, where many Colored families picnicked. Theresa sat by his side, watching Jonathan and Benjamin searching the nearby reeds for treasures important only to little boys.

David laughed softly as he watched the boys, but periodically stared off into the distance, something that did not go unnoticed by Theresa.

"What are you thinking?" she asked.

He shrugged, picked at a wildflower. "We'll be graduating in two weeks."

"Regrets?"

"No regrets."

"Then, what?"

There was a long pause. "I'm trying to imagine what Jonathan and Benjamin will look like when they are grown men."

A bolt of fear suddenly gripped Theresa. "I don't want

to hear that kind of talk." She looked away quickly, not
wanting him to see the fear in her eyes.

"It's something we have to talk about, Theresa. All soldiers have to have this talk with their wives when there's a
war to be fought."

She had thought about David and the war even though
she had never uttered a word about it. She wondered what
would become of her if he were killed. How would he die?
Where would he be buried?

She thought of the dark curtain that stood between the
temporary and the permanent.

She thought of how powerful men could cause so much
anguish to innocent people.

"I prayed you wouldn't receive your appointment to officer's training."

"I know," David said.

She looked at him with surprise. "How did you know?"

He touched her hand. "You acted too happy when I received the appointment."

"I'll have to learn to be less enthusiastic in the future."

"No, don't change. I don't want to have to start learning
about you all over again. I like you just the way you are."

Theresa leaned forward and kissed him lightly on the
lips.

Not far away Harwood sat with Alice, little Joseph on
his knee. He handed the child to his wife and watched as
Alice opened her blouse and guided the child to her breast.

Harwood stood and stared out over the pond. She could
see there was something on his mind. "What's bothering
you, Joseph?"

He picked up a rock and skipped it across the water, setting the mallards to flight.

He sat back on the blanket. "I'm worried about you and
Little Joe going back to Tennessee. I don't like the idea of
you living with your aunt Esther."

Alice shifted the baby to her other nipple, then said, "We don't have to go to my aunt Esther's."

This caught Harwood by surprise. "What does that mean? Of course you have to go to your aunt's. There's nowhere else to go."

"We can go to Arizona."

"Arizona."

"Miss Selona and Augustus have invited—have insisted—that me and the baby go with them to Arizona until the war is over and you return."

Harwood had never given this the remotest thought. "Arizona. My God, that's so far away."

"I'll be safe and there's plenty of room."

"Are you sure?"

"Well, room enough. But there could be one more coming along on the journey."

Adrian now walked without support. His main thoughts were on the upcoming march and returning to the barracks at the end of the day.

But he had other thoughts as well.

"You know," he said to Hannah, "my mother will be closing up the boardinghouse and returning to Arizona with Theresa and the children when we receive our commissions."

"I think Alice and baby Joseph will be going with them. Your mother has her mind set on looking after them," Hannah said.

Adrian looked past Hannah to a tree where his father and mother sat.

"Nothing that woman does surprises me," he said. "What are your plans?"

Hannah shrugged. She had been on her own so long, thinking only of surviving the moment, she rarely gave thought to tomorrow. "Stay here, I imagine."

Adrian leaned forward and ran his fingers through her hair, then lightly kissed her cheek. "You could go to Arizona."

"I couldn't do that. I would be a burden."

"Not if you were family."

"How could I be—" Her words froze on her lips.

"I don't offer much promise to a woman. I know I'm a lot older than you, I'm not much to look at, and I'm going to war."

Hannah smiled. "What's that got to do with anything?"

Adrian's mouth suddenly felt bone dry. "Do you think you might like to go to Arizona?"

She threw herself into his arms, kissed him long and deliciously, and sighed, "I'd love to go to Arizona."

Selona watched them approach, and her thoughts flashed back to Indian Territory, the day she and Augustus had wed and slept together on the prairie on the very same buffalo robe she and he now sat upon.

They had made love together beneath a carpet of stars, giggled from moonlight to sunlight, oblivious to the danger that lay just beyond. If given the option to relive her life, would she again endure the days, even weeks of loneliness, wondering if her man would come home alive? Would she raise her children in the shadow of savagery and privation?

Yes, she thought. Yes.

21

✯ ✯ ✯

The shrill horn blast of reveille broke the following morning's quiet at Fort Des Moines, as Adrian swung his feet over the edge of his cot, stood carefully, and began to dress in his field uniform, trousers, blouse, and socks. Finally, he pulled on his brogans, laced them, and wound his puttees around his ankles.

The instant he stood he felt dizzy and for a moment thought he would drop to his knees.

"You all right?" asked David.

Adrian nodded, then began making up his bunk.

"Ten-hut!"

The men snapped to attention as the heavy boots of Major Graves moved smartly along the aisle, followed by Surgeon Carrington. When he reached Adrian's cot, Graves stopped.

"Candidate Sharps, are you well this morning?"

"Yes, sir. Quite well. Thank you, sir."

Graves smiled with delight, then turned and marched back along the aisle. Reaching the front entrance to the barracks, he encountered Kozak, who was staring past him to Adrian.

On Kozak's face was the look of respect.

Graves passed by Kozak, who then barked, "After morning mess, fall out with full field packs. This will be your final forced march. Any candidate who does not complete the march will be dismissed from the regiment."

From the beginning of the march Adrian felt pain shooting through his ribs with each step. The pack was not filled with rocks but issued gear, and each man carried a wooden rifle.

The cool October air was invigorating, and though his chest ached, at least the stifling heat and humidity no longer bore down on him.

By the time the company reached the pond where Adrian and his family had picnicked only the day before, the pain was no longer endurable. He slumped to the edge of the water and removed his pack and turned to see Kozak sitting astride his horse.

Adrian watched Kozak walk the horse to the tree where he had told his mother and father that he and Hannah were going to marry—something that seemed to have happened long, long ago.

Twenty minutes later the rest period ended and the men rose to the sound of Kozak's whistle. Two columns were formed on the sides of the road; Kozak mounted and rode to the front of the column. He raised his hand and shouted, "Forward!"

As the column started to march, Kozak suddenly dismounted from his horse and stood at the side of the road. When Adrian reached the sergeant, Kozak shouted, "Candidate Sharps, fall out of formation."

Adrian stepped from the column and stood at attention as Kozak said, "Candidate Sharps, do you wish to fall out of the march?"

Adrian straightened. "No, Sergeant, I do not."

Kozak studied him, as though looking for a crack in his demeanor.

The sergeant's next words startled Adrian. "I understand you rode with the Rough Riders and Buffalo Bill Cody's Wild West Show."

"Yes, Sergeant."

Kozak grinned as he handed Adrian the reins. "Then you must know how to ride a horse."

Adrian took the reins, his mind numb from the words, and didn't notice Kozak take his rifle and remove his pack. The sergeant swung the pack over the saddle horn, slung the rifle over his shoulder, then marched off without a word.

Adrian stood dumbfounded. A voice from the column finally broke through. "Get on the horse, man."

Adrian climbed into the saddle, then lightly coaxed the horse forward with a tap of his heels to the animal's flanks.

That night the barracks celebrated, as the candidates now knew they had passed the final, difficult stage of their training and would soon become officers in the United States Army.

Equipment was to be returned the following day, with the rest of the week focused on the paperwork every soldier would encounter at least once in his tour of service: the forms certifying transfer from one duty station to another.

Adrian lay on his bunk trying to work the puzzle in his mind.

"I don't understand the man," he said.

"I've never tried to figure a white man," said Harwood. "But you're right. This is a puzzle."

In the background a harmonica played lightly; a deep voice hummed a gospel song.

There was a commotion near the front entrance of the barracks, where a clerk was tacking sheets of paper to the wall. The candidates were watching in silence, when Kozak stepped through the door and shouted, "Well, do you gentlemen want to know your rank—and your next posting?"

There was a split second of silence, then everyone rushed from their bunks, swallowing Kozak in a black sea of men who were about to learn of their future.

Adrian pulled himself to his feet and followed, watching the others gradually return to their bunks after learning of their destination. Some wore grins, some were disappointed, but all looked relieved to at least know they were leaving Fort Des Moines.

David found his name on the sheets, turned, and grinned at Adrian. "Second lieutenant. Three-Seventy-Second Infantry Regiment."

Harwood, too, had a big grin. "Second lieutenant. I've been assigned to the Three-Seventy-Second Infantry Regiment."

Adrian read his orders. He turned, and with a broad grin said, "First lieutenant! Three-Seventy-Second Infantry Regiment!"

David and Harwood snapped to attention and saluted Adrian, who returned the salute smartly; then all three came together in one great hug, and despite the pain, Adrian danced with the two in an awkward circle, nearly falling, but was caught and righted by a pair of strong hands. He looked into the face of Kozak, then stepped back and straightened. "Thank you, Sergeant."

Kozak nodded, then started to leave the barrack room, when he was stopped by Adrian's voice.

"Sergeant, I need to know something."

Kozak turned and faced Adrian. "You need to know why I helped you today."

Adrian nodded.

"I served with Captain Charles Young in the Ninth Cavalry back in eighty-seven. He saved my life in a scrap with the Sioux at the Milk River. I figure I owed one good Colored officer a favor. I think you'll set the books straight for me."

Adrian extended his hand, saying, "I'll set the books straight for you."

That night the barrack walls fairly shook in celebration, a loud hubbub of noises—talking, laughing, singing, shouting, dancing—among men who had endured the punishing training and were soon to be commissioned as officers in the Army of the United States.

22

One week after the postings, on October 14, 1917, Colonel W. T. Johnson, chief of the Division of Training Camps, War Department, arrived by train in Des Moines with commissions for 639 officers: 106 captains, 329 first lieutenants, and 204 second lieutenants.

Colonel Johnson was met by Major Graves and two enlisted personnel, who quickly loaded the senior officer and his belongings into a military automobile and sped off toward Fort Des Moines.

Several hours later a train arriving from Omaha stopped at Des Moines. A tall man wearing a business suit and western hat stepped from a passenger car.

The white man hailed a taxi, loaded his suitcase, and gave the driver instructions.

Fifteen minutes later, the cab carrying the white man stopped in front of the Sharps boardinghouse. The man got out, walked to the door, knocked, and waited patiently.

Augustus answered the door and his immediate reaction was joy. Not surprise—joy.

"Ernst! I had hoped you would come."

He removed his hat. "I recommended two fine men from Arizona to become officers in the United States Army. The only two from the whole state of Arizona—and both Colored. Do you think I'd miss their graduation?"

Augustus shook his head in amazement.

The next morning the 639 officer candidates assembled on the parade field in front of a reviewing stand where Colonel Johnson, the camp commander, and the regimental commander stood to conclude a historical undertaking in American military history.

Adrian stood at attention at the head of his platoon along with Kozak; Graves stood at the front of the company.

At the edge of the parade field, hundreds of family members had arrived for the ceremony, including the Sharps family and Alice Harwood.

At the center of the group stood Augustus and Ernst Bruner, who watched with pride as the presentation began.

The second lieutenants were commissioned first, followed by the first lieutenants, then the captains.

When the ceremony was concluded, the band struck up "Stars and Stripes Forever," and the full complement of the 17th Provisional Training Regiment passed in review before the officers and civilians.

Standing to the side, Selona felt Augustus's big hand grip her arm lightly, and as she turned and looked into his face, she saw a glimmer in his eyes that only she understood.

Selona despised the thought of her sons going to France, and she certainly made no secret of that. But at this moment, watching this great occasion, she felt Augustus's pride.

Sergeant Major Augustus Sharps's military career had begun as a young trooper of the 10th Cavalry on the frozen plains of Kansas in the late 1860s, and now, over five decades later, he stood on the parade ground at Fort Des Moines to watch his sons receive commissions as officers in the army. He had known and served with Colonel Benjamin H. Grierson, the first commander of the 10th; served with and become friends with Lieutenant Henry Ossian Flipper, the first Colored man to graduate from West Point; and ridden with the Congress of Rough Riders with William F. Cody to tell the world of the buffalo soldiers on the western frontier. He had never dreamed of becoming an officer himself, and never dreamed of what he now witnessed: Not one or two token Colored officers, but 639—an entire regiment of Colored officers!

That evening in the parlor of Selona's boardinghouse, all gathered for the final ceremony of the day.

Dressed in his uniform, Adrian stood beside his father; wearing a white gown, Hannah stood by Selona as a local minister read from the Bible and joined the two in marriage. With the exchange of vows and rings, the bride and groom turned to the gathering.

At that moment, Augustus pulled his sabre from its scabbard, David pulled Darcy Gibbs's, and the two joined the tips of the swords above the bride and groom.

First Lieutenant Adrian Sharps and Hannah Simmons Sharps passed beneath the steel arch to the applause of friends and family to begin a new life.

PART 3

★

THE 372ND INFANTRY REGIMENT

23

∗ ∗ ∗

On the morning of April 14, 1918, a low, gray sky hung over Saint-Nazaire, France, barricading the rising sun from the soldiers aboard the troop transport U.S.S. *Susquehanna*, an old German freighter formerly named the *Rhine*. Nearby, what appeared to be a fleet of American cargo ships sat in anchorage in the harbor and at the port of the town that lay 225 miles southwest of Paris, where the Loire River met the Atlantic Ocean.

Beyond the dock, on the cobblestone streets of the centuries-old port city, hundreds of anxious men, women, and children stood awaiting their first glimpse of the new arrivals.

Word had spread like wildfire the night before, when the giant transport had cruised into its anchorage with 5,500 men who had traveled across the Atlantic to assist France in its hour of need.

An old man stood at dockside with a little girl, his eyes red from shedding tears for men he had never seen; a young woman watched expectantly, holding a small American flag

she had made the night before. Banners read, VIVE AMÉRI-
CAINS! WELCOME 372ND INFANTRY REGIMENT!

There was even a band and a group of dignitaries, all ig-
noring the early morning chill to honor the new arrivals.

Through the thin light, movement could be seen on the
quarterdeck of the *Susquehanna*. Dark shapes moved toward the lowered gangway, shadows set against a gray
background.

And when it seemed the suspense could no longer be tol-
erated, a single doughboy suddenly appeared at the apex of
the gangway.

In his hands he held aloft a long pole bearing the Stars
and Stripes, which flapped in the dockside breeze.

Now the bank struck up "The Washington Post March"
and the tumultuous welcome began.

The tall, black-skinned soldier, wearing combat gear,
pack, and steel helmet, marched smartly down the gangway
to the thunderous cheers; then two more soldiers appeared,
shoulder to shoulder, carrying the standards of the 372nd
Infantry Regiment and the 93rd Division.

Down they came, eyes straight ahead, and the moment
the boots of the soldier carrying Old Glory touched French
soil, the cheers rose to a deafening pitch. Then, slowly,
steadily began a drumming sound. The ship seemed to tremble at its mooring, the dock to vibrate as all eyes moved
from the standard-bearers to the deck and gangway of the
ship, the source of the low drone of stamping feet marking
time in heavy hobnailed boots, now sounding like a herd of
thundering buffalo.

The standard-bearers marched to the waiting line of dignitaries and made a slow turn until they faced the ship;
behind marched Brigadier General Roy H. Hoffman, the
regimental commander, who saluted the mayor of Saint-
Nazaire, shook hands, then turned to review the arrival of
his troops.

Down they came in a column of twos, carrying full field packs, Springfield rifles slung on their shoulders, their black diamond eyes straight ahead.

Appearing at the head of A Company, First Battalion, marched Captain Robert Chauncey, tall, blond-headed, with blue eyes that peered coldly from beneath the rim of his steel helmet. He appeared unimpressed by the commotion, showing no emotion whatever. But that was not the case of the officer who followed at the head of the First Platoon.

First Lieutenant Adrian Sharps's first thoughts were of his father, and how he wished the old buffalo soldier could be marching at his side this very moment. How proud he would have been to see the outpouring of love from a nation of strangers.

The rumors were true, he realized, about the reception given the 369th Regiment, a part of the 93rd Division, upon its earlier arrival at Brest.

Adrian heard a familiar voice from behind, as Second Lieutenant David Sharps, at the head of Second Platoon, reached the cobblestones and ordered a column right turn.

Behind him would be Second Lieutenant Joseph Harwood, at the head of his troops.

The column wound along the street, past screaming spectators, small stores, and bread vendors, and began to move up a hill toward the center of town.

Adrian's gaze remained steady to the front until he saw a flash of red from the corner of his eye. A young girl in a red dress rushed to the side of Private James Kenny, a tall, thin eighteen-year-old from Richmond, Virginia.

The woman threw her arms around the startled Kenny, hugged and kissed him, and caused him to break step in the march.

Adrian yelled, "Eyes front! Stay in formation, Kenny! No fraternizing with the civilians while marching."

The private glanced at platoon sergeant Rufus Hatch, who marched at the outside of the column. "What does 'fraternizing' mean, Sergeant?"

Hatch looked severely at Kenny, then barked, "He means ... keep your eyes to the front, and no mixing with the civilians!"

Just then an old man grabbed Hatch's hand and kissed his knuckles. Hatch appeared stunned at this, could only grin and nod.

Marching beside Kenny was Private Franklin Tibbs, an eighteen-year-old from Washington, D.C., who fancied himself a ladies' man. Tibbs turned slightly and found a pretty young woman giving him a tantalizing smile. He smiled back, then snapped his head to the front, awaiting the wrath he knew would follow.

"Tibbs, eyes front!" growled Hatch. "You're a soldier now, not a street-corner pimp!"

Tibbs looked straight ahead, still grinning, as the platoon passed Captain Chauncey, at street-side reviewing the men. Beside Chauncey stood First Sergeant Vince O'Doul, a red-headed Irishman and twenty-year veteran who had served with Chauncey in the 9th Cavalry in the Philippines.

Adrian glanced at O'Doul as he marched by. The Irishman's green eyes fixed on him for a hateful moment before he spit on the cobblestones.

At that moment it all seemed to come together. His rank! Since receiving his commission, Adrian had been treated with contempt by white brother officers, even those subordinate to him. But he took it, like his father had when he'd served in the army. The Colored soldier, officer or enlisted, had to take it. There was no other option.

To hell with them, thought Adrian. He was as good a soldier as any of them, and as the column wound through town and into the lush green countryside, he knew that while many things would never change, the debarkation would change the lives forever of every sable doughboy—the name fondly given the Colored American soldiers by the people of France—and perhaps the lives of those who commanded them.

24

Like a long, undulating snake of steel and khaki, their fixed bayonets glistening in the afternoon sun, the column marched at route step along a narrow road fringed by an endless rock wall. To the doughboys, the sight was more than impressive; it was like something out of a dream.

In the countryside, as in the town, farmers and their families and workers from the fields lined the rock walls, shouting and throwing flowers in their path. Although pack straps cut into their shoulders, and the weight of rifles added to the burden, the soldiers appeared to glide across the road as though strolling in the park.

Adrian noticed with silent glee that the spirit of the men had risen since they were now marching in full combat gear after being aboard a cramped troop ship for two weeks.

He especially noted Private Kenny, who appeared still in shock at the way they had been received.

Then he overheard Franklin Tibbs say to Kenny, "What's wrong, young soldier—ain't you ever seen white folks glad to see Coloreds before?"

Kenny shook his head in amazement. "Not unless it was time to chop cotton."

Tibbs chuckled. He had formed a brotherly fondness for young Kenny since their training at Camp Stewart, Virginia. "I wouldn't know about chopping cotton," he told the private. "But I do know something about women, especially when a woman tells you you're welcome."

Sergeant Hatch shook his head. "Shut up that fool talk. We come here to fight Germans, not chase women!"

He turned away without seeing Tibbs chuckle, or hearing him whisper, "There'll be time for both."

Adrian saw Hatch approaching, and sensed there was something on the man's mind. "Sergeant?"

He sighed heavily. "The men are in good spirits, sir."

Adrian nodded. "That's clear. I doubt many of these men have ever experienced anything like that reception."

"I sure as hell haven't," the sergeant said.

Adrian chuckled. "There's more to come."

"Sir?"

"I learned it in Cuba. Changes, Sergeant. We've just walked from one world into another. It always creates problems."

"We already got one."

"Oh?"

"The men. They've been aboard that ship for two weeks. You understand what I'm saying, sir?"

"Female companionship."

Hatch nodded his head severely.

Adrian straightened his pack and adjusted his rifle. He said to the sergeant, "Did you know that during the Civil War, General Hooker brought along a caravan of prostitutes to service his men?"

"No, sir. I didn't know that." There was a pause. "Did we bring one of those caravans?"

Adrian laughed, and pointed to a nearby hill. "We didn't have to."

On the hill, standing around a wagon, were a dozen young French women.

Sergeant Hatch stared for a moment. "I think I might like this war."

Hatch walked back to the platoon, and as Adrian walked on he passed Sergeant Vince O'Doul, who was standing by the road, glaring at the prostitutes.

The rain began at noon, turning the road into a quagmire. The columns of heavily equipped soldiers carved two great furrows, nearly a foot deep, along the sides of the muddy road, making the march an annoyance. But even more annoying were the trucks moving along the road from Saint-Nazaire to the east, spraying the soldiers with a thick, black mud.

"Good farming land," said Kenny, wiping the muddy slime from his face. He examined a clot closely. "Thick and black, not red like in Alabama."

"Shut up, boy. Going on with all that country talk about dirt. Hell, I've eaten more of it this afternoon than they got in Alabama," Hatch snapped.

The sergeant joined Adrian. "How much farther, Lieutenant?"

Adrian's face was ashen from the dried mud. "I can't say, Sergeant. Just keep the men moving."

Adrian looked down the road and saw a motorcycle with a dispatch rider stop and talk with Captain Robert Chauncey. The courier then roared along the center of the column, spraying the men with more mud.

Chauncey raised his arm and pointed to a field on the other side of the rock wall.

Adrian turned and motioned to his men, who climbed the wall and sat in the lush grass.

It appeared, for a time at least, that the march was over.

*   *   *

By sunset, the countryside was dotted with tents for as far as the eye could see. For Adrian's platoon, the luck of the draw gave them a small stable for their bivouac.

The smell reminded him of the stable at home in Arizona.

"Dreary but dry, Sergeant Hatch."

Hatch looked around skeptically. "Beats sleeping in the mud."

Suddenly, Kenny shouted, *"Ten-hut!"*

Adrian turned to see Sergeant O'Doul enter the stable. The man's green eyes flashed as his nose nearly pressed against Kenny's. O'Doul pointed at his stripes and shouted, "You tree-climbing monkey, you call 'attention' when an officer enters. I ain't no goddamned officer. I'm a senior NCO. You call 'at ease' when a senior NCO enters. Do you understand me, boy?"

Kenny managed to sputter, "Yes, First Sergeant."

O'Doul wheeled and pointed at Adrian. "You, boy, come with me."

A sudden quiet fell over the stable as the first sergeant walked outside. Adrian felt a rush of anger as he walked uncomfortably past his men.

Outside, a soft rain was falling; O'Doul lit a cigarette as Adrian approached.

O'Doul took a drag, then said, "Now, boy, you know me and the captain come to the company just before we shipped over here from Newport News, so there's something you best learn right off—"

Adrian interrupted. "First Sergeant, I am Lieutenant Sharps, platoon leader of First Platoon, A Company, First Battalion, 372nd Infantry, 93rd Division. Don't ever call me 'boy' again."

O'Doul reddened and looked at Adrian as if he had been slapped in the face.

"I'm going to let that remark pass this one time, First

Sergeant, but be warned: If I hear 'boy,' 'nigger,' 'tree-climbing monkey,' or any other slur out of your ignorant mouth in the future, you will answer to it."

Adrian looked past the slack-jawed first sergeant and could see Hatch watching through a crack in the door.

O'Doul stepped back and gave Adrian a long perusal. "You sure are one uppity nigger."

Adrian stepped close to O'Doul, close enough to smell his cigarette breath. "Make that 'You are one uppity nigger, *sir.*' "

O'Doul mashed his cigarette under his boot, then spit, and said, "There'll be hell first." He started away, then stopped and turned to face Adrian. "Your platoon has just volunteered for perimeter guard and every other dirty detail I can find."

After Adrian watched O'Doul walk toward a nearby farmhouse where the white officers and NCOs were billeted, he turned and started back to the stable and spotted Hatch still watching. "Come here, Sergeant," Adrian said.

Hatch stepped out of the stable and closed the door.

"You heard all of that?"

Hatch replied uncomfortably, "Pardon me, sir. But you got to be the craziest Colored man I ever seen in my life."

"Why?"

"You can't talk to a white man like that, sir."

"Why is that?"

Hatch looked like a man with a bad case of indigestion. "It just ain't done."

Adrian faced Hatch, his eyes blazing. "I'm not a nigger. I'm not a boy. So I guess I can talk to a white man like that."

Hatch nodded slightly. "I reckon I best get started on posting the guards."

25

O'Doul kept his word to make life miserable for Adrian's platoon. After pulling a night of guard duty, the formation the following morning brought another detail as O'Doul announced, "First platoon is assigned to stevedore duty at the port in Saint-Nazaire."

Adrian was fuming as he approached Captain Chauncey. "Sir, this isn't right. My men have been on guard duty all night. They need rest."

Chauncey seemed to stare through Adrian. "The first sergeant assigns work details, Lieutenant. I have to respect his authority."

Adrian had learned the adage long ago that while generals ran the wars, first sergeants ran the army.

At the stable the men were in a sullen mood.

"This is a bunch of crap, sir," said Hatch. He was eyeing Adrian with a contempt that couldn't be concealed.

"We've been given our orders, Sergeant. Get the men fed, then we'll form up at the company command post."

Adrian walked off under the baleful eyes of his men.

He had fought, and lost, his first battle in the war in
France. An hour later two transport trucks arrived and the
men of first platoon were loaded. Adrian climbed into the
cab of one transport while, to everyone's surprise, O'Doul
climbed into the cab of the other.

Saint-Nazaire no longer pulsated with the cheering
crowds who had lined its streets to welcome the American
soldiers. The single trace remaining of that joyous tumult
were the trampled flowers in the street. Now the port city
hummed with the more mundane business of unloading
cargo.

Twenty lorries sat in a long line waiting to be unloaded
with food supplies shipped to France from the United
States. Since America had not been on a vast war footing
since the Civil War, it had no large foundries making cannon and other weapons. Such armament would be sup-
plied by the French and British. America would provide
men and food.

O'Doul jumped down from the transport vehicle and
swaggered over to Adrian. He pointed at the string of lorries, saying, "Your platoon has been detailed to fill those
trucks. I expect that'll take you most of the day. You'll be
picked up at seventeen hundred hours. If you're not finished,
the drivers have been instructed to wait until your detail is
completed. Those are Captain Chauncey's orders."

The sergeant wheeled and climbed into the first transport,
motioning the driver of the second to follow.

The driver of the first lorry, a young Colored private
from one of the Service of Supply units, approached and
saluted.

Of the more than 400,000 Colored men who had joined
the army or been drafted, more than half that number were
in Service of Supply. Adrian had learned that 200,000 Coloreds were serving in France, most in butchery companies,
stevedore regiments, engineer service battalions, labor battalions and companies, and pioneer infantry regiments—all

of which were military terms for units of common laborers. Only a small percentage of these Coloreds were combat troops.

"What's the routine, Private?" Adrian asked.

The private pointed at a crane extending from the ship, attached to which hung a large cargo net filled with bags of grain. "Sir, the nets are lowered to the deck and unloaded. Then another net comes in a few minutes later. We just unload and load. When a truck is filled, it parks over yonder and waits for the rest to be loaded. When all the trucks are full, we leave in a convoy."

"What if we load two trucks at once from two cargo nets?"

"Lord, sir, you'll kill your men if you try loading two trucks with only the men you've got."

Adrian said, "My men can handle it, Private." Just then he heard the whirr of the crane and saw the cargo net lowering to the dock.

Adrian looked at Hatch, then said, "Sergeant, get this first net loaded onto this private's lorry. I'll be back in a few minutes."

Adrian turned and walked toward the brow leading onto the cargo ship.

He returned twenty minutes later, as the net was nearly empty.

"Sergeant Hatch, get two lorries alongside each other. We're going to load them at once."

Hatch shook his head. He was dripping sweat from the work. "You'll kill us all, Lieutenant."

"No, Sergeant. We'll work twice as hard and there'll be a reward in it for the men."

"What reward?"

"Our transportation will return at seventeen hundred hours. The sooner we get these trucks loaded, the more time the men will have to go sightseeing in town."

Hatch smiled broadly and saluted. "Yes, sir."

Adrian's father once told him that there was a great difference between an officer and a leader of men, and that the key for an officer to become a leader was to command by example.

He removed and folded his blouse, then did the same with his undershirt, and placed the garments in a neat pile. The other men did the same as the two cargo nets settled onto the dock. Two lines were formed, and in bucket-brigade fashion, the loading began with a fury.

When the two trucks were filled and roared away, another pair replaced them just as a new set of cargo nets arrived onto the dock.

Throughout the loading Adrian sensed a rising resentment among the men, which he understood, for he felt the same way.

As usual, it was Frank Tibbs who began the complaining. "I thought we came to France to fight Germans, Lieutenant." He hoisted a heavy sack to Kenny, then turned to receive the next one from Hatch.

"We'll fight Germans, Tibbs. First, let's get these trucks loaded."

"He's right, Lieutenant," said Kenny. "We didn't come here to load cargo."

Hatch had heard enough. "Shut your mouths and work. You ain't ducking the boss today. Not with me in this goddamned line."

Adrian chuckled. "Ducking the boss" was a southern Colored's term for dodging work. In the army it was called "goldbricking."

Hatch looked at Adrian. "What kind of orders puts infantrymen on the docks unloading ships?"

"Chauncey's orders," Adrian said as he hoisted a fifty-pound sack into Hatch's waiting arms.

"More like O'Doul's," said Tibbs.

Hatch worked behind Adrian, and as each sack was passed along, their eyes would lock for a moment. Finally, the stocky sergeant said, "I told you, you can't talk to a white man like that, sir."

Adrian forced a smile. "If I'm going to take these men into combat, they have to know that I'm the one they must follow."

"You niggers stop the talking and keep at your work," a loud southern voice barked.

Adrian froze, then slowly allowed the sack to slide from his hands. He straightened up and massaged the small of his back.

"You there. You, boy. Get back to work," Southern Drawl said.

He turned to see a tall, lanky naval petty officer pointing at him. Adrian tapped his chest. "Are you talking to me?"

The sailor nodded. "Yeah, I'm talking to you. Get back to work."

Adrian stepped out of the line and slowly walked to where his blouse lay. Slowly, carefully, he slipped the blouse on, his back to the petty officer.

The sailor, by now furious, snapped to the soldiers, who were watching Adrian, "The rest of you niggers, get back to work."

Adrian turned just as the petty officer stepped within arm's length.

The sailor's eyes widened. "Well, I'll be damned. You're an officer."

"That's correct. And you are an enlisted man. These men are soldiers, not 'niggers' and not 'boys.' Is that clear?"

The sailor's head slowly nodded.

"Don't enlisted men salute officers in the navy?" demanded Adrian.

The petty officer said, "Who told you to lower two cargo nets at a time? I'm the dockmaster. I give the orders around here on how things are run on this dock."

"The ship's captain said it wasn't a problem. He said if my men could handle the pace, it was fine with him."

The sailor hawked and spit, then walked off cussing.

For the next three hours the lorries were being loaded faster than anyone had ever seen, including the petty officer, who stood watching with amazement.

The last truck was loaded by 1300 hours, and since there was no more work to be done, and the troop trucks would not arrive until 1700 hours, there were four hours to spare.

Sergeant Hatch approached Adrian, sweaty, his hair in a tangle, but a smile spread across his face. "What now, Lieutenant?"

"Get the men dressed and into formation. We're going to town."

A roar rose from the dock as the platoon scrambled for their blouses and undershirts.

The streets of the old port city had a different feel than any Adrian had ever known. But the strangest feeling he had was that of being alone. For the first time he wasn't in training, or with his wife, or overseeing the welfare of his men. For the first time since leaving Arizona, he felt like an individual. If for only a few hours, it was, he realized, an exhilarating feeling.

He had decided not to accompany the other men, leaving them in the charge of Sergeant Hatch, for he knew there was the distinctive line that separated officer from enlisted man. He wanted to be friends, especially with Hatch, but that was not possible. His father had taught him that another aspect of leadership was to remain separate, for someday he would lead them into battle, and he could not let his judgment be swayed by friendship.

Suddenly, he stopped, and his eyes were riveted to a glass case inside a small shop. He went inside, where he found an old man sitting at a table, a pair of jeweler's lenses mounted on his metal glasses. Adrian went immediately to the case and pointed at an object that he found captivating.

Adrian did not speak French, but by pointing he made the man understand. He was handed a small case no more than nine inches long and three inches wide. A miniature guitar was inside the case, and before he could ask, was told, "Posette."

Adrian held the tiny case in his large hands and noted the exquisite craftsmanship, then glanced to the table where the old man had been working and saw musical instruments of all types in various stages of manufacture.

Then he laughed aloud as he realized this tiny man with friendly eyes and soft hands was the craftsman.

He took out a tiny book that translated English into French and asked, "How much?"

The craftsman laughed at his poor French, then took five francs from his cash drawer. Adrian understood and removed five francs from his purse and gave it to the man.

They shook hands and Adrian left, carrying with him the only piece of beauty he had seen since arriving in a country wracked with the ugliness of war.

A piece of beauty to be sent to his wife, another piece of beauty.

At 1700 hours, Sergeant Vince O'Doul returned with the transports, and the look on his face made the work of the day all the more worthwhile. He stepped down from the transport expecting to find the first platoon looking like death warmed over. Instead, he found the men standing in formation, all their faces wearing broad grins.

"Get aboard, men," Adrian ordered.

During the trip to the camp, voices from the two transports competed with each other for the high ground in singing,

"Over there, over there, send the word, send the word over there. That the Yanks are coming, the Yanks are coming, the drums rum-tumming everywhere.

"So prepare, say a prayer, send the word, send the word To beware. We'll be over, we're coming over, and we Won't be back till it's over over there."

26

The mood in the regiment went from jubilation on the first day of landing at Saint-Nazaire to one of near riot by the third day, when companies of the new arrivals were being sent to work on railroad repair, road construction, and more stevedore work at the docks.

In the opinion of the enlisted men and officers, the men of the 372nd were being treated like slave labor gangs, not like soldiers.

One company even went so far as to go on strike to voice its total disgust with the situation.

"Why shouldn't the men be angry?" David seethed as he washed the grime from his hands and face. He had spent the entire day with his platoon in the hold of a cargo ship loading the huge nets with wooden crates filled with ammunition.

Harwood was exhausted as well, after his platoon had spent the day working in the railyard at a small village a few miles from Saint-Nazaire. "I thought working the slaugh-

ter house was hard work. Man, today nearly killed us all,"
he said.

Adrian began adding his own complaint when Sergeant
Hatch suddenly appeared, accompanied by two other
sergeants, neither of whom Adrian recognized.

"Lieutenant Sharps, sir. May we speak with you?" Hatch
said.

Adrian joined the NCOs outside the stables. He had been
an enlisted man and knew that when sergeants from various platoons got together, it spelled trouble.

"Sergeant?"

Hatch fumbled around for a moment, then got to the
heart of the matter. "Sir, this is Sergeant Jefferson from second platoon, and Sergeant Holmes from third platoon."
Adrian shook their hands.

"What's this about?"

"It's about the labor details, sir. The men in the ranks are
getting restless. There's talk about going on strike if something isn't done, and done damn quick."

"Do you know what you're saying, Sergeant Hatch?"

"Yes, sir. We know that we can be executed. Me and
Sergeants Jefferson and Holmes represent the men of the
company, and we thought you'd be the one to speak with
since you've had more experience in the army."

" 'Represent'?" Adrian said the word with such empha-
sis, it made Hatch step backward.

"Yes, sir. We're soldiers, sir, not labor gangs. The men
came here to fight Germans, not work as stevedores and
railroad repair crews."

At that moment David and Harwood stepped outside and
listened. Hatch continued, "We speak for every enlisted
man in the battalion, sir. The men are not going to be used
as common labor. What we want to do is avoid a big ruckus.
That's why we're here. To ask you to speak with Captain
Chauncey on our behalf and ask him to speak to the battalion commander."

David looked severely at Jefferson. "Do you understand what you're getting yourself into, Sergeant?"

Jefferson nodded. "All the men agree, Lieutenant."

Harwood looked at Holmes. "Sergeant Holmes, do you understand?"

Holmes also nodded. "We'll follow you anywhere, Lieutenant. Right through the gates of hell, if necessary, and put out the fires—as soldiers! But we won't work on labor detail. All the men agree, sir."

"Do you understand you are talking mutiny? You could be executed," Adrian said.

Hatch volunteered the answer. "It wouldn't look good back in the States if three thousand Colored soldiers of the 372nd were executed for wanting to fight the Germans, sir."

"You're saying this is a regiment-wide feeling?"

Hatch nodded. "Yes, sir. There's a few that don't want to go along, but not many."

Adrian looked at David and Harwood. Both looked dumbfounded. "You men get back to your troops. I'll speak with Chauncey."

Adrian found the flap of Chauncey's tent closed. He spoke through the canvas. "Captain Chauncey, this is Lieutenant Adrian Sharps. May I speak with you, sir?"

There was a rustling inside the tent, the sound of low voices, then the flap opened. Chauncey stepped out, followed by O'Doul and another captain Adrian recognized as the commander of B Company. All three looked nervous. Adrian's eyes drifted to Chauncey's hand. The captain had a Colt .45 pistol in his fist.

"What do you want, Lieutenant?"

Adrian got to it. "I'm afraid we have a problem, sir. The men are talking about going on strike."

Chauncey looked around nervously. "I know. What's your part in this, Sharps?"

"I have no 'part,' sir. I have been asked to speak to the battalion commander on behalf of the men. They have grievances regarding the use of the men for labor details. They want to fight Germans, not unload ships and repair railroads."

Chauncey's empty hand swiped at his sweating forehead. "They'll be court-martialed."

Adrian glanced quickly at the ground to hide his smile, then looked at Chauncey and said, "An entire battalion, sir? An entire regiment? These men have come to fight the enemy. I doubt the French government would stand silently by while fighting men are court-martialed for *wanting* to fight."

Chauncey wore the look of a hurt dog, which said he didn't know which direction to turn. And he was frightened, thought Adrian, otherwise, why the Colt? Were the other white officers sharing this same fear?

"Will you see the battalion commander, Captain?" Adrian asked after an uncomfortable second of silence.

Chauncey holstered his pistol and walked off in the direction of battalion headquarters.

The next morning, the officers and NCOs of A Company stood at the front of their respective platoons. Down the line the reports echoed, "All present or accounted for!" until Sergeant Vince O'Doul turned and saluted Captain Robert Chauncey and said, "All present or accounted for."

Then Chauncey ordered, "All platoon leaders will report to the company command post. Dismiss your troops and have them report to the chow wagons. That is all."

Adrian turned to face his platoon. "Sergeant Hatch, dismiss the men and have them report to the chow wagon. When I return from the meeting with the company commander, be prepared to receive training orders for the day."

Adrian had emphasized the word *training*.

Hatch sputtered, "You mean . . . "

Adrian clapped him on the shoulder. "I can't promise, but I think so."

The lieutenant made the short walk to the command post, where he found the other officers and noncoms waiting. No one said a word. Then Chauncey appeared from inside his tent, and he sat at the table. "Colonel Hoffman has instructed the battalion commanders that the regiment is to resume training exercises."

"There'll be no more labor details, Captain?" asked David.

Chauncey shook his head. "Labor battalions from Support of Services will assume all labor details."

A collective sigh of relief rippled through the group.

"You'll start with physical training, then a ten-mile march with full field packs. The troops appear to be in sorry condition after the boat trip from the United States. The next order of business will be close-order drill, then bayonet practice. There will be no respite. The men will train from sunrise until dark, and after evening chow there will be cleaning of equipment and guard duty."

27

They marched in every direction like ants stirred from their hill, each platoon given a specific heading and ordered to march for two hours, rest for thirty minutes, then return.

Adrian noticed that the mood of the men had changed. Once again they were acting like soldiers, not common laborers. But they were the lucky ones. Most Colored soldiers in France had nothing to look forward to except the dreariness of unloading ships and repairing roads, while the white infantry could at least feel as though they were in France to do a soldier's job and could at least walk through the lush countryside.

Adrian had broken his eighty-man platoon into ten-man squads, and the squads into five-man sections, starting the sections on the march in three-minute intervals. Within an hour, the platoon stretched nearly a mile in a westerly direction, moving at a pace set by the first section.

The hike felt good to Adrian; his leg muscles were still

stiff but they gradually began to loosen and his body seemed to be coming alive again. The platoon walked in the morning sun, the men chattering, joking, and singing.

"Oh, Mademoiselle from Armentières, parley-vous?
Oh, Mademoiselle from Armentières, parley-vous?
Oh Mademoiselle from Armentières,
Will you wash a soldier's underwear?
Hinky Dinky, parley-vous."

Then came a livelier version.

"Oh, the General got the Croix de Guerre, parley-vous?
Oh, the General got the Croix de Guerre, parley-vous?
Oh, the General got the Croix de Guerre,
But the son-of-a-gun was never there!
Hinky Dinky, parley-vous."

By noon the first section had reached the edge of a farm a few miles east of Saint-Nazaire, its turnaround point.

The squad leader was a young minister named Willie Dawes, a heavyset young man from Washington, D.C., who had been a member of the First Separate Battalion of the District of Columbia National Guard, a battalion that now constituted the bulk of the First Battalion/372nd Infantry Regiment—more than nine hundred men.

The regiment's motto was *Fidelis et Paratus*—"Faithful and Prepared."

Most of the men had known each other before the war, with the exception of soldiers like Hatch, Tibbs, Kenny, and many of the officers. These men had been assigned after volunteering to fill the complement required under the existing U.S. Army Table of Organization.

Willie Dawes, a meticulous man who practiced his ser-

mons as he marched, found himself walking through a field
of blue flowers. "Lord," he shouted, "what a beautiful piece
of heaven you done put on this tormented land!" He
reached and pulled a bloom to his nose, inhaled the soft fra-
grance, chewed on the light yellow stem, then threw his
arms to the sky and shouted, "Thank you, Lord! Thank you
for this wonderful moment."

What Dawes heard in response was a steady buzzing
noise and, in a flash, the young preacher and his flock were
being stung and tormented by a swarm of bees.

Had Dawes been closer to nature than to God, he'd have
recognized the blue flowers as flax, and had he been a farm-
boy instead of a city preacher, he'd have known that flax,
which is used in the making of linseed oil and textile fiber,
is annually pollinated by bees—thousands of bees.

The men of the first squad saw Dawes running toward
the top of the hill and, slapping and yelling, began following him. The second squad followed, infested by the angry
swarm, disturbed at its work, as did the next squad, and the
next.

Adrian was no luckier, and swatting his face, ears, and
the air, ran like the others, not looking back.

After twenty minutes, the platoon reached the safety of
a large pond on the far side of the hill, and peeling off
clothes, equipment, and cursing like sailors, all eighty men,
including the platoon leader of First Platoon, A Company,
First Battalion, 372nd Infantry Regiment, 93rd Division,
had their first baptism by fire and were trying to put it out
in a scummy pond. "One thing's for sure, Lieutenant," said
Hatch.

"What's that, Sergeant?"

"The men won't be dreaming about women tonight.
They'll be having nightmares about them bees!"

The platoon had returned to their tents with swollen
hands and faces, some with their eyes puffed nearly closed,

but in high spirits despite the lost battle with the flax bees.

Guards were posted that night and the platoon slept in and around the stables, blissfully unaware of the changes that would soon take the 372nd on a unique—and historic—path.

28

* * *

David Sharps and Harwood found Adrian in the bivouac area with his platoon after reveille on the morning of the fifth day. He and his men were standing with their mess kits in a long line waiting for their rations from the chow wagon.

David grinned. "Let's go to the officers' mess."

Adrian looked puzzled. "What officers' mess?"

Harwood said, "It's set up at regimental headquarters."

Adrian preferred eating with his men, since a soldier's stomach was a quick barometer check on morale, but, then again, he thought, he was an officer and rank did have some privileges.

The three walked to a large farmhouse a quarter mile down the road, where regimental headquarters had been established and an officers' messhall set up in the barn.

"What the hell is that?" asked Harwood, pointing at the seating area.

Adrian shook his head in disbelief. A long rope had been strung down the middle of the barn and on it hung large blankets dividing the seating area into two sections. On one side sat the white officers and white NCOs; on the other, the Colored officers.

The three sat down and waited. Within a few minutes, enlisted waiters brought French bread, a thin vegetable soup, fried potatoes, and hard-boiled eggs.

Adrian looked at the food and asked the server—called a striker—"What's this, Private?"

"Breakfast, sir."

Adrian shook his head. "Where's the fatback, the fried eggs, the biscuits and molasses?"

"I don't know, sir."

Adrian looked around and spotted the mess sergeant. He walked to the head of the serving line where the thin, wiry noncom with deep ebony skin was watching over the strikers.

Adrian pointed to the rope and blanket. "What is that, Sergeant?"

The mess sergeant looked nervous while stirring a large vat of soup. "General's orders, sir. He wants the whites and Coloreds to eat separate from each other."

Adrian was fuming. "What about this chow? You're feeding us French rations."

"Yes, sir. From now on, the breakfast meal will be from French rations, the evening meal from American rations."

"By the general's orders, no doubt?"

"Yes, sir."

"What about those American rations? Are our supplies that low?"

The sergeant shook his head. "No, sir. Our supply depot is busting at the seams with American chow, especially now that there's more coming in every day."

Adrian went back to the table and sat down angrily and told them what he had learned.

"Why feed us French rations when there's tons of American rations sitting at the port and in our own regimental supply depot?" David asked.

"Logic says that you feed the rations of the army you're in," Harwood said.

"Exactly," Adrian said. An uneasy suspicion gnawed at his stomach. He stood, took his bowl of soup, and walked to a large garbage can. In full view of the entire mess, he dumped the soup, bowl, and spoon into the can and left.

One immutable fact exists in the army: If an officer needs an answer, he speaks with the sergeants.

Adrian found Hatch sitting outside the stable running a cleaning rod through the barrel of his rifle. "How was morning chow?"

Hatch pulled the rod out of the barrel and removed the cleaning patch. "Nothing like I've ever had before, Lieutenant."

Adrian eyed him warily. Hatch was a quiet man, a no-nonsense man who had earned the respect of the men while serving in the National Guard before his unit was assigned to the 372nd. The sergeant also had close ties at regimental headquarters.

"I believe you've got a friend at regimental. A clerk?"

"Yes, sir. Sergeant Paul Withers."

"Do you think Withers might be able to answer a few questions?"

"What kind of questions?"

"Questions about what's going on as far as the future of the regiment."

Hatch grinned. "If there's anybody who knows what's going on, it'll be Withers. He's General Hoffman's clerk and knows most everything before the general."

"Do you think we might talk to Withers about something involving future plans?"

Hatch's mouth tightened. "No, sir. We couldn't."

Adrian's disappointment could not be hidden.

Then Hatch grinned. "But I could. One sergeant to another. Withers don't trust officers. He's surrounded by them."

Adrian understood. "Sergeant Hatch, I'd like you to speak with Withers—sergeant to sergeant."

An hour later Hatch returned to the stable. He wore a strange look on his face.

Adrian wanted to speak to him before platoon leaders' call. So he was waiting at the company command post when Chauncey arrived with O'Doul.

Adrian realized he and Chauncey had never spoken alone, not even aboard the ship from Newport News. He didn't know the man, but hoped that he was a good leader. A good leader listens to his men and tries to settle problems before they escalate.

He knew that if the Colored soldiers were to be amalgamated with the French, there would be trouble among the ranks.

Chauncey saw Adrian, whispered something to O'Doul, who walked off, then went to the portable desk he had set up in front of his tent.

"What can I do for you, Lieutenant?"

"It's about the food, sir."

Chauncey sat back, studied Adrian for a long moment, his blue eyes never flinching. "What about the food? Aren't you a connoisseur of the local cuisine?"

"The soup was flavorful but not filling. I just wonder why we're eating French rations."

"You only had one ration, Lieutenant."

"The mess sergeant said our meals are to be divided into French and American rations. I wonder why. Are we short of supplies?"

"We have ample supplies."

"That was my understanding."

Then Chauncey caught Adrian off-guard. "You served with Roosevelt and the First Volunteer Cavalry, didn't you?"

"Yes, sir, all the way to Kettle Ridge."

"Then you know a soldier often lives off the supplies of the local government."

"In Cuba, we had no choice in the matter, sir."

"What exactly is your question, Lieutenant Sharps?"

Adrian took a deep breath. "Is the 372nd going to be attached to French forces?"

"What makes you ask that?"

"The food, sir. There's no reason to change our diet unless the diet becomes of military significance."

"You're very perceptive, Lieutenant." Chauncey reached into his map case and removed a letter. He handed the letter to Adrian.

Adrian recognized the letter as an order, Number 7589/3, dated April 14, 1918, the day the 372nd had arrived in France. It had been issued by General Raquenrau, chief of the French military mission with the American Army, to the commander in chief, American Expeditionary Forces.

The order read:

SUBJECT: Assignment of the 370th Colored Regiment to the 7th Army, and the 371st and 372nd to the Second Army.

I have the honor to inform you that the 370th Colored Regiment will be attached to the 40th Army Corps, which forms part of the 7th Army.

The 371st and the 372nd will be attached to the 13th Army Corps, which forms part of the 2nd Army.

None of these three regiments will be sent to the 4th Army, contrary to the verbal information which had been given you.

By Order of Chief of Staff
(signed) DUTILLEUL

Adrian released a long, deep, and angry sigh. "This isn't right, Captain. We're Americans. We should be fighting alongside American soldiers, not attached to French command."

Chauncey reached over and took the field telephone. He lifted the receiver and held it out to Adrian. "If you wish, I give you permission to contact General Pershing in Paris and discuss the matter with him. I'm sure he'll be interested in what you have to say. After all, he did approve the order."

Adrian stood helpless. "That's not necessary, sir. Can we assume that we will be near the front?"

There was a mischievous look on Chauncey's face as he said, "That's where the French are, Lieutenant. At the front."

"Then we're going to the front? When?"

Chauncey rose and stomped his boots hard, as though trying to shake the blood back into his feet. "In a few days, Lieutenant. Now, if you'll excuse me, I have to prepare a briefing for the other officers in this company, officers who, I must say, are not as perceptive as you."

Adrian saluted. He turned and walked away with mixed emotions of anger and exhilaration. The 372nd wasn't going to fight with American soldiers, but they were going to the front.

That meant—by God!—they were going to fight the Germans!

"We're eating French rations because the brass is getting ready to put us with French forces. They're getting us used to the food."

"We won't have our own separate division?" David asked.

"Remember this?" Adrian asked: " 'Once let the black man get upon his person the brass letters of "U.S.," let him get an eagle on his buttons, and a musket on his shoulder, and bullets in his pocket and there is no power on earth which can deny him his citizenship in the United States of America.' "

Harwood recognized the quote. "Frederick Douglass, during the Civil War."

David sighed heavily. "The American government is so scared that 200,000 Coloreds are rifle-carrying soldiers, they don't want us to be seen as our own organized and disciplined fighting division."

"So they hide us among the French."

29

The regiment was to be transported by train in battalions, and since A Company was in the First Battalion, it would be among the first to depart by train from a point east of Saint-Nazaire.

On the morning of April 18, the battalion arrived at the entraining point to await boarding.

The A Company troops sat in the warm sun, resting against their packs as Chauncey and O'Doul checked each platoon. Adrian noticed that the captain and ever-present sergeant went first to David's and Harwood's platoons, and that made him wonder.

He found out the reason just before entraining, when O'Doul came up and said smugly, "Your platoon is riding up top for security."

The trains were composed of hundreds of "40 and 8" cars, which meant each car could transport either forty troops or eight horses. The cars were low-ceilinged in comparison with their American counterparts, and very narrow, with wooden windows that folded down. The heat inside promised to be unbearable.

Riding in the cars will be hard enough, thought Adrian, but up top!

Atop each car were two sandbag-fortified positions, each designed for two men. Since he knew his men would not fill all the positions on the train, other platoon leaders who spoke out would now join him in having the Lords of Rank exercise their administrative muscle.

The first few hours of the journey, which was scheduled to take two days, weren't as bad as Adrian expected. His men were forced into cramped positions but at least they could feel the wind against their faces and had a panoramic view of the countryside.

At each village they passed, the train slowed, and townspeople lined the tracksides, waving, shouting joyfully at the soldiers—much different, thought Adrian, than when the 9th and 10th cavalries had passed through the south enroute to Tampa for the voyage to Cuba. While the Rough Riders were treated with fanfare, the 9th and 10th were jeered and heckled, bombarded with rocks and bottles, and prevented from leaving the train when there were required stops for water and fuel.

Not in France. Colored soldiers were being treated with courtesy, dignity, and even love—by foreigners. The journey allowed him plenty of time to consider the irony of it all.

He sat at the front of the train with Hatch, and although the noise was much too loud for conversation, their eyes seemed to reflect the same thoughts as they waved at the cheering people of France.

The train stopped at 1900 hours and the troops were fed in short order, since the two remaining sections were traveling behind in one-hour intervals.

Hatch said, "Give me your mess kit, Lieutenant. I'll get you some chow."

"Thank you, Sergeant. I'll check on the men."

Adrian hurried along the top of the train, chatting briefly with his men, who were now feeling the bruising effects of riding on the unyielding roofs of the cars.

Kenny stood, stretched, and did what all the men riding up top sorely needed. From each car along the length of the train the security personnel relieved themselves, looking like dark water fountains against the fading sunlight.

As usual, Tibbs was the first to begin complaining as Adrian approached his position. "How long we going to ride on this damn train, Lieutenant?"

"Our estimated time of arrival at Souilly is nineteen hundred hours the day after tomorrow."

"Day after tomorrow! Lord, Lieutenant, how far are we from the front?"

"A long ways, Tibbs. So get your mind—and your young ass—used to the idea of being miserable for two more days."

Tibbs stepped back angrily as Adrian walked toward his position. Hatch handed him his mess kit. Adrian looked at the food and shook his head. "More soup."

"Don't these French people eat cornbread?" asked Hatch. "Or meat?"

The train lurched, spilling Adrian's soup. He and Hatch started laughing and emptied their soup over the side.

The next day the train moved farther east, through Tours, and reaching Orléans turned north toward Paris. As darkness fell, the men were tired and sore from the travel, but as dawn approached on the morning of April 20, when the train stopped for chow and a rest break, Adrian stood, and for a moment he was grateful to O'Doul.

He pointed to the east, where a bright smear of color lit up the horizon.

"What is it?" asked Hatch.

"Paris. The City of Lights."

"I ain't never seen so many lights, not even in Washington, D.C."

Adrian understood how Paris got its name. From their vantage point atop the cars, he and his men had a better view than the troops below and saw millions of lights highlighting the outline of the city, which appeared like some great wheel, with the streets running spokelike to the center.

Hatch pointed to a tall structure in the distance that stood high above the city. "What's that tall thing, Lieutenant? The one with all the lights on top."

"That 'thing,' Sergeant Hatch, is the Eiffel Tower."

And for a long, glorious moment, the men stood staring in total silence.

"How's the view?" a voice called from below.

Adrian looked down and saw David and Joseph. "Magnificent. Come see for yourself."

The two officers climbed the 40 and 8, and stood staring at the lights. "It is magnificent," David said. "Too bad we won't get to walk down the Champs-Élysées."

After chow, the men of first platoon stretched out in the morning sunlight and slept in the soft grass—those who *could* sleep.

Adrian sat with his men and was soon joined by David and Joseph.

Tibbs broke the silence. "Lieutenant, what exactly is the front?"

"It's called the Hindenburg Line. Some call it the Siegfried Line," Adrian said.

"Don't mean nothing to me, sir. What I mean is—what is the *front?*"

Adrian thought for a moment, then lay his helmet on the

grass and said, "Think of the helmet as Paris." He then placed his rifle a foot away, the trigger housing on a perpendicular line with the helmet. "Think of this rifle as stretching a distance of approximately four hundred miles. The butt is the mountains of Switzerland, where it borders with Germany; the muzzle ends at the North Sea, about fifteen miles southwest of Zeebrugge, in Belgium."

Hatch shook his head in disbelief. "That's a whole lot of ground for one army to cover, Lieutenant."

Adrian looked at David. "You want to take over, Lieutenant Sharps?"

"The Germans have occupied all the towns along and behind the line, but that's mostly for command, supply, training, and artillery. The fighting soldiers live in a network of trenches that stretch along the line."

"What do these trenches look like?" Kenny asked.

"Big slits in the earth about ten feet wide, sometimes wider, sometimes narrower. But they don't run in a straight line. The trench runs a hundred yards or so, then zigzags."

"Why?" Tibbs wondered.

"To prevent enfilading fire," David said.

Kenny looked dumbfounded.

Adrian said, "That's when an entire column can be swept with enemy firepower. The zigzagging of the trench exposes only a certain section to the firepower."

"Then there's the barbed wire, the minefields, the tank traps all lying between the Allied and enemy trenches. That part is called no man's land," Harwood added.

"How far apart are the trenches?" someone asked.

Adrian tapped the rifle butt. "As much as a mile." Then he tapped the barrel. "Or as close as ten yards."

"Where do we billet?" Tibbs wanted to know.

"In the trenches. There'll be holes carved into the walls called dugouts. Some are big enough for a squad; some are small and can only fit a few men, or only one man."

"We are going to live in the dirt?" asked Kenny.

"In the dirt, the rain, the mud, and with the lice. Over here they are called 'cooties.' It comes from the Malaysian word *kutus*. A lot of Brits fighting over here served in Malaysia before the war. They gave them the name."

"But don't worry," added David. "You'll be deloused once a month."

Kenny pointed to the rifle. "Tell us more about this Hindenburg Line."

Adrian again tapped the muzzle. "It was started accidentally by a German count named Von Schlieffen. He decided it best to invade France through the wide flat plains of Belgium, thus avoiding the well-defended French-German border and the Alps. That's where it all began, in 1914."

"What came next?" Kenny asked.

"The Germans roared in from all directions with the lights of Paris dancing in their eyes. Especially from Belgium, where the largest army advanced, but instead of wheeling behind and to the west of Paris—as the Von Schlieffen plan called for—the Boche moved to the front and east and were pushed to a river called the Marne. That's where the Brits and the French stopped them along this long line."

"After the Allies stopped the Heinies along this line, that's when the trench warfare began. Advancing warfare became too costly in men and material," Harwood said.

"It's been going on that long?" asked Tibbs.

"Four years. There have been a lot of big battles, such as Chemin de Dames—on the Aisne River—seventy-five miles east of Paris, where the French took back a little ground and the Brits took a lot of casualties."

Adrian touched between the trigger housing and the front sling swivel. "But the worst was along the Somme River, with more than one million casualties on both sides."

Tibbs looked around nervously. "The Germans sure like to fight near rivers. I hope we don't have to fight them in no river: I can't swim!"

The men had a brief laugh before David resumed the

track-side talk on the war. "In 1915, in Belgium, about twenty miles from the sea, the Heinies tried to break through again, at a place called Ypres. That's when they first started using poison gas."

David added, "Verdun—where we're going—was one of the most devastated sectors along the line. But the town itself was never taken by the Germans, despite years of intense bombardment."

"Speaking of artillery," Harwood said, "from just east of Verdun the Germans brought in a cannon called the 'Paris Gun.' It could fire a 276-pound shell seventy-five miles. And did, right into the streets of Paris.

"Now *we're* here," Hatch said.

"The Americans have already done their share since we arrived in 1917." Adrian picked up his rifle. "Now we're here and there's still plenty of fighting left for the 372nd."

30

Throughout the day the stark reality of war began to rise from the ground as the train pressed closer to the front. Gone were the lush fields of crops, replaced by wasted land that had felt the impact of battle. Towns and villages bore scars of artillery attacks; houses stood partially destroyed, many no more than smoke-darkened skeletons.

But it was the people, Adrian noticed, who were most affected. There was no cheering as the train passed through the villages, no flag waving, only empty stares.

At 1900 hours, on schedule, the train reached Sainte-Menehould, twenty miles east of Verdun, a town that sat on the banks of the Meuse River some 150 miles east of Paris.

The men slowly detrained and formed into their platoons near the depot, in silence, as hundreds of wounded soldiers lay on the wooden platform waiting to be transported to hospitals in Paris.

Private Kenny froze when he stepped down from the top of the 40 and 8. He stared at a row of soldiers lying on stretchers, their faces and hands covered with blood-soaked bandages, and at one man with both legs amputated. Hatch felt ill as he looked at a row of men wearing bandages over their eyes and heard their rasping coughing.

"Mustard gas," Adrian said, anticipating the question.

Tibbs watched a nurse—one of a score—in her blood-stained uniform light a soldier's cigarette, which he held between two bloody bandages covering both his hands.

Suddenly, all eyes of the first platoon were jerked to the east, to the rumble and flash of artillery fire coming from the front.

Chauncey approached in the company of a French officer. Adrian saluted. "The company is formed, Captain."

"Very good, Lieutenant." He nodded toward the French officer. "This is Captain Bouchardon. He has been assigned as our company liaison at the training center at Conde-en-Barrois."

Bouchardon extended his hand. He was tall, dark-haired, of an indefinite age—no more than thirty, perhaps, but appearing much older, his eyes sunken, his face haggard.

Adrian looked beyond the platform and saw nothing but darkness.

"Where are the transports, sir?"

"There are none available," Chauncey said wearily. "We are going to march to Conde-en-Barrois tonight. It's approximately twenty miles from here and we should be there in about seven hours."

Adrian stared at him, then blurted out, "Seven hours! These men can't march for seven hours, sir. They're exhausted. Why can't we go by trucks?"

Bouchardon answered the question. "The transport trucks are being used to transport wounded, and to transport reinforcements to the frontline trenches."

Chauncey's face hardened. "We have our orders, Lieutenant."

*   *   *

Within minutes of the march, the rain began, turning the road into a quagmire. At 0200, the battalion arrived at the training center of the French XIII Corps, situated on the outskirts of Conde-en-Barrois, a small, nearly deserted village in the Argonne forest.

Entering the town first, Adrian's platoon was directed by Captain Chauncey to billet in an empty house. The men fell out of formation, and trudged into the spacious two-story house. There every man collapsed to the floor and immediately fell asleep.

With the second platoon, David Sharps saw an old woman standing in the window of the house where Chauncey had directed the platoon. When they entered they found the old woman holding a candle. She watched them for a moment, then shrugged and disappeared up the stairs.

Throughout the town the soldiers of the First Battalion found shelter where they could, in shops, stables, buildings, and houses.

From the front, the rumble of artillery fire disturbed the night, but it was heard by only a few.

31

The first day at the training center in town was spent cleaning equipment and taking a needed rest. Latrines were dug by each company, long trenches in the earth, and as expected, the task for A Company fell to the first platoon.

The dirt from the new latrines was wheelbarrowed to the old slit trenches, where a coating of lime was added, then dirt.

By the afternoon, the chore of repairing the platoon's billet was underway, with each man finding his place in the house.

After the last formation, Adrian chose a spot near the fireplace, sat down, and wrote a few lines to Hannah before the evening mess. He told her some of the things that were bothering him, but avoided making charges and naming names, knowing the letter would be read by censors.

Franklin Tibbs had found a small trap door in the kitchen, and opened it carefully. Below lay a cellar, deep and dark. "Give me a candle, Kenny," Tibbs said.

Kenny found a candle, lit the wick, and Tibbs eased down

the small steps into the musky odor, the light dancing off mortared walls. Suddenly, he stumbled and fell, extinguishing the candle.

"Give me another match," he yelled to Kenny behind him.

The match flickered and the candle glowed; then, seeing what tripped him, Tibbs's eyes grew wide. "Lord have mercy, look what we done found."

Minutes later the two climbed up the steps and hurried into the main room, where Adrian sat writing his letter. "Lieutenant, look what we found," said Tibbs.

Adrian looked up and chuckled. Tibbs and Kenny stood, big grins on their faces, holding six bottles of wine.

"Can we keep it, Lieutenant?" Kenny asked.

Adrian nodded. "I think you men deserve a little relaxation after that trip from Saint-Nazaire. But we have to keep this to ourselves. If Captain Chauncey or Sergeant O'Doul find out, they'll probably confiscate the whole lot."

"For themselves," Sergeant Hatch snarled.

Nothing more was said and the first of the bottles was uncorked. Soon the men were sitting on the floor of their billet slugging down wine from dark bottles while the sound of artillery rumbled in the distance.

In the midst of it, a voice shouted, *"Ten-hut!"*

The men jumped to attention; Adrian didn't move. He stared past his men to see David and Joseph Harwood standing at the door.

"At ease," David said calmly, then motioned Adrian outside, where the three laughed as Adrian related the discovery of the wine.

"All my platoon has discovered is an old woman in the upstairs," David said.

Harwood then asked Adrian, "Are you hungry?"

Adrian patted his stomach. "Let's hit the officers' mess. But first let me speak with Sergeant Hatch."

He went inside and returned several minutes later carrying his rifle and helmet.

The officers' messhall lay a short distance from the billets, in the city hall of Conde-en-Barrois.

While walking to the mess hall the trio saw one of the strangest sights they had encountered since arriving in France. Four lorries slowed in the muddy street, and soldiers suddenly began unloading packs and rifles. They wore white kepis, long blue overcoats, dark trousers, and carried field packs and rifles. And they were of many races—white, black, Oriental, others unidentifiable.

"What nationality are they?" David wondered aloud.

Harwood recognized the uniforms. "They have no nationality. They are in La Légion Étrangère."

"What does that mean?" David asked.

"The French Foreign Legion."

They stood watching as the legionnaires, nearly fifty in number, all looking battle weary, formed into ranks. A tall white officer stepped forward, walking with a slight limp and carrying a riding crop. Then another tall man, his skin a rich ebony, stepped in front of the company, turned, and saluted the officer.

When the officer returned the salute, the sergeant barked an order and the legionnaires began marching. As the company passed the three, the sergeant turned, saluted, and in perfect English said, "Welcome to France, gentlemen."

The three returned the salute, startled by the words of the legion sergeant.

Adrian said, "One moment, Sergeant."

The big sergeant halted his men and came to Adrian. "May I help you, sir?"

The sergeant was tall, reminding Adrian of his father, with a thick, bushy mustache. A deep scar ran from the outer edge of his eye to the corner of his mouth.

"What's your name, Sergeant?"

"James Watts, sir."

"You speak very good English."

Watts said nothing as the legion captain walked up to them. The captain spoke to Watts in French, then the big man nodded politely and returned to his men.

The captain's hand extended to Adrian, and with a broad smile on his face, he said, "Good evening. I am Captain François Girard, La Légion Étrangère."

"Good evening, Captain. I'm Lieutenant Adrian Sharps. This is Lieutenant David Sharps and Lieutenant Joseph Harwood."

Girard shook hands with David and Joseph, who were still staring at the departing sergeant, listening as the legionnaires sang in dirgeful voices:

"Nous sommes soldats de la Légion;
La Légion Étrangère;
N'ayant pas patrie,
La France est notre mère."

Girard noted Adrian's curiosity as he continued to watch the legionnaire sergeant. "You are surprised to see a black legionnaire?"

Adrian nodded.

Girard lit a cigarette. "He is one of your countrymen."

"Why is an American in—"

Girard interrupted. "Lieutenant, one question that is never asked of a legionnaire is why he joined the legion. We have a saying in our illustrious unit: 'The legion is our country.' "

"Fair enough," Adrian said. "We were on our way to the officers' mess. Would you care to join us?"

Girard bowed slightly and motioned the Americans to proceed. They crossed the street and entered the mess, where two long rows of tables were divided by a blanket, white officers and NCOs seated on one side, Colored officers on the other.

The four walked toward the Colored section, when Chauncey stood and said to Girard, "Captain, won't you join us?"

Girard looked at the blanket with contempt, then said, "*Merci,* Captain, but I will sit with my new friends."

Girard passed into the Colored section, where Adrian politely offered him a chair. Girard placed his riding crop on the table, then graciously bowed to the Colored officers and said, "Gentlemen, welcome to my country. We are delighted to have you here in this time of great need."

As they ate, the animated Frenchman fielded questions about the war, the front, and the strength of the enemy, while on the other side of the blanket not a word was spoken.

Late the next afternoon, as the sun was fading, the company was assembled in full field gear, including rifles. Standing with Captain Chauncey and Sergeant O'Doul was Captain Girard and several of his legionnaires, including the Colored sergeant. Chauncey came directly to the point while motioning to Girard. "This is Captain Girard of the French Army. Captain Girard and his company have been assigned to the battalion to train our troops in trench warfare. Beginning today, you will be issued French equipment, including rifles, packs, and helmets. The uniforms will be American, but all other equipage will be French."

An uneasy murmur rippled through the company; confusion marked all the faces over this stunning announcement as Girard stepped forward.

"Gentlemen, your battalion has been attached to the French Thirteenth Corps. It is a very proud corps, and I am certain you will be an important part of that proud tradi-

tion. We are called 'the Territorials,' which means we are
composed of military units from all over the world where
France has national interests."

Girard motioned and several lorries eased to a halt in
front of the company. The tailgates dropped and a number
of French soldiers suddenly appeared. The company stood
and watched as rifles, helmets, overcoats, and packs were
unloaded into stations.

Chauncey ordered, "Form a single file. At each station
remove your American equipment and receive the French
equipment in exchange."

The distribution began with Chauncey and O'Doul placing their rifles in a pile; they received a French bolt-action
Lebel rifle and bayonet and walked on to the next station.

The bile rose in Adrian's mouth as he lay his Springfield
in a pile and was issued the French Lebel.

Hatch followed, took a Lebel, then looked at the French
bayonet and said, "The only good thing about this is the
French bayonet is longer than the American."

"Take off your soup bowl, Lieutenant," Chauncey ordered.

At each station, Adrian felt himself gradually lose his
identity, and by the time he reached the last, where he received the type of helmet worn by the French soldiers—a
blue helmet with a smaller brim than the doughboy "soup
bowl" helmet—Adrian said to Hatch, "I feel more like a
French *poilu* than an American doughboy."

Hatch plopped the blue helmet on his head, then growled,
"We still got one thing American the French will not dare
take from us even if we try to give them up: our dirty drawers."

PART 4

THE RED HAND

32

On May 26, the 372nd Infantry Regiment ended their training phase with the French XIII Corps.

On June 1, orders were received attaching the American regiment to the French 63rd Division.

On June 4, the regiment was ordered to occupy a subsector in the dense Argonne forest. Fifteen miles east sat Verdun, between the Meuse and Aire rivers, less than fifty miles from the point where Belgium, Luxembourg, and Germany bordered France.

On June 12, the 371st, the 372nd, and the French 333rd were formed as the 157th "Red Hand" Division.

Adrian soon learned there was no historical certainty on how the division became known as the Red Hand, or Le Main de Sang. There were two conflicting theories.

The division had once used a brewery for its headquarters, and the manager of the brewery was murdered by a person who left only a bloody handprint. It was rumored that this was the reason for adopting the symbol, for the manager was truly adored by the soldiers, though more for his spiritual support than his patriotism.

The second theory is similar—that a member of the 157th was killed at a French roadhouse by an unknown assailant during an evening of merriment. As was the custom when a soldier was killed at one of these inns, a red hand was painted over the entrance. Upon seeing the symbol, comrades of the slain soldier used it in remembrance of their dead comrade.

Adrian did not know if either were true; however, one thing he did know was the division's recent combat history: The Red Hand had been literally decimated in May and the first week of June during the German offensive at the second battle of the Aisne River, when German Field Marshal Erich von Ludendorff sent twenty-eight divisions across the Aisne, sweeping west to Château-Thierry and Belleau Wood, coming within fifty-five miles of Paris before the offensive was stopped by French and American soldiers.

The Red Hand, a part of the French 4th Army, was commanded by French Brigadier General Mariano F.J. Goybet, a tough field commander who did not believe in giving up ground without a fight.

Goybet sent the 372nd from its relief position near the Meuse to defensive positions in the front lines of the dense Argonne forest.

The regiment had moved closer to the front in increments from Conde-en-Barrois to near the small village of Les Senades in the Argonne forest, where each man reduced his equipment load to a maximum of thirty pounds.

The artillery no longer rumbled in the distance; now the ground vibrated and the dark sky lit up with each salvo from the German emplacement on the heights of Montfaucon, overlooking the forest—thick woods and mountainous terrain that was an infantryman's nightmare.

The bitter ground was composed of a northwest-running hogback range of hills with ridges, deep saddles, and steep ravines. The woods at the rear of the front comprised a thick tangle of vines and trees; to the front of the trenches the trees stood stripped of branches by the constant artillery fire.

Adrian's platoon had marched from Les Senades toward their subsector along the Argonne, the men alert and apprehensive as they drew closer to the thundering artillery fire.

The soldiers marched in two long columns on separate sides of a dark road made visible only by artillery flash. With each step the men knew they were nearing the labyrinth of trenches threading through the forest, most of which had traded hands several times over the years between German and French troops.

At 0200 hours the 372nd received its baptism by fire.

Adrian heard the whine of the first artillery shell and shouted, "Take cover!"

The round struck in the middle of the road, destroying a French cook wagon after lifting it awkwardly into the air. Through the momentary flash of light, Private Willie Dawes saw one of the mules drawing the wagon blown to red meat by the blast.

Instantly, the road was consumed by two enormous fireballs that leaped into the sky, licking the night with orange-white tongues that momentarily transformed the darkness into bright copper. When another shell struck an ambulance, the two medics in the front were shredded by the flying shrapnel; when the gas tank ignited, a soldier who was marching near the ambulance was set aflame and then fell twisting in the road.

The barrage continued. Hatch found Adrian huddled near a splintered tree and shouted, "Lieutenant, the Germans have the road bracketed. We're getting slaughtered!"

Through the flashing light, Adrian could see his men running crazily along the roadway.

"Get off the road!" he shouted.

But none seemed to hear through the din and fury of the cannonade.

One soldier, running along the center of the road, was suddenly blown into the darkness above the light, then fell back to the earth, crumpled like a rag doll.

Adrian suddenly realized that stark fear had overcome all training and discipline and that chaos had now taken command.

"Come with me!" he ordered.

Adrian and the sergeant ran to the road and saw one soldier kneeling in the mud.

"On your feet, soldier! Get off the road!" Adrian yelled above the din.

The young soldier was holding the mule's severed head in his lap and looked up at Adrian with eyes as empty as the mule's. He nodded metronomically; then, when another flash lit up the road, Adrian and Hatch recoiled in horror. The man's legs had been blown off at the knees.

The two grabbed the soldier by his pack and began dragging him from the road.

Another explosion shook the ground so fiercely, Adrian was knocked off his feet. Hatch took charge of the wounded soldier and disappeared into the darkness.

When Adrian rose to his feet he saw a French soldier trying to control a mule that had been pulling a light artillery caisson. The mule bellowed, then ran at an angle, charging Willie Dawes, who stood paralyzed with fear nearby. In the last instant Dawes saw the mule charging toward him and tried to run, but it was too late.

Adrian watched helplessly as the animal plowed over him, dragging hundreds of pounds of iron cannon and caisson across his body.

Then, suddenly, the howl and whine of incoming artillery

ceased, and in the blackness new sounds could be heard: the screams of the wounded and dying.

The stretcher bearers—the French called them *brancar-diers*—arrived after the barrage ended and began the gruesome task of loading the dead and wounded for transport to hospital trucks. Adrian and Hatch began assembling the platoon and taking human inventory when Captain Chauncey appeared.

"What's your count, Lieutenant?"

"Two dead, four wounded." Adrian sighed. "What about the rest of the company?"

Chauncey shook his head in disgust. "I estimate between seventy and eighty dead. Third platoon took it the worse. They were nearly wiped out."

Adrian felt his throat constrict. "What about second platoon?"

"Your platoon took the lightest casualties. The main barrage fell behind your position. Second and third platoons took the brunt of the barrage."

My brother!

Adrian saluted Chauncey, and jogged back down the road, a death chill seeping into his soul.

He reached the second platoon area on the run, half stumbling as he reached a soldier who sat motionless on the roadside, smoking and gazing absently at the sky.

"Where's your platoon leader? Where's Lieutenant Sharps?"

The soldier took a drag on his cigarette and said nothing. Adrian grabbed him and pulled him to his feet, shouting in his face, "Where's Lieutenant Sharps!"

Just then a familiar voice said, "I'm over here, Adrian."

Adrian found David kneeling beside a wounded soldier. "Are you hit?"

"No," said David, his voice trembling.

"What about Joseph?"

David's quivering voice said, "I don't know. But they got hit the heaviest."

Adrian looked down the road. Lanterns danced wildly as stretcher bearers, looking like ghoulish apparitions in the eerie light, raced along the road. He patted David gently on the shoulder. "I'll check on Joseph."

He hurried along the road through the pleas and screams of the wounded, past the barking of NCOs trying to organize their men. When he neared a hospital truck, he saw Vince O'Doul standing by a litter, writing on a notepad. Adrian saw him tear off the note and reach down to the soldier lying there.

"First Sergeant O'Doul?"

O'Doul turned as Adrian stopped in the dim glow of lantern light by the truck.

"Where's Lieutenant Harwood?"

O'Doul growled something unintelligible, then took a lantern and lowered it to the stretcher. "He's gone west."

Gone west! Adrian shivered at the doughboy phrase for "dead."

Lieutenant Joseph Harwood lay on the stretcher beside the muddy road, his huge body now looking small and frail, his pink, splotched skin no longer visible beneath the mask of blood covering his face.

33

Rifles at the feet of the dead soldiers, bayonets shoved into the mud, helmets hung by their chinstraps on the stocks stood as markers for the bodies awaiting transportation to the rear.

Adrian sat beside Joseph's body, holding his hand as though he might come awake at any moment.

But he was dead, the booming laughter silenced forever, the friendly smile gone west with the rest of him.

What did he see? Adrian wondered. Did he feel pain? Did he think of Alice? Little Joseph? Did he have time for one last moment of reflection, or was everything erased suddenly?

David appeared out of nowhere, looking worn and haggard. He knelt in the mud beside Adrian and placed his hand on his shoulder.

"How are you doing?"

David nodded but said nothing. Captain Girard came up to them. "Get your men ready to move out in five minutes. We've still got a long march ahead." He looked for a moment at Harwood's body, then turned sharply and walked away, slapping his riding crop against his leg.

David looked down at Harwood. "I can't leave him like this, Adrian."

"Get on your feet, Lieutenant Sharps. Your men need you," Adrian said as he pulled his brother to his feet, hoisted the pack onto his back, and handed him his rifle. "Just like in Cuba . . . one foot in front of the other."

The two stepped into the muddy road and joined the column walking toward the front.

Where there had been cursing and complaint on the march, now silent men watched as the approaching dawn drew a gray stripe on the horizon. Gradually, the beauty and slow awakening of sunrise unveiled a cruel and tortured landscape pockmarked with deep craters and laced with trenches weaving along the front lines.

The trenches in subsector Argonne west were long, hideous, zigzagging narrow slits in the earth, threaded through the huge mounds of dirt piled on the edges. Between the Allied and enemy trenches lay a tract of open country called no man's land. The trenches provided protection from machine-gun and rifle fire, but none from artillery or gas attacks. Wooden ladders poked from the trenches intermittently; when it came time to charge the Germans across no man's land, the ladders were the means of going "over the top."

Adrian's platoon filed silently into the deep trench and walked toward what was called the 700 Dugout section.

The dugouts were where the men would "live" during their occupation of the trenches. They were primitive burrows dug in the trench wall and covered with branches. Most dugouts were crude, but a few had wooden floors and, sometimes, the luxury of sleeping cots.

The deep, baritone voice of Watts boomed, "Keep moving, men. Don't stop until you hook up with the second platoon. Maintain a ten-foot separation from the man to your front."

The soldiers of first platoon followed Watts like puppies following their mother. He had been here before. They were new residents and did not even know the address.

Except that it was located in a deep groove carved into the earth.

When the two platoons linked up at last, Adrian saw David down the line and waved, but got no response.

After the platoons linked up Watts pointed to one of the many periscopes stationed beside the ladders. "The first rule at the front is never stick your head above the trench. You want to eyeball, you do it through these periscopes."

The periscopes were strange-looking devices, like binoculars that had been stretched several feet long. They were erected on telescoping poles, and the lenses barely peeked above the top of the trench.

Adrian stepped to the periscope and peered through. In the gray distance lay the German lines, where machine-gun nests with interlocking avenues of fire covered every inch of ground.

Adrian felt a chill creep along his spine as he thought about all that open ground with no cover except for a scattering of deep shell craters. He visualized the moment his platoon went "over the top": They would climb the ladders and advance across no man's land under heavy artillery fire until they reached the barbed wire. Once through the needlelike wire there would be the minefields, and those who survived that would come under the raking fire from Maxim machine guns and mortars. Those who survived the wire and the mines would face more machine guns, mortar fire, and the rifle enfilade of the Germans occupying their trenches and gun emplacements. Those who survived all this would spill into the enemy trenches, where the fighting would be hand to hand with bayonets and rifle butts.

The assault would take them through the gates of hell itself and many would not return.

34

On the other side of the world, Augustus Sharps sat at attention on his horse, facing the predawn Arizona darkness, as he often did when he wanted to recapture his youth or clear his mind of burdensome thoughts.

The stallion showed a momentary restlessness, throwing his great head forward, then trying to rear up, until he was settled by the tightening of the reins. The horse snorted and tried to crane his head away from the empty space that began beyond the rim of the deep canyon.

"It's almost time," Augustus whispered.

He was watching the eastern sky as the sun began to filter through the crackback ridges of the mountains northeast of Bonita.

Moments later, the sun broke over the horizon; a red flood of light swept the land and seeped into the canyon, running like fast water across hard ground.

Augustus spurred the horse, stood in the iron stirrups, and leaned forward as the stallion bolted over the edge into the redness of the canyon.

Down the stallion plunged, the speed building. Augustus held firm to the reins, checking the power of the animal. He felt the tightness of fear as he leaned precariously over the neck of the charging stallion.

He pulled the reins taut, leaned back as far as possible, but weight and poor balance brought more stress to the saddle than the cinch could withstand and it snapped. Augustus felt the momentary sickness of knowing he was helpless, felt himself falling forward as the horse continued down, leaving him suspended for a moment in the air. When he hit the hard ground, still gripping the reins, he heard a loud crack when the horse's hooves pounded against his head, then felt nothing as he was swallowed by blackness.

Hannah Simmons loved Arizona, especially in the morning before the heat began rising. She was now in her fifth month of pregnancy and wore the glow of a woman expecting her first child.

She was hoeing in the garden when she heard the sound of hooves pounding on the hard-packed desert ground.

"Miss Selona!" she shouted, dropping the hoe and running for the house.

Selona came out immediately, and her heart raced with fear as she saw the saddleless horse slow to a trot, then stop in front of the hitching rail.

Selona's mind reeled, then instinct took command. She took the horse's bridle, ran her hand along his sweating neck, patting him softly. The red, wet dust on her palms told her all she needed to know.

Theresa and Vina Gibbs suddenly appeared, both looking frightened. Selona looked quickly to Vina. "Saddle me a horse." To Theresa she said, "Hitch up the buggy."

Selona looked into the horse's dark eyes, wishing the creature could speak. But she knew that something was wrong. Terribly wrong.

Vina brought a horse and Selona climbed into the saddle.

"Do you want me to go with you?" asked Hannah.

Selona shook her head, then turned to Vina. "You and Theresa follow me."

"Where are we going?" asked Vina.

"To the canyon."

She kicked the horse's flanks and bolted from the yard, unaware that her calico rag and hairpiece had flown from her head.

Selona reached the canyon and jumped from her horse, then stopped cold where she saw the trail disappear over the rim. She slowly inched her way to the rim, then peered down.

"Augustus!"

He lay at the bottom, his artificial leg skewed grotesquely, like a limb broken from a tree.

Selona mounted the horse and rode for the mouth of the canyon as Vina arrived with the buggy. Selona motioned them to follow and she rode down the narrow, steep incline to where her husband lay.

Dr. Tyler Summers had seen more than his share of broken backs in his forty years of practicing medicine on the western frontier. He could set legs, mend bullet wounds, deliver babies, but he was treating a fractured skull, and massive brain damage was out of his realm of practice.

For two days following the fall, Selona sat by her husband's bedside in their home, holding his hand, cooling him with damp towels, and talking without let-up into the late hours of the night.

She was tired as her eyes teared and she said, "Do you remember that clump of piñons at Fort Davis where we used to sleep under the stars on them buffalo robes?" He said nothing, nor did he move. He had not twitched a muscle since she found him at the bottom of the canyon.

She reached into the pocket of her apron and withdrew an envelope. With near reverence she opened it and began reading the first letter from Adrian, dated May 2, since his arrival in France:

Dear Mom and Pop,

Hope this finds you all doing well. David, Joseph, and I are fine.

We have moved closer to the front and can hear the heavy artillery being fired from both sides. I can't tell you exactly where we are, except to say we are close to the action.

The men are in good spirits despite the constant training and movement from place to place. We seem to be always on the move, and no sooner do we get settled than we move again.

The only real highlight at this point came today when we were inspected by General Pershing. He was most impressed and said we "have the makings of a very fine regiment."

There have been several Colored newspaper reporters who are covering the war, and when they file their stories you'll learn more details of what is going on.

Enclosed is a letter for Hannah. Please tell her I love and miss her and look forward to holding our baby.

I better go. Like you always said, Pop, "When the bugle blows . . . "

Love, Adrian.

Selona folded the letter and tucked it away. She took a cloth, dampened it in a basin, and wiped the perspiration from Augustus's brow. Then she patted his face and throat. She realized something strange: In the more than forty years of their marriage she had never really studied his face in detail.

She sat looking at him—his high forehead, the skin darker beneath the area where his hat shaded his head; the tiny scar within the folds of his eyelids she had never noticed before. She wondered where it came from. In a battle? In a fall from a horse? His broad nose and thick porkchop sideburns truly did give him the look of a buffalo, appropriate for a buffalo hunter and a buffalo soldier.

It was nearly dawn when he sighed deeply, giving her a momentary start.

"Augustus?" she whispered. "Can you hear me?"

He said nothing; his eyes opened for an instant, then his body stiffened and fell still.

The moment the sun rose over the eastern horizon, marking the beginning of a new day, Sergeant Major Augustus Sharps, 10th Regiment of the United States Cavalry, died.

Selona found herself walking from the stable, carrying a shovel. Later, she couldn't remember leaving the house.

Vina was standing on the porch feeding Theresa's baby when she saw Selona walking toward the cemetery. "Oh, Lord God. No." Vina hurried inside and placed the baby in the crib and ran to the graveyard.

Selona was standing, studying the layout of the cemetery, looking as though she were trying to solve a problem.

"Selona?" Vina whispered.

Selona shook her head, as though in conversation with some unseen person. "I think you'd want to lay next to Darcy and Sergeant Major Brassard." Then she nodded and dug the first shovelful of dirt as Vina looked on with tears.

"Selona, let me dig the grave."

Selona shook her head. "He was my man. I'll dig the grave. Same as he done for his momma and poppa."

Vina watched and after a time said, "Theresa said she would write to David."

Selona stopped her work and pinned Vina with a flash of her eyes. "No! I don't want them to know. They've got enough on their minds. I don't want them to know! Not until they come home."

That afternoon the ranch overflowed with visitors who had heard of Augustus's death. Selona stayed in the house, washing his body, then carefully dressed him in his best cavalry uniform. Ernst Bruner arrived with a coffin, and with the help of two men placed Augustus into the wooden box.

The coffin was placed in the front room for several hours, draped with an American flag, as visitors passed through the house to pay their respects.

Later that afternoon Augustus was buried beside two old friends he had served with throughout the Indian campaigns.

Selona sat by the grave well past midnight, reminiscing beneath the stars. Then she went into the house, and left a lantern burning in the front window.

As she had always done when Augustus was away from home.

35

Adrian's platoon spent its first day in the trenches with the ordinary tedium of soldiering. The men cleaned equipment, adjusted to the dirt and mud, and talked with nervous bravado while trying to ignore their common fear: the first night on the line.

To keep his troops occupied, Adrian had each man clean and oil his rifle and bayonet, and strip his field packs of clothing, personal effects, and anything else that was not needed in the event of an enemy assault. What was not needed for battle was stored in duffel bags in the dugouts.

At the entrance to the trenchline, cook wagons arrived and the men were sent in small groups to fill their mess kits.

As Adrian approached one of the wagons, he recognized the mess sergeant from the first bivouac outside Saint-Nazaire.

The sergeant saw him coming and smiled, asking, "Have you gotten used to French cooking yet, sir?"

"I'm getting used to it, Sergeant. But I still prefer ham and lima beans to *potage à l'Andalouse.*"

The soup was delicious, and Adrian had grown to enjoy the concoction of vegetables, spices, and rice.

The sergeant looked at him warily, saying, "You been eating too much French food. You're even starting to say it like a Frenchman."

Both laughed, then Adrian looked at the French bread piled high in dozens of wooden crates. "Cornbread would taste good right about now."

The mess sergeant said nothing as he reached into a compartment in the wagon and pulled out a black iron skillet covered with a damp cloth. He lifted the cloth to reveal golden cornbread. He took a huge slice from the skillet and placed it in Adrian's mess kit. "Enjoy, Lieutenant."

Adrian's eyes danced with joy, then he said, "Thanks, Sergeant. I'll pay you back someday."

He sat beneath a tree, its limbs shredded by years of artillery fire, watching the soldiers come out of the trenches, go through the mess line, then return carrying their rations as though they were ants leaving their nest in the ground and returning with forage.

Then he heard a familiar voice and looked up and saw his brother.

"Want some company?"

David sat down and took a long pull from his canteen. Then he reached into his coat and handed a letter to Adrian. "Hannah sent you this along with my letter from Theresa. Of course, she didn't write it, but I recognize Momma's handwriting."

Adrian leaned on his elbow and read the letter, only two pages, but long enough to hear what he wanted to know. "She says everybody's doing fine and that she's getting bigger with the baby." He noticed a short note from his mother, but not from his father.

"I wonder why Pop doesn't write," said David.

Adrian shrugged. "You know Pop. He's not much for letter writing."

Adrian studied David for a moment. "Have you written to Alice?"

David shook his head. "That's going to be the hardest letter I'll ever have to write."

Adrian understood. He had two letters he had yet to write to the families of his two men killed in the artillery barrage.

Finally, both stood, hugged each other, and returned to their trenches. They both paused, turned at the same moment, and looked with the same wondering stare: Would this be the last time they saw each other alive?

One hour before sunset and one hour before sunrise—prime times for enemy attack—the men were required to be in a complete state of readiness for combat.

Adrian knew what to expect that moonless first night and had prepared himself for the inevitable: When darkness fell, the thick, tangled woods would come alive. If not alive with actual Germans, tree stumps would suddenly resemble the enemy crawling toward them; the sound of barbed wire rustling from the wind would signal an approaching soldier; the moon would draw shadows across the ground, would creep toward the American trenches, suggesting the enemy preparing to fall upon them at any moment.

The night, to the untested soldier, could pose as great a threat as an enemy soldier with a rifle.

Nerves were pushed to the limit of endurance.

Adrian knew this, and the knowledge prompted him to do something he had learned from his father: Turn the night into an asset. Take the night from the enemy.

That afternoon Adrian had seen a wide, deep crater fifty yards to the front of the American trenches, and after "stand to" had been called down, and the sentries begun their watches and the men were in their dugouts, he set his plan in motion.

He walked quickly along the line, tapping the shoulders of men not assigned to a watch. He said nothing, just pointed to the center of the platoon's line of defense.

He took ten men, motioned them to the centermost ladder, and said, "Follow me. We're going to crawl fifty yards to a crater in front of our platoon. Stay low, and don't make a sound. Leave your rifles. You won't need them."

The ten men looked at him as though he had lost his mind, but when he climbed the ladder and rolled over the lip of the trench, they followed.

They inched forward on their bellies, moving snakelike from their trenchline toward the enemy. Adrian reached the crater first and slid over the edge and down into its depth. When the last man slid to the bottom, he motioned them to move close.

"I'll be back in one hour," Adrian said cryptically as he crawled toward the top of the crater, Kenny at his side for the first few feet.

"What if our own men start shooting at us? Or the Germans?"

Adrian grinned, and even in the darkness his teeth gleamed. "Keep quiet and no one will know you're here."

Then he climbed from the crater and disappeared.

Kenny and the others sat and listened; not a man moved. An hour passed, and at last Adrian appeared with ten more men, who slid into the crater like drops of rain down a window.

He gave the new men their instructions and crawled to the top of the crater, followed by Kenny and the nine others from the first group. They crawled toward the trenches, where he placed the ten men on guard positions along the line.

Throughout the night Adrian continued the exercise until every man had spent an hour crawling and lying in silence, trapped between American and German guns.

That night, the first platoon was the only one in the battalion that did not fire a shot at shadows and ghosts.

36

At 1000 hours the morning after the shell crater exercise, Adrian was summoned to the command post.

Chauncey, in a dugout carved in the back of the trench, had a map stretched out on a table. Girard and Watts were also present, along with David, who stood talking with a new officer.

Chauncey motioned toward the officer. "This is Second Lieutenant Frederick Thomas. He's going to take command of third platoon."

Thomas, a tall, sapling-lean young man, nodded to the others as Chauncey continued.

"Captain Girard has suggested we all visit another area of the front. I think it's a good idea."

Girard stepped to the map and pointed his swagger stick at a spot that was circled in red ink. "Gentlemen, this is Hill 295. We French call it Mort Homme."

Adrian was standing by David and whispered, "What does that mean?"

David shrugged, and overhearing the two brothers, Lieutenant Thomas said, "Dead Man's Hill."

Chauncey grabbed his rifle. "We'll load into a lorry at eleven hundred hours. Be certain you bring your gas masks. That's all."

Adrian turned to Thomas and offered his hand. "I'm Lieutenant Adrian Sharps. This is my brother, David." They all shook hands and began walking along the trenches toward their platoons.

"Where are you men from in the States?" asked Thomas.

Adrian replied, "Bonita, Arizona. You?"

"Baton Rouge, Louisiana."

"Is that where you learned to speak French?"

He nodded.

"That'll come in handy when you go on leave."

David added, "If we ever get to go on leave."

An hour later all were assembled, and the lorry awaited.

The trip took nearly two hours, the lorry moving along a narrow road that wound its way to Avocourt, a small town ten miles west of Verdun. At 1300 hours the truck turned north toward another sector facing the Hindenburg Line.

The countryside was greatly different from that around the Argonne. There were open spaces and tall hills, rivers and streams, and for the first time since arriving at the front, Adrian realized the vastness of the terrain held by the Germans.

The lorry stopped, and all climbed down and entered the labyrinth of trenches.

The trenches wound upward, then emptied into an observation position that overlooked a vast valley. From the top of the hill they could see in the distance the heights of Montfaucon, held by the Germans. Hundreds of miles of German trenches sat beneath Montfaucon, threading through a no man's land separating the French from the German troops.

Huge, high-powered telescopes were stationed in sand-bagged positions. Girard pointed to the east, to the German lines. "Gentlemen, there are the enemy!"

Through the telescopes, German artillery could be seen on the heights, barely visible through canopies of camouflage.

Adrian saw the first German soldier, a man who raised and lowered his hand. In the next instant the onlookers saw an artillery piece belch a white cloud of smoke and heard the rush of the incoming round.

Adrian quickly adjusted the telescope. The round struck the trenches below the observation post, raising a shower of dirt.

"They're firing on the Moroccans," Watts shouted.

Adrian heard another whine as another round exploded in the trenches occupied by the 2nd Moroccan Infantry. In an instant, four Moroccan soldiers disappeared, blown to atoms in a tremendous explosion.

Girard pointed to another sector coming under fire. "That is where the Senegalese are positioned."

Adrian looked through the telescope and saw the African soldiers, their distinctive red turbans wrapped around their helmets.

The steady *crump* of the big German guns was advancing westward through the trenchline.

Watts yelled, "Rolling barrage!"

Girard shouted, "Take cover!"

The hill suddenly came alive with the whine of incoming artillery, concussion, and a sucking wind that drew the air from the lungs.

Both Adrian and Fred Thomas were blown off their feet by the blast and found themselves lost in a punishing cloud of smoke and dirt.

"Gas!" Watts screamed.

The acrid taste of the gas burned their mouths, then their lungs with every painful breath they took as they reached to the canvas bags containing their only hope for survival: the gas masks.

Adrian strapped his mask on and saw, through the yellowish haze, that Thomas was fumbling frantically with the awkward device. Then he saw Watts crawl toward Frederick, grab Thomas's mask, fix the mask on the lieutenant's head, and pull the straps tight.

The soldiers huddled together, their eyes wide with fear even through the lenses of their masks. No one said a word; no one moved. They sat like children in a corner after being scolded. They listened. They prayed.

37

The ambulance stopped at a field hospital in Sainte-
Menehould. The hospital consisted of a few surgical tables and cots lining the walls, where wounded soldiers
waited to be transported to Paris.

Adrian was supporting Frederick Thomas, who had a
slight shrapnel wound in his leg. He gently assisted him to
a table, then spotted a nurse wearing a bloodstained smock
over her uniform. She was kneeling by a Senegalese soldier,
dressing a wound on his leg, when she looked up and saw
Adrian. The Senegalese began babbling rapidly in French.

"He said his eyes are on fire," Thomas said from his
nearby table.

The African soldier's face was puffy, his eyes nearly
swollen shut.

The nurse took a pan of water that contained a murky
solution, held the soldier's head back, and flushed his eyes
with the liquid. He moaned, then lay back, whispering
something to her.

She bandaged his eyes and walked over to Thomas. Her

hands moved quickly, cutting away his trouser leg as Adrian watched her, seeing the fatigue in her eyes.

"I'm Mary. Are you wounded, Lieutenant?" she asked while continuing to work on Thomas.

Adrian shook his head. "Just a little disoriented."

She took a pan of water, dipped a thick gauze in it, squeezed it to dampness, then began washing the wound.

Adrian was amazed at her speed and dexterity, her steady hand, as though she were working instinctually.

She took a forceps and said to Thomas, "This will sting."

She closed the jaws of the forceps on a shard of shrapnel jutting through the skin. With a quick, sure motion she cleanly removed the twisted piece of metal, then stanched the bleeding by pressing gauze to the wound.

Adrian looked up and saw Watts enter. His face was a grotesque, swollen mask. Frederick tried to sit up and speak to Watts, but was reprimanded by Mary. "Lie back, Lieutenant."

Watts nodded at him, saying, "You heard the lady, Lieutenant. Lie back on that cot and do as she tells you." He paused, and smiling, added, "Sir."

The nurse looked at Watts, and before she could say what she was thinking, he said, "Yes, ma'am. I'm an American."

Captain Chauncey and David came through the door, followed by Captain Girard. Like Watts, David had a swollen face.

Chauncey looked at Frederick's wound. "Just a scratch. You'll be up and around in a few days."

Frederick shrugged. "Helluva way to start off the war."

Girard laughed. "You were lucky, Lieutenant. More than you can know."

Frederick raised up and lowered his feet to the floor. "How's that, Captain?"

"You're officially in the French Army. French soldiers receive a three-day pass to Paris for being wounded."

Watts released a long sigh of relief. "I'll get to see my family for a few days."

Adrian looked at David. "Too bad we didn't get wounded."

Even Chauncey laughed.

38

✫ ✫ ✫

The truck groaned noisily and moved snail-slow along the main street of Bonita, as though the driver was searching for something and didn't know where to find it. He was a young lieutenant with blond hair; sitting beside him was an older officer who wore a cross on his collar.

The truck stopped at the sheriff's office, where the younger officer went inside for a moment, then reappeared on the front step with a deputy.

The deputy pointed down the street, and the officer climbed back into the truck and drove to Selona's restaurant.

She was sitting in the front of her building when the door opened and a hot blast of dust roared in, followed by the two officers.

She froze as she looked into their eyes and shook her head so violently her buffalo hairpiece nearly fell off.

"No!"

The chaplain put his hand on her shoulder and asked gently, "I'm told you can help me find Mrs. Joseph Harwood."

For a moment there was an uneasy relief in her eyes;
then the tears flowed down her face as she heard the second officer speak.

"Do you know where we can find Mrs. Joseph Harwood?"

Selona nodded numbly but could say nothing. She stood
and walked limply to the door, where she paused for a moment, staring through the window at the military truck sitting in the street.

"She'll be feeding the baby, I expect."

The chaplain asked, "Can you take us to where she
lives?"

Selona nodded, wiped at the tears. "I don't want to. But
I will."

The moment she saw the truck through her bedroom window, Alice became nervous; when she saw Selona get out
of the truck, followed by the officers, she became terrified.

They didn't walk to Selona's house, where Hannah was
standing on the porch; they were headed toward Vina
Gibbs's house, and the moment their heavy boots met the
front steps, she knew in her heart that her world—or
Theresa's—was about to be destroyed.

Before she stepped into the parlor, Alice looked in the mir-
ror, rubbed the tears from her eyes, and took a deep breath,
mustering all the courage within her.

The moment she saw Selona's eyes she knew the truth.

The younger officer removed his campaign hat, as did the
chaplain. At that moment Theresa came to the front room
from the kitchen. Both women stood staring at each other.

The chaplain looked at Theresa and asked, "Are you
Mrs. Joseph Harwood?"

Theresa shook her head.

Alice collapsed.

The rain fell in torrential sheets and none of those gathered at the small family cemetery could remember when it had last rained so hard. There was no grave, just a white marker to remind the world that Joseph Harwood had existed.

Selona could only stand and look helplessly at Alice. What could she say?

The marker read:

LIEUTENANT JOSEPH H. HARWOOD
Born May 2, 1894
Killed in France, June 13, 1918
372nd Inf. Regt., 93rd Division (Colored)

The memorial service over, Theresa led Alice into the house, where Vina had prepared a meal.

Selona went to a wooden box that sat on the porch and returned to Joseph's marker. She looked at the grave of Augustus, and recalling that Joseph and he were about the same size, used his dimensions as a guide for her work.

Then, in the driving rain, she knelt and began planting flowers in such a way as to fashion an outline of the empty grave.

39

One week after the artillery attack on Mort Homme, Adrian was ordered to report to the command post. There he found Chauncey in conference with Captain Girard.

"Your platoon is going on night patrol along this part of the sector, Lieutenant Sharps," Chauncey said peremptorily. "The purpose of the mission is to bring back a German prisoner. Is that clear?"

Adrian smiled nervously. "Yes, sir."

"Take one squad. I'd suggest, since it's your first venture into no man's land, you handpick the best men you have."

Girard then stepped forward and said, "Your patrol will be accompanied by one of my men, Sergeant Watts, an experienced soldier in this sector."

Adrian had had little contact with Watts since their first meeting but thought him a strange man, an American who, outwardly, at least, did not like serving with American troops.

"We welcome Sergeant Watts's experience," Adrian said. Girard nodded at Watts and both legionnaires left the dugout.

Chauncey waited a few seconds and said, "Strange one, that Watts. He's an American, you know."

Adrian nodded. "I know. I wonder why he's in the French Army."

Adrian was walking through the trenchline chatting with his platoon members, when he saw Frederick Thomas approaching. The young officer looked glum—and angry.

"You don't look like a single young man that is about to see the lights of Paris."

Thomas shrugged and handed a folded sheet of paper to Adrian.

"This was given to me at battalion headquarters when I picked up my pass. It's something you should know about. The order was issued yesterday."

Adrian read.

"My God. This will cause a riot among every Colored unit in France," he said. As if to confirm the nightmare order, he read it aloud. " 'From Headquarters, Ninety-Third Division. The issuance of this order, titled Order Number Forty, bars Colored American soldiers from speaking to, or fraternizing with, white French women. Any member of the division found in violation of this order will face general court-martial for misconduct.' "

Adrian handed the paper back to Thomas and stomped away toward the command post.

Chauncey was sitting at his desk when Adrian returned. He saluted the captain but there was no protocol, merely anger.

"Captain, why didn't you tell me about Order Number Forty?"

Chauncey stood and rested his hand on his holster. "I intended to discuss the matter tomorrow with the officers. I only received word of the order this morning."

Adrian shook his head in disgust. "How could Allied Command do something like this to American soldiers?"

Chauncey seemed delighted in pointing out the obvious. "The order is directed only at the Colored soldiers in France."

"That's my point, sir. It seems a crystal clear act of prejudice directed at my people."

"Are you questioning this order, Lieutenant?"

"Yes, I'm questioning the order, along with two hundred thousand other Colored soldiers when they learn of it."

Chauncey's eyes narrowed. "You have a patrol to lead tonight, Lieutenant. I suggest you prepare your men."

There is a special silence among men who are preparing for combat, and so it was with the six men chosen by Adrian for the night patrol.

In the trench, Sergeant Watts whispered, "Tighten the slings on your rifles and remove your helmets."

"What about our ammunition?" asked Hatch.

"If you need more than what you've got in your rifle, you'll be dead before you can reload," Watts said.

"Gas masks?" Adrian asked.

"Leave them. There won't be time to use them if we're caught in the open. Take your bayonets and shove them inside your boots and pull your socks over the handles. When we move, we will move at right and left angles, never in a straight line. Is that understood?"

"What about mines?" asked John Carter. He was a thin man from Virginia with a drooping mustache, and he wore a harmonica around his neck on a bootlace.

Watts grinned, teeth gleaming. "The mines in this sector have been cleared."

"By who?"

"By fools like us."

Watts started up the ladder, followed by Adrian, then paused and looked at Carter. "Leave your harp, son. You won't be needing it where we're going."

The men of the first platoon who were staying behind watched their comrades ease up the ladders into the rich darkness of the Argonne forest, aware that the patrol would soon be alone in that open space that lay between their guns and the guns of the Germans: no man's land.

Watts took the point, crawling over the shell-pocked terrain with the confidence of a combat-hardened soldier; the others followed less assuredly but no less swiftly into the moonless night.

Adrian had selected Hatch, Tibbs, Carter, Kenny, Private Andre Levette, and Private Jefferson Satter, his six best men, all who now followed Watts ten yards from the trench.

Bent low, Adrian could hear his heart pounding but no other sounds.

When they reached the first strands of barbed wire, Watts knelt and waited for the others to catch up. Adrian dropped quietly beside him and wiped at his sweaty brow while the legionnaire raised the lower strand of wire and motioned Adrian to crawl under. Adrian rolled on his back with his rifle cradled across his chest and slithered backward under the looped wire into the clear air. He knelt and held the wire while Hatch and the others, and finally Watts, had crawled into the open.

Watts whispered, "Now we crawl on our bellies. Very slowly."

They snaked forward to a huge shell crater and slid down the edges of it.

They heard German voices. Adrian felt Watts pull at his shoulder. "Leave two of your men here to cover us. We'll leave our rifles."

Adrian tapped Levette and Satter and whispered his orders, then followed Watts as he began crawling toward the voices.

There were three Germans in the nest—two awake and one sleeping—when the four Americans spilled into the machine-gun position.

Watts's giant frame loomed over the others as he shoved his bayonet into the throat of the German gunner. Adrian heard a muffled, gargling sound as he dove at the second, startled gunner. His hand clamped over the German's mouth, then he slid his bayonet beneath the man's sternum. He felt the soldier tremble, felt the man's legs flail.

Hatch meantime had slammed the butt of his bayonet against the sleeping German's head, who snapped awake just as he saw the black silhouette of his attacker.

Watts took a handkerchief and gagged the unconscious gunner as Adrian and Hatch pulled leather thongs from their belts to tie the man's hands and feet.

Minutes later, Levette and Satter stared wide-eyed at Watts and the German prisoner when the men reached the crater.

"What now?" Adrian whispered.

"Move out. Stay low, and if the shooting starts—run like hell." Watts caught his breath, then draped the German over his left shoulder and started toward the American trenches.

They moved faster now, feeling the safety of their lines drawing closer with each step. Bent low, it was now a footrace before the Germans discovered the machine-gun emplacement had been deactivated and a prisoner taken.

To cross the wire Watts laid the German over it, and the others stepped onto Watts's back and dropped to the other side.

He pulled the German upright and again hoisted him onto his shoulder. The patrol moved in a straight line toward the trenches, praying they would not be shot by the enemy—or their own men.

Adrian was amazed at the stamina of Sergeant Watts, who kept moving, bent low, saddling the German without so much as a grunt.

Adrian heard the staccato of the German machine guns raking the trenchline, the gunners using interlocking fire, probing for human flesh.

"I'm hit!" one of the soldiers shouted.

Adrian turned as a flare exploded overhead; he saw, in the eerie, dancing light, Private Carter dragging his leg.

Adrian heard another chatter from the enemy Maxims and watched helplessly as Carter suddenly spun, like a ballerina performing a pirouette, then straightened, his dark face turned upward to the flare light overhead that momentarily gave the black hell of no man's land a special brilliance.

In that moment, Adrian ran—but not toward the trenchline, as did the others. He ran toward the young soldier, knowing the futility of it, the foolhardiness of it, but inescapably compelled. He charged back toward the dancing light and to Carter to fulfill a promise he had made to all his platoon: *I will not leave you behind.*

He reached Carter, who was lying on the ground, the reflection from the dwindling light of the drifting flare mirrored in his dead eyes.

Then he hoisted the dead soldier on his back and stumbled toward the trench.

Adrian sat against the wall of the trench where the light at sunrise bent unevenly through the shattered trees of the Argonne. He stared at his bloodstained hands and thought about Private Carter and how he loved to play the harmonica.

"Adrian, are you all right?"

Adrian glanced at his leg. His pants were torn and it was then he realized how close the German bullets had come.

"I'm fine." He motioned for David to sit beside him on a blanket in the muddy trench.

"I heard you lost one of your men."

Adrian nodded. "His name was Carter. He was a good kid."

"I know what you're going through." David shook his head sadly. "I can't get Joseph out of my mind. I started writing a letter to Alice, but I don't know what to say."

"Tell her the truth."

"That he was walking down a dark, muddy road in France when he suddenly died?"

"Tell her that he died a soldier's death, that he knew it could happen. He knew that when he joined the army. Tell her that he was walking tall and proud in a land where people needed his help and that he died unselfishly, which is a helluva lot more than most men can say when they die."

"We haven't talked like this since we were much younger. Not at all since we joined the army," David said.

"We're brothers. We don't have to talk. We know what each other feels."

David reached into his tunic, took out an envelope, and handed it to Adrian. "This is for Theresa. Should anything happen to me. I don't want it mailed. Give it to her in person."

Adrian took the envelope, stared at it long, then reached to his map case and took out a sealed envelope. "Give this to Hannah if I go west. Seems like we've been thinking along the same lines—like brothers do."

David chuckled. "One of my privates asked me last night, 'Lieutenant, what are we doing here?' "

"What did you say?"

"Real simple. I told him we're fighting a war."

"Did he buy that?"

"For about two seconds. Then he said, 'That's a bunch of crap. We're here because we're all trying to prove something to the folks back home.' "

Adrian broke into a wide grin. "Sounds like the kind of soldier Pop would be proud to meet."

David thought a moment. "I wonder how Pop's doing."

"I expect he's doing fine."

David looked at the sealed envelope. "Well, brother, what was it like out in no man's land?"

Adrian released a long sigh. "It wasn't like Cuba. Hell, we never knew who we were shooting at half the time. Never even knew if we killed anybody. Last night, I *saw* the enemy. I could taste his breath." His voice trailed off.

"How do you feel?" asked David.

Adrian took a deep breath. "I feel like I went to the edge of the world and stared into the darkness below."

"What did you see?"

Adrian's eyes teared as he looked nervously around the trench. To the ladder. The periscope. The muddy blanket on which he sat. "I enjoyed it, David. I shoved that knife into that German soldier's heart and it made me feel good, God forgive me."

David said nothing. Again he looked at the sealed envelope addressed to Hannah, and remembered when they were boys living at Fort Davis and had encountered a rattlesnake in the desert. David had stood frozen with fear.

He remembered the brother who took a stick and chased the rattlesnake away.

40

Later that afternoon, Adrian was studying no man's land through a periscope when he noticed a man walking toward him. The man was short, wore wire-frame spectacles, was dressed in a rumpled business suit—and was Colored. He stopped beside Adrian and asked, "May I take a look?"

Adrian motioned to the periscope. The man looked into the lens and breathed softly, "So that's what it looks like."

"Not much for scenery."

The man stared for a long moment, then turned away from the periscope and extended his hand. "I'm Andre DuBois."

"I'm Lieutenant Adrian Sharps." Adrian shook his hand, then asked, "What are you doing in France, Mr. DuBois? You're obviously not a soldier."

DuBois shook his head and laughed. "No, I'm obviously not a soldier. I'm a journalist with the *Pittsburgh Courier.*"

"An outstanding newspaper. I've enjoyed it for years."

"Thank you. I'm here on assignment to do a story on Colored doughboys at the front."

"What kind of story?"

"I want to focus on life in the trenches."

Adrian smiled, then pointed to his dugout. "Care for some coffee?"

DuBois nodded and slipped into the dugout and sat beside Adrian on his blanket. Glancing around, he noticed the sabre lying on Adrian's duffel bag. DuBois pointed at the sabre, then asked, "May I?"

Adrian nodded as he gathered two tin cups. Dubois ran his hand along the scabbard. "This is most interesting. I didn't know men in the infantry carried swords."

"It belonged to my father. He served in the Tenth Cavalry."

"I'm impressed. You're a second-generation soldier in the army."

"I have a brother who is also an officer in this company." Adrian poured the coffee and watched with some glee as DuBois's face wrinkled in distaste.

"My God, this is awful." DuBois spat out the coffee. "Tastes like boot polish."

"Boot polish would taste better."

Both men laughed as DuBois lay the sabre onto the duffel. He then grew serious. "What are your feelings on Order Forty?"

Adrian grew sullen. "I think it stinks."

DuBois took out a notebook and began writing. "Can you be more specific?"

Adrian grew cautious. "I could get into a lot of trouble for questioning an order."

DuBois put down his pencil. "You're an officer. I should think you would question an order that will have an impact on the morale of your men."

"An officer follows orders, Mr. DuBois. No matter how disgusting the order."

DuBois nodded knowingly. "Have you seen any effect on the morale?"

Adrian waved his arms about the dugout. "This is tough enough on the morale. Besides, there aren't any women in the area."

"What about when the men go on pass?"

Adrian's eyes narrowed. "Then they will have to obey the order or suffer the consequences."

"No matter how unfair?"

"No matter how unfair."

Just then Hatch appeared at the entrance of the dugout. "Lieutenant Sharps, may I speak with you?"

Adrian rose and followed Hatch to the periscope.

"We got a problem, sir."

"What problem?"

Hatch nodded down the trenchline. "It's Private Tibbs, sir. He refuses to report to his position."

In his squad's dugout, Tibbs lay curled against the wall, his face buried in his hands. Adrian slipped inside and knelt by the soldier.

"Private Tibbs?"

Tibbs said nothing, nor did he move.

Adrian gently put his hand on Franklin's head. "Private Tibbs, you have to report to your position."

Tibbs shook his head, then a sob broke from his throat. "I can't, sir. I can't."

Adrian gripped him by the arms and turned him until both men faced each other. "You have to report to your position."

"I can't," he repeated.

Suddenly, a voice boomed from the entrance.

"What the hell is going on here, Sharps?"

Adrian looked up to see Chauncey and O'Doul standing at the entrance.

"Just a case of nerves, Captain," Adrian replied.

Chauncey looked at Hatch. "What's going on, Sergeant?"

Hatch shrugged and looked helpless. "Private Tibbs refuses to report to his position, sir."

There was fury in Chauncey's voice as he said, "Nerves, hell. Sergeant O'Doul, get this coward on his feet and at attention."

O'Doul came into the dugout and reached past Adrian and gripped Tibbs's arm. With a heavy grunt he dragged Tibbs from the dugout and jerked him to his feet.

Tibbs stood crumpled, his eyes staring at the muddy ground.

"Private, you have thirty seconds to get your equipment and report to your position. Is that clear?"

Tibbs shook his head.

"By God, you will, soldier, or I'll have you court-martialed for cowardice."

Again Tibbs shook his head.

Chauncey looked at O'Doul. "First Sergeant, take him to the provost at battalion headquarters." He looked at Hatch. "You accompany the first sergeant."

O'Doul pulled his .45 pistol and prodded Tibbs in the back. "Move out, you piece of garbage."

Adrian stood, looking helpless.

From a short distance, DuBois wrote furiously in his notebook.

Nearing sunset, Hatch returned looking shaken to the core. He was dragging his rifle by the sling, his eyes appearing empty and lifeless. He stopped in front of his squad's dugout, where he sat on the ground and removed his helmet.

Adrian came out of his dugout to get his platoon ready for "stand to" when he saw Hatch and walked to the sergeant. He placed his hand on his shoulder and said, "Tibbs'll be all right. Once he's examined by the medics he'll be given medical treatment, not a court-martial."

Hatch shook his head, then his chest heaved. "There won't be no court-martial, sir."

"I know."

Hatch shook his head and began sobbing. "No, sir. You don't understand. Private Tibbs has gone west."

Adrian pulled Hatch to his feet and shook him by the shoulders. "What are you saying?"

Hatch shook his head disconsolately. "He's dead, sir."

"Dead? How in the hell could he be dead? My God. How?"

"First Sergeant O'Doul shot him in the back, sir. Tibbs started howling and screaming, looking like he was tetched. When we got to battalion headquarters, he broke loose and started running. O'Doul shot him down like a dog!"

Adrian went straight to Vince O'Doul's dugout and found the man sitting on his cot. He gripped the sergeant's harness and jerked him to his feet.

"What the hell are you doing?" O'Doul demanded.

"You murdered one of my men," Adrian snapped.

"Get out of here! He did it to himself by trying to escape."

"Escape! Escape to where?"

"There were dozens of witnesses, including Hatch. He saw the whole thing happen."

Adrian's face twisted into a mask of rage. "You murdering bastard."

Adrian was reaching for the flap on his holster when he felt strong hands close on his shoulders and guide him into the open trench.

"What did you expect?" asked Sergeant Watts calmly. They stood staring for a long moment. Watts continued, "You might be in France, but the white man brought a piece of America along."

"What would you know?"

Watts lit a cigarette. "I know more than you will ever know."

Adrian stood nose to nose with the legionnaire. "What do you know, Sergeant Watts, if that is your name?"

Watts didn't flinch. "My real name is William Brown. I'm from Harlem."

"Why are you in the legion?" Adrian demanded.

"Five years ago, I killed a white policeman in New York City." He turned and started to walk away.

Adrian said, "Wait. I should have known it was something like that. You want to talk about it?"

Watts shrugged. "Nothing to talk about. Two cops started beating me with their nightsticks. I fought back. One went to the hospital, the other to his grave. I came to France aboard a freighter and joined the legion in order to survive."

Watts took a few steps, turned, and said, "You best start getting your mind right, Lieutenant. We're going into combat."

"How do you know?"

The legionnaire smiled mysteriously. "I know. Believe me, I know."

"When?"

"Soon. Very soon."

Adrian stormed away, chased by O'Doul's howling laughter.

41

★ ★ ★

At Sabre Ranch, Selona sat on the front porch staring off into the night, her thoughts as distant as the moon. The pain of Augustus's death had not quite begun; she was too numb to hurt.

"Too many deaths in too short a time," she whispered to the moon.

She heard something in the yard and looked to see Vina and Theresa approaching.

"Evening, Miss Selona. May we join you?" Theresa asked.

Selona motioned them forward. The women sat on the steps, saying nothing as they joined Selona in star gazing.

"Beautiful night," Selona said.

"Sure is," replied Vina.

There was a long quiet, then Selona asked, "Vina, where do you think the stars was the most beautiful?"

Vina was quick to answer. "Fort Davis, Texas. It seemed those old stars burned like torches."

"I think you're right," Selona said.

"Which fort did you enjoy the most?" asked Theresa.

"Wherever Augustus was posted."

A long silence followed, then Vina said, "He was a good man. He always gave you what you wanted."

Selona grumped. "Yes, but not always without a fight."

Vina understood. "Your cooking business."

Selona nodded her head.

Theresa asked, "You mean Augustus was against your starting your cooking business?"

Selona and Vina both laughed wildly.

"Child, that was the closest that man ever came to leaving me."

Selona looked up at the stars, the same stars that had hung above Fort Davis, Texas, in 1882.

Need brings about yearning, yearning brings about dreams, and Selona had had a dream she never spoke of because she knew it would never come true: to own her own business.

Then history changed all that with the arrival of the Southern Pacific Railroad, giving Selona an idea to fulfill her dream.

By the summer of 1882, the San Antonio–El Paso Mail had been put out of business, the stagecoaches replaced by the Iron Horse, which rode on rails stretching as far as the eye could see. This new entry into west Texas kept the buffalo soldiers out on the desert, protecting the various watering holes and the long stretches of isolated track, which Mexican bandits found ideal for train robbing.

Although the railroad bypassed Fort Davis, freight companies and the Overland stage line operated between the fort and the closest railroad depots, at Marfa to the southwest and other towns to the north and east.

The reason Fort Davis was important was because of water.

She was standing in the sutler's two days after Augustus's

confrontation with Armitage, noticing the throng of passengers milling about while the stage took on fresh horses.
That's when the idea came to her.

The next morning Selona rose early and cooked an un-
usually large breakfast, so large that Augustus was astonished at the feast.

"God Almighty, woman. I can't eat all that!"

She merely said, "Eat to your fill. We'll have the leftovers
for dinner."

The table was heaped with biscuits, sorghum molasses,
fried fatback, eggs, hot coffee, fried tomatoes from her garden, and a variety of tortillas stuffed with rabbit meat and
venison. She had made two apple pies from apples purchased at the sutler's. When Augustus was full he finished
dressing and reported to the orderly room.

When he had left, Selona selected a variety of the leftovers, filling two plates. She wrapped the plates and carefully placed them in a basket. She left Adrian and David
with Vina and walked across the parade ground straight to
the sutler's and stood in front of the counter.

Conniger could see there was something different this
morning in the way she smiled. But first he went to his
ledger, skimmed to her name, and noted her credit was up
to date.

"What can I do for you, Mrs. Sharps?"

Selona placed the basket on the counter and carefully removed the plates. "I want to talk a little business with you,
Mr. Conniger. But first . . . I want to show you something."

Frank Conniger was in his sixties, with a long beard and
gentle eyes as green as the hills of Scotland, which he had
left as a boy to come to America. He had a government con-
tract as the sutler, providing a combination of grocery store,
dry goods shop, saloon, and stage depot. He eyed her warily, then looked at the plates. "That's a mighty fine-looking
spread, Mrs. Sharps."

She smiled and handed him a fork. "My husband says I'm

the best cook in the west. Judging by his size, not many will argue."

She watched Conniger begin to taste the various selections. In a moment, he was eating heartily.

"I have a proposition for you, Mr. Conniger."

Conniger nodded his head and kept eating, motioning with his hand for her to continue.

"Augustus can't stay in the army forever. That's just a natural fact. And you know Colored folks in the army can't save enough money to buy a piece of land. When he retires, and we own a piece of land, we'll have somewheres to go."

"A man should think about the future," Conniger agreed, wolfing down a biscuit dipped in molasses.

"So I was thinking. We like west Texas, and it's starting to settle down. There's land around here to be bought—"

"Land takes money," Conniger interrupted.

"Yes, sir, I know. That's why I'm here."

Conniger's mouth stopped. He wiped his hands on his apron. "Are you looking to borrow money, Mrs. Sharps?"

"No, sir. I ain't looking to borrow money. I'm looking for a business partner."

Conniger laughed. "What do you have to offer for your side of the partnership?"

Selona pointed at the plates. "You're eating it, Mr. Conniger."

That afternoon was the first meeting of the new school at Fort Davis.

Marcia O'Kelly arrived early, setting up chairs and washing the chalkboard; then she set out chalk and slate-boards given her by the chaplain, and the primers used to educate the young troopers. She had not slept the night before, thrashing about and keeping Jon awake, who wound up sleeping in a rocking chair on the front porch.

The atmosphere was childlike though there were plenty

of adults sitting in the back of the room; the six laundresses had worked furiously that morning to finish their washing in order to attend class, and Selona was the first to arrive, with David and Adrian.

"We'll begin with learning our letters, then our numbers. Once you've learned the letters, you'll begin learning how to form words, and that will help you to learn to read."

The process began with Marcia, chalk in hand, scrawling the alphabet on the board. With each letter she would have the class repeat the letter aloud, then write it on the slate boards.

Something of exultation swept through Selona as she watched David and Adrian scrawl the letter *a* on their slate boards. She realized that on that day she had done two things in her life she never dreamed she could do.

She had begun a small business, and she had taken her children to school.

That evening Augustus returned home to an astonishing surprise. He had to step over pots and pans, metal plates, cutlery, and several baskets filled with vegetables, eggs, and smoked hams. His eyes bulged as he tried to count the money he would owe the sutler.

Sitting at the table with Selona was Vina. Selona wore a Cheshire grin; Vina was her usual solemn self.

Before Augustus could speak, Selona was out of the chair, saying, "Now, honey, before you bust a gut, you got to hear me out."

Augustus was silent. He sat on the edge of the bed and nodded.

"I got me this idea, honey. I've been trying to sort through everything until it was ready before I told you."

"You got everything sorted through, Selona?"

She nodded.

"Then you can tell me why you've taken leave of your

senses and bought all this food on credit. You have enough food here to feed the regiment."

"Not the regiment . . . passengers on the stage and the men who haul freight to the railroad."

Augustus stood and walked around the small room, studying the baskets of food. "Go on, Selona. I'm listening."

"This idea come to me. You said I was the best cook in the west."

"That I did. There's no doubt about that."

"I took Mr. Conniger some of my cooking. He loved it. I told him my idea was to set up a little stand at the stage depot. When folks come through on the stage they always get off and stretch their legs. Why not have food for them to buy? Good food. My food! The best in west Texas!"

Augustus started laughing and clapped his hands. "Girl, you have to be crazy."

"Crazy like a fox, Augustus. Mr. Conniger thinks it's a wonderful idea. He's going to supply the food. I do the cooking and we split the money. You know when word of my cooking gets around we'll be swimming in money."

Augustus sniffed at a large onion. "What about the laundry? If you give that up we'll lose our quarters and have to move off the fort."

"I'll keep my laundry job."

He shook his head. "You're going to cook all day and wash at the same time?"

She shook her head and pointed at Vina. "Vina's going to do the laundry. She'll use my kettles and have my washing folks. We'll split the money."

Augustus looked worried. "That doesn't sound fair. She'll be doing all the work and you'll be getting half the money."

"Augustus, me and Darcy and the kids could sure use more money. I'm willing to take on the extra work."

Selona added, "She'll be my partner. Mr. Conniger suggested it to me. He said it's good business, just like me and him being partners."

Vina nodded in agreement.

"I make ten dollars a month doing the laundry. I'll make that every week with my cooking. In a few years we'll have enough money to buy us a piece of land."

This statement surprised Augustus. "What piece of land? You haven't said anything about a piece of land."

She patted him on the hand. "I was getting to that, honey."

"You best get to it real fast, Selona."

She started off slow. "All my life I've wanted a home. A place I could call my own, on my own land, for us and the children. We ain't ever going to get that land off your army money. And what are we going to do when you're too old and tired to soldier? What will we live on?"

Augustus stood slow, wearing a look of shame. "Are you saying I can't take care of my family?"

She stepped against him and felt his back stiffen. Her voice was no more than a whisper, a pleading whisper. "No, honey, I'm not saying that. I'm asking you to let me help."

He pushed her away slowly and walked to the door. "I'm going back to the orderly room. It appears you don't need my advice."

Selona stood there, tears in her eyes, watching him until he disappeared through the front door.

Augustus had walked no more than ten feet from the porch when he heard the clatter of hooves thundering across the ground behind his house. He stopped and turned just as the silhouette of a rider appeared in the darkness, riding at full gallop.

Selona had just closed the door when she heard the horse, then the sound of the glass in the back window breaking.

Her eyes filled with terror, then she screamed, "Vina . . . run!"

Augustus was nearly to the porch when Selona and Vina came running through the door, with Selona screaming, "Run! Run! Someone threw dynamite into the house!"

Augustus grabbed her by the hand as Vina ran past him, and started running, dragging her as far from the house as possible.

They ran, stumbling; then, suddenly, Augustus stopped. He turned and looked at the house.

There was no explosion.

"Stay here, Selona."

"What are you doing?" her frantic voice called as he started for the house.

Augustus said nothing as he stepped onto the porch and carefully peered through the open door.

A stick of dynamite was lying on the bed, but there was no fuse. He walked to the bed and picked up the explosive, noticing a piece of paper tied around it. He removed the paper and began reading as he heard Selona call, "Are you crazy! Come out of there."

Augustus walked outside, where he found dozens of people had collected from Suds Row. Darcy was running, carrying his pistol in one hand while pulling up his suspenders with the other. He stopped next to Augustus and, seeing the stick of dynamite, said to the frantic Selona, "Nothin' to worry about, Selona. There ain't no fuse in the dynamite."

Selona collapsed to her knees, then Vina knelt beside her, and both women began trembling uncontrollably.

Augustus handed the dynamite to Gibbs, telling him, "Take this to the sergeant major. Tell him what happened."

Gibbs nodded and started off, but paused as Augustus unfolded the paper and read the message scrawled in pencil: " 'Touch a white man again . . . you die.' "

Augustus crumpled the note and looked around, but saw nothing.

Sergeant Major Brassard read the message for the third time, then said to Augustus, "We got to get you off this fort. I'll transfer you to Fort Concho in the morning."

"Fort Concho!"

"You'll be safe there. Besides, there's an opening there for a first sergeant."

Augustus's jaw suddenly set like it was made of iron. "I'll get out of the army before I'll let that bastard run me and my family like a dog."

"You better come to your senses, Augustus. You've got a wife and children to think about."

A hard glint came into his eyes as he stared first at Brassard, then at Selona, and said, "I *am* thinking about them. For the first time, maybe, and I'm thinking real hard. This is our home, and we're going to buy us a piece of land near here for when I retire."

Brassard stared at him incredulously. "Piece of land! What piece of land?"

Augustus grinned at Selona. "Whatever piece of land we want."

Brassard pointed out the immediate problem with the idea. "That takes money. You can't buy a piece of land on a soldier's pay."

Augustus reached over and put his arms around Selona. "Selona has her own business now. We'll get that piece of land, and there ain't no man on earth that's going to chase us off."

Selona went to the bed and picked up the red dress she planned to wear on her first day of business, and asked Augustus, "Now that I've got a business, do you think I can get a pair of shoes to go with this dress?"

Augustus laughed aloud, saying, "You can buy two pairs of shoes."

Both were laughing wildly as Brassard looked around at all the food filling their quarters and said, "What you plan on doing, Selona—feed the whole regiment?"

Selona and Augustus looked at each other quickly, then burst out laughing again and started dancing around Brassard, who could only stand there looking dumbfounded.

* * *

"You got you that piece of land," Vina said softly.

Selona nodded and said, "It sure does seem like an empty piece of land at this moment."

"And that Texas Ranger captain that threw that stick of dynamite got his piece of land," said Vina with deep laughter.

That got Selona to laughing. "He sure did. Six feet of land."

"Yes, ma'am. Shot and killed by Injuns."

All three women laughed again, knowing the truth.

"I often wonder what happened to Juanita Jackson and her son, Chihocopee," said Selona.

"I reckon she's in Mexico with her people. After Captain Armitage killed Trooper Jackson, and she killed him, she couldn't stay in Texas," said Vina.

Selona lightly slapped her knees, then stood, saying, "I guess I better get to bed."

Vina and Theresa said good night and left as Selona went inside.

She stopped at a small room and opened the door and peeked inside. A lantern burned low, illuminating Alice and baby Joseph, who slept together.

Her heart ached for the young woman, knowing they now shared the same emptiness.

But at least she and Augustus had more than forty good years together.

She did have that.

PART 5

THE MEUSE-ARGONNE OFFENSIVE

42

The tedium of the wait wears at a soldier more than facing the enemy. Adrian and his platoon had grown irritable and even sloppy in the previous two months waiting for the "big push," as the anticipated offensive along the Hindenburg Line was called.

The 372nd had been moved so many times from the frontline trenches to the rear for further training, the men no longer believed there would be a big push.

September 23 found the 372nd at Dommartin-sur-Yvre, ten miles east of Sainte-Menehould, where the anticipation of the big push ran high.

That afternoon, Adrian and his platoon were bivouacked in the woods outside the village, cleaning their equipment in preparation for another move, this time toward the lines of the Boche.

Walking among his men, Adrian stopped and began chatting with Hatch, when O'Doul appeared. He was carrying a Chugach gun, a French automatic weapon that was drumfed and heavier than sin. O'Doul motioned for Adrian.

He stood with the Chugach perched on his hip. "Lieutenant Sharps, the company is moving forward at zero-two-hundred. Your platoon will take the point." He walked away with a grin.

Adrian walked back to Hatch. "Get the men to ready their gear. We're moving out at zero-two-hundred." He looked around. "I've got something I need to take care of. I'll be back shortly."

Adrian picked up his rifle and removed his sabre from the back of his field pack. He made the short walk to where the second platoon was positioned, some two hundred yards away, and found his brother.

David looked excited. "I guess this is going to be the big push."

Adrian nodded. "I think you're right. O'Doul has my platoon on point. He wouldn't do that unless we were going into a ruckus."

"I think you're right. God, that man hates you, Adrian."

"Not as much as I hate him." He paused, then held out his sabre. "I think we need to do something before we get moving."

David looked at the sabre and seemed to understand. "What do you have in mind?"

Adrian saw David's blanket laying on the ground. "Grab your blanket and come with me. I know someone who might help."

The two brothers walked a short distance to the village, where headquarters was located. The buildings were in typical frontline condition—mostly blown to hell—but served as a reference point for the companies.

The legionnaire company had been assigned to stay with the battalion command post and were easy to find. The building they occupied had no roof and only two walls.

Adrian found Captain Girard and Sergeant Watts with their men, making final preparations for the move north toward the front.

"Good evening, gentlemen. I hope you are prepared for the evening's activities."

Adrian shook hands with Girard. "We are, Captain. We sure as hell are."

"*Bon, très bon.* It will be, as you say, a 'real ruckus.' "

Watts added, "A hilacious street brawl."

Adrian looked at Watts. "Sergeant Watts, I would like to ask you a favor."

Watts nodded carefully. "If possible. What do you need?"

"We're going to be at the point, and I'm sure you know what that means."

Watts nodded.

Adrian held out his sabre and said, "My brother and I want these to get back to our family in Arizona should something happen to us."

Watts looked at the sabre. "What would you suggest?"

Adrian knelt and spread the blanket on the ground and looked at Watts. "Do you have a spade?"

"I'll get one." Watts left as Adrian took his sabre and lay it on the blanket. He touched the scabbard affectionately, then looked at his brother. David knelt and laid his sabre next to his brother's. Adrian folded the blanket around the sabres, wrapping them tightly, then took a piece of heavy twine and bound the bundle.

Watts returned with a small spade and handed it to Adrian, who looked around and stared at the corner where the two remaining walls joined. He walked to the corner and began digging where a large chunk of the flooring had been blown away.

When finished, he placed the bundle in the hole and covered it, then tamped down the dirt. He looked at Watts, then took a folded piece of paper from his pocket and said, "Send them to this address."

Watts took the paper and nodded, saying, "I will, if I am able."

Girard turned to the legionnaires and spoke in French

while pointing at the corner. When finished, the men shouted in unison, *"Oui, mon capitaine!"*

Adrian looked confused. Watts smiled, then said, "At least one of us here should survive. Your precious sabres will be returned to your family. You have the promise of La Légion Étrangère."

Girard said, "I will write for each man the address of your family."

Adrian shook hands with Watts and said, "When this war is over, you could possibly return to America. Perhaps under another name."

Watts replied with sincerity, "No, my friend. The legion is my home—my country. I am treated with respect. My race does not matter in France."

Adrian held his hand for a long moment and stared deeply into his dark eyes, then said, "I understand."

Adrian shook hands with Girard, David with Watts. *"Au revoir, mon ami,"* Adrian said.

Then the two brothers turned and walked away, never looking back . . . not even to the corner.

43

At 1130 hours, September 25, 1918, 2,700 artillery pieces of the Allied Expeditionary Forces commenced firing along a line that stretched northeast from Verdun to Vouziers, a thirty-five-mile stretch of the worst terrain known to an infantryman.

The centerpiece of that area was the Argonne forest.

After two days of marching through forest and devastated terrain, the men of the 372nd were being held in reserve at Somme-Bione, a small town nine miles south of Ripont on the west flank of the Argonne forest, the 157th Division's first objective.

The roads had been jammed through the night with troops marching in columns of twos, and equipment being moved to the frontline trenches. Trucks groaned constantly, hauling field artillery pieces, machine-gun batteries, ammunition, and ration carts, forming a parade with intermingling tanks and ambulances.

Adrian's platoon was spread out through a treeline near

the village, each man stripped down to rifle and bayonet, extra rations and canteens, and extra ammunition. Nothing was to be carried that each soldier couldn't eat, drink, or use for killing.

The noise from the barrage was deafening, and the men sat silently, watching, listening to the destructive force preparing the ground they would travel en route to the enemy.

Adrian moved through his platoon chatting briefly with each man, calming him as best he could. He found Rufus Hatch and James Kenny kneeling by a tree, smoking cigarettes, trying to act nonchalant.

"Sure is a thunderous noise, Lieutenant." Hatch crushed out his cigarette, never taking his eyes off the artillery flashes at the front.

"Can't imagine what those Germans must be going through right now," said Kenny.

"No worse than what our boys will be going through come morning," Adrian replied.

Finally, Kenny spoke the words all the men were thinking. "What are we doing here, Lieutenant?"

Adrian replied, "Preparing to fight Germans."

"No, sir. I mean, why are we here in France fighting for white people's freedom when we ain't got freedom for ourselves back in the States?"

He could only answer the way his father had when asked that same question. "If the Colored man is going to stand shoulder to shoulder with the white man, we've got to make the same sacrifices. Our people have come a long distance since Emancipation, and there's a long way to go. But it'll come. You'll see. It'll be men like us who will make the country change its way of treating us."

Hatch shook his head. "I think I'm going to stay here in France when the war's over. I'm treated better here than by Americans."

Adrian knew there were hundreds of Colored troops who had the same plan.

"Not me," said Kenny. "I want to go home to my momma, and I ain't ever going to leave Alabama."

Adrian thought a moment. "I'm going back to Arizona and take my wife and baby on a camping trip up in the mountains. I'm going to stand at sunrise and look out over the land that my family defended for nearly fifty years. I'm not letting hatred or anything else strip me of my birthright."

A howitzer salvo streaked across the sky, and the three watched the flash.

Adrian continued along the line, stopping to talk with every member of his platoon.

At 0530, the barrage lifted and the 157th Red Hand Division began its first assault, using a tactic called a wave formation, the troops rushing forward, using the fresh shellholes for momentary protection before racing to the next line of craters.

The initial assault by the 369th, the 161st French, and the 2nd Moroccan comprised some of the most fierce fighting known along the Hindenburg Line.

That afternoon, the 372nd marched forward to Butte de Mesnil, south of Ripont, where the Germans had dug in and were putting up stiff resistance.

On both sides of the narrow road lay a wall of carnage: immense piles of corpses, severed limbs, hundreds of dead horses, some still harnessed to artillery caissons—all rotting in the sun, the bodies bloated.

Hundreds of German prisoners were marched toward the 372nd in a long column, footsore, eyes sunken, bent from fatigue. The French and Moroccan guards prodded the stragglers with boots and rifle butts.

It was nearly dusk when the regiment was ordered to a new position on the right flank of the 371st, to fill in a gap left by the 161st French and 2nd Moroccan. The 372nd reached that position at 0200 on September 27, and was ordered into shellholes to await further orders.

44

At 0400 on September 27, the First Battalion of the 372nd Infantry Regiment heard the dreaded whistles amid the artillery barrage. Then phosphorescent flares thumped into the dark sky, signaling the men from the shell-holes and forward toward the German trenches.

A rolling barrage was the most devastating form of attack known to any soldier who had ever served on the FEBA—forward edge of the battle area. Artillery shells were fired along the line to the front of advancing soldiers, falling dangerously close to the men, who would constantly adjust their eyes to the changing light as the projectiles slammed into the earth, turning the darkness ahead into a momentary point of brilliant reference that faded quickly to pristine velvet blackness.

From every hill the German Maxims opened fire, raking the 550-yard front where the 372nd charged.

Adrian heard the screams, but shouted, "Keep moving! Keep moving! Keep moving!"

Ahead of their advance, the earth exploded, then shuddered, spewing huge clumps of dirt and human bodies into the air.

The screams intensified as the interlocking bands of machine guns chattered their deadly firepower and scores of men fell, alone and in clumps and in clusters, as the incessant fire continued.

Only one hundred yards separated the American and German trenches, but it was the longest one hundred yards any of the Americans had known, all of it covered beneath the dancing flares fired by enemy mortars.

Adrian ran, fired, reloaded on the run, then fired again. Glancing to his left, he saw one of his soldiers stiffen beneath the eerie light, then stagger and look upward before pitching forward into a crater where several German soldiers lay dead.

The next enemy soldiers he saw were not dead; they were alive and firing. Now he realized the barrage had ceased, and the fighting would be man against man.

Like a great wave crashing onto a beach, the troops of the 372nd poured past German rifle fire and sharp bayonets and into the enemy trenches.

Hatch was among the first to leap into the trench and landed on an infantryman with such ferocity, the soldier dropped his rifle. Hatch, eyes wide with fear and exhilaration, lunged forward, driving his bayonet through the German's chest. When he tried to withdraw the blade, it held fast to the man's rib cage, and the sergeant had to fire his rifle and slam his boot into the man's chest to free the bayonet.

"Kill them!" came the collective screams of the American soldiers, who were now fighting as much from rapture as fear.

A German officer raised his pistol to take aim at Adrian, who fired his revolver from the hip and, in a lucky shot, blew a piece of the soldier's head away.

Throughout the German trenches, soldiers of America

and Germany fought one another in fierce hand-to-hand combat. There was no time to reload, and rifles became nothing more than brutal clubs.

"Use your knives!" a doughboy shouted.

Kenny quickly removed his bayonet and fell onto a German soldier, slashing, grunting, growling like an animal. He ripped away the soldier's throat and was nearly blinded as the blood spewed into his eyes.

Beside him, Hatch's fingers clawed the throat of a German soldier. Then he drove his knee into the Boche's groin, picked up a rifle, and slammed the weapon into the man's head with such force the German's teeth disintegrated.

More flares ignited the night and the trench took on a ghoulish appearance, as though it marked where the earth had opened and exposed an entrance into the bowels of hell.

Just when it seemed the situation could not become more horrific, there came the stammer of a Chugach automatic weapon.

Adrian looked to the top of the trench, where he saw Vince O'Doul, his face a demonic mask, firing wildly into the trench, sweeping German soldiers in the storm of bullets, as well as several Colored soldiers of the first platoon.

Adrian saw O'Doul's insane mask of a face and screamed, *"No! No!"* But the first sergeant did not hear or ignored Adrian's shout and continued to fire until the weapon's magazine emptied, then reloaded and shouldered the gun to aim again into the swarming trench.

Captain Chauncey arrived on the scene at the moment Hatch raised his rifle and fired a single shot into O'Doul's brain. The NCO spun wildly, one leg kicking out, then dropped to his knees. His body slowly slumped forward, his face buried between his knees.

Chauncey was bug-eyed as he raised his pistol toward Hatch, but four men who were following close behind the company commander slammed into him, knocking him into the trench. He disappeared beneath the dead, dying, and fleeing as the enemy were forced out of their trenches and began running to their next line of trenches.

"Keep going!" Adrian shouted, waving his arms and pointing. "Keep going! To the next trench. Next trench!"

The remnant of the platoon pursued the Germans through what was once their hard-won ground. Those who stumbled, died, as knives slashed throats, bullets tore into chests, rifle butts cracked skulls.

Defending the next line of enemy trenches were more machine-gun nests, but the 372nd soldiers swarmed forward into the hail of bullets like men pursued by demons.

Adrian tasted the bile in his throat as he caught a German from behind and drove his bayonet into the man's back.

Screams in English and German mixed with the Chugach's steady *b-b-b-r-r-r-r* and the *rat-a-tat-tat* of the Maxims, creating a symphony of horror beneath the constant flarelight.

In the next trench, the blue helmets of the Red Hand and gray helmets of the German soldiers became the only weapon the men had to use. Jaws broke, teeth shattered, blood ran from cracked noses.

Nearing the dreaded Maxim positions, Adrian could see the German infantrymen were dead or wounded, and only the machine guns stood in the way of the doughboys.

"Look!" a doughboy shouted.

Adrian looked to see the German machine-gunners raise their arms in surrender.

The Americans slowed their advance and Hatch found Adrian. "They're whipped, sir! We've done it, by God! We've done it!"

The Germans were standing sullenly behind their machine guns, their arms raised; some stood with their heads and upraised arms bobbing above the positions.

As the soldiers of the 372nd advanced, each step made

Adrian's skin crawl. Something was terribly wrong and his mind flew back to Kettle Ridge in '98.

"It's a trap!" Adrian yelled. "Hit the dirt!"

From their left flank, dozens of unseen enemy machine guns opened fire on the Americans as they advanced toward the trench. Doughboys fell, thrashing and screaming, as red tracer bullets weaved and licked like a hot flame through the ranks.

Despite the intensity of the fire, the Americans charged on step by bloody step, refusing to relinquish ground, jumping and yelling over fallen bodies, comrade and enemy alike.

The moment the survivors reached the machine-gun emplacements, the doughboys threw themselves at the enemy gunners with such fury there was no force on earth that could stop them from taking the trench.

Hatch charged empty-handed into an emplacement, knocking over both gunner and the Maxim. The two men rolled, kicked, gouged, and tore at each other's throats. Hatch felt his fingers grip the German's larynx; then with all his strength he squeezed until he felt the cartilage break.

Hatch slung the body away and righted the Maxim and began firing into the German emplacements.

The Boche were now running in full retreat, chased by doughboys, who showed no mercy to any German they caught. The Germans began a counter-barrage to cover the retreat of their fleeing soldiers.

An artillery round struck nearby and Adrian shouted, "Take cover!"

Just then David Sharps suddenly appeared. "Where the hell did you come from?" Adrian shouted in his brother's ear.

"The German guns pushed us in your direction. Are you hit?"

Adrian made a quick check. "No."

"Good. We've got to fall back."

"Fall back! Like hell. We just got here and the trench is ours. I'm not ordering these men to fall back! Not after what they've been through. We're going forward!"

"Chauncey's orders," David said with a shrug.

"To hell with Chauncey's orders. We're going forward!" He stood and, as he straightened, heard the crack and whine of an artillery round. As if in slow motion, he felt a tremendous rush of air, hit the ground, saw David's head—a surprised look on his face—surrounded by a red mist, and saw his brother crumple to the ground.

45

In the morning sunlight, his head reeling from the concussion of the artillery round that had exploded near his position, Adrian sat staring at the carnage.

David lay twisted on the ground in a bloody mass of rags and flesh, his head nearly severed from a piece of shrapnel.

Adrian was holding David's hand when Kenny suddenly appeared. The young soldier sat beside Adrian, a distant look in his eyes; eyes that slowly brimmed with tears as he absently puffed on a cigarette.

"Are you all right, Private?"

Kenny angrily exhaled a cloud of smoke. "Yes, sir." He looked at David, then placed his hand on Adrian's shoulder. "I'm sorry, Lieutenant. Your brother was a good man, and a helluva soldier."

Adrian ran his hands roughly over his face. "He was a prankster as a kid. Always pulling some crazy stunt. I keep waiting for him to sit up and tell me this is just another one of his pranks."

"We've lost most of the men, nearly all the squad leaders. We need you, Lieutenant. There ain't no time for grief."

Adrian said nothing. He removed one of the two dog tags from around David's neck and slipped it into his pocket. That afternoon, the remnants of A company were ordered north and east of Séchault, where the troops took up positions in abandoned German trenches. Near dusk, after a much needed meal, Adrian's platoon had just gotten settled when a runner approached him.

"The captain wants you and Sergeant Hatch to report to battalion headquarters, sir."

Adrian glanced around and saw Hatch, who was cleaning his rifle. The look on Hatch's face suggested the sergeant had an idea of what was coming.

The two walked through the trench, often climbing over piles of dead German soldiers, until they reached the makeshift battalion headquarters in a recessed bunker. Inside, Lieutenant Colonel John Stiles was talking with Captain Chauncey.

Stiles had come up through the ranks of the regular army, and though in his forties, he now looked in better shape than his men, most of whom were half his age, despite the fact that he had a bandage on his left arm.

Adrian started to report but was stopped by Stiles's halting hand. "Have a seat, Lieutenant. I'll be with you in a moment."

Adrian looked around and, to his surprise, saw DuBois sitting in a rickety chair, looking in as pitiful shape as the infantrymen—his clothes filthy, trousers and shirt torn, disheveled and worn out.

DuBois motioned to a chair beside him. "I'm glad to see you, Lieutenant," he said. "I'm sorry about your brother."

Adrian said nothing. Hatch sat on the ground beside him, cradling his rifle.

The reporter took a flask from his pocket and offered it to Adrian. "I've never seen anything like what I've seen this morning."

Adrian took a sip and passed the flask to Hatch. "Neither have I. But what are you doing here?"

"I need to get permission from the battalion commander to interview some of the troops."

Adrian said, "There aren't many left."

Chauncey approached, a mean look in his eye. "Colonel Stiles wants to talk to both of you."

Adrian and Sergeant Hatch walked up to a map table at which Stiles sat and saluted. "That was a fine job your men did this morning, Lieutenant."

"Thank you, sir."

Stiles straightened and looked at Hatch. "However, there is the matter of First Sergeant O'Doul."

Adrian glanced quickly at Chauncey, who looked away.

Stiles asked, "Captain Chauncey, did you see Sergeant Hatch kill First Sergeant O'Doul?"

"Yes, sir. In cold blood."

Stiles glared at Hatch. "Very serious charges, Sergeant."

"Yes, sir."

Adrian quickly came to his defense. "Sergeant Hatch did what was necessary at the moment, sir."

Stiles glared at Adrian. "Captain Chauncey claims you and O'Doul had been feuding ever since the regiment arrived in France."

"On many occasions, sir. O'Doul was brutal, insubordinate, a racist, and a murderer . . . sir!"

"He's also been recommended for the Medal of Honor for saving our troops in that trench."

Adrian couldn't believe his ears. "What! Recommended by whom, sir?"

Chauncey answered the question. "By me, Lieutenant."

Adrian looked at the captain incredulously. "You can't be serious. That bastard murdered American soldiers!"

Stiles snapped back, "Did you see him kill a specific American soldier?"

"There were soldiers being killed in every inch of that trench, sir."

"But did you see him kill any *American* soldiers?"

"There were Americans being shot, sir."

"Captain Chauncey claims O'Doul was in the act of killing only Germans when Sergeant Hatch killed him."

Adrian exhaled heavily. "That is not what happened, sir."

Stiles said angrily, "I don't have time to sort this out. We're advancing again, and there's no time for an investigation now."

"Is Sergeant Hatch under arrest, sir?"

"No. I need every man I can get my hands on. But when this offensive is over, Sergeant Hatch will be sent to Paris to stand court-martial for murder."

"Sir, Sergeant Hatch will need an attorney. May I represent him?"

"Do you have formal legal training?"

"No, sir. But as an officer I am qualified to assist in his defense, and I was there, sir."

Chauncey spoke to Stiles. "That might not be a bad idea, Colonel. The French are upset enough over Order Forty, and the newspapers are making a lot of it in the States. Newspaper people will cover the court-martial, and if Hatch is represented by one of his own kind, it might create less controversy."

Stiles gave this some thought. "You may be right. I've got a Colored reporter waiting to speak with me right this minute."

The major turned to Adrian. "Very well, Lieutenant, you may represent Sergeant Hatch. In the meantime, return to your platoon. Get them ready for the advance."

*   *   *

Kenny saw the two approaching and could sense something was wrong. "Trouble, sir?"

"Sergeant Hatch is going to be court-martialed for killing O'Doul."

Kenny looked at Hatch. "This is crazy."

Adrian laughed dryly. "Chauncey nominated O'Doul for the Medal of Honor!"

Kenny went limp for a second, then said, "First we can't talk to white women and now they're going to decorate white noncoms for killing Coloreds! Why should we fight for white people anymore, sir?"

Adrian had no answer.

They began cleaning their rifles and bayonets, readying for the advance.

46

At 1000 hours the First Battalion moved north from the trenches near Séchault toward Monthois, an important link in the German railroad system. Adrian's platoon marched in columns of twos along a road that led to their assigned position on the right flank of the assault echelon.

At noon, the ambulances began filling the road, returning with wounded from the front.

The white doughboys—the first Adrian and his platoon had encountered—who were ambulatory walked like zombies, their eyes dead.

One soldier, stumbling down the center of the road, suddenly fell into Private Kenny's arms. Kenny caught the man and realized it was the first time in his life he had ever touched a white man. He gently lifted the young soldier to his feet.

"Thanks," the man—or boy—said. "You got a smoke?"

Kenny took his pack of cigarettes and shook out the last one.

"You best keep it. You won't find any in the trenches up ahead."

Adrian watched as Kenny shook his head. "It's okay, take it."

The soldier took the cigarette and Kenny struck a match and touched it to the tip. The two said nothing as they traded drags on it.

The young doughboy took a final draw, handed it to Kenny, got to his feet, and said, "Good luck, buddy. I hope you do well."

"Take cover!" a voice called from somewhere on the road.

The German triplanes dove from the clear sky like the bees that had swarmed the first platoon in the field of flax. Down they came, their machine guns chattering, stitching the road and anything in it.

Adrian saw a spray of bullets slap Captain Chauncey in the back, spinning him forward onto the road, and in the next moment saw the young doughboy turn and look up the instant a bullet tore through his chest, pitching him backward.

Adrian pulled himself upright and walked to where Chauncey lay. A thin smile spread across his face as he looked at his dead company commander.

Kenny approached, saying, "I guess the captain won't be testifying at the trial."

By 1300 hours the first platoon had taken their position along the broad line of American and French trenches south of Monthois. To the front of their position, the men could see the splintered remnants of a farmhouse.

A rolling artillery barrage told each man that within minutes they would be out of the trenches and again in the fury of no man's land.

When the signal came, there were no overhead flares, just a wave of men rising from the long slits in the earth and running forward, screams bursting from their lungs, deadly steel tipped to their rifles.

Adrian felt the ground vibrate, felt the heat from the explosion, and saw dirt rise in a brown cloud that rendered the charging soldiers dim shapes in a ruined landscape. Ghosts, he thought. My men look like ghosts.

The enemy machine guns raked the advancing doughboys with a withering fire, shrouding them further in a pall of smoke and dirt.

Adrian could dimly see the farmhouse and the German gun positions. To the front lay the barbed wire, and as the first platoon reached the wire Adrian shouted, "Kenny! Hit the wire!"

Kenny threw himself onto the wire and became a human bridge. The soldiers that followed stepped onto his back and plunged toward the German guns, their faces ashen from terror and dust.

The screams of the wounded and dying were incessant, and indistinguishable as to friend or enemy, as the few remaining men of the first platoon crossed the barbed wire and closed on the farmhouse.

From the windows there, Maxim guns maintained a blistering fire.

Adrian turned to motion his men forward. He saw Private Kenny trying to untangle himself from the barbed wire, then, suddenly, spin wildly and fall beneath a hail of bullets.

"Kenny!" he shouted, his stomach churning.

He saw Sergeant Hatch stop, bend over as though picking up something he had dropped, then saw a German soldier step from the side of the house, raise his rifle, and fire a bullet into Hatch's head.

"No!" Adrian screamed and ran toward the enemy, who reloaded his rifle and fired at Adrian.

The bullet struck Adrian in the left shoulder, sending a hot flash of pain through him and spinning him off his feet and onto the ground. He got up, never knowing how or even remembering, running into the German with his bayonet. They stared at each other for what Adrian thought was a long time. Brown eyes and blue eyes filled with wonderment.

Then the light faded from the blue eyes and shadows dulled the brown ones.

47

☆ ☆ ☆

His arm was gone, high up at the shoulder; waking, he tried to move, but a bolt of lightninglike pain shot through his shoulder, then his body, driving him back onto the bed.

Through a haze he saw a white apparition approach and thought it might be an angel, and that he had gone west straight to Doughboy's Heaven.

"Lieutenant Sharps, I'm your nurse. You've been severely injured and you must remain quiet."

"How long—"

"You have been here four days. But you spent three days at a field hospital at the front before you could be transported to this hospital."

"A week?"

He then felt the cool, damp cloth wiping the perspiration from his face and felt the dryness in his mouth when he tried to speak. "Where am I?" he said in a hoarse whisper.

"In Paris. You're at the army hospital at Casernes de

Vincennes. Now please, don't talk. You've lost a lot of blood."

He couldn't talk but he could think, and he remembered David, Kenny, and Hatch, and the agony was far worse than any bullet could cause.

The stench of gangrenous flesh and the pitiful agony of the maimed and wounded filled the hospital ward. Adrian had been conscious for four days and had yet to accustom himself to the stench or the screams.

Hour after hour, more men were brought onto the ward until many were sleeping fitfully or rolling in agony on pallets strewn about the floor.

He had come to realize that there was no glory in war.

Four days later the nurse came to Adrian's bed. "I think it's time you got on your feet and moved about the ward, Lieutenant Sharps."

The nurse's voice pulled him from deep thoughts.

He shook his head and the lightning bolt shot through the arm that was no longer there.

"I don't want to do anything except lie here," he said.

She perused his chart quickly. "You're not eating. You refuse to get out of bed. What do you want, Lieutenant Sharps? Do you want to die?"

He stared at her through hollow eyes. "You have others to take care of."

Her eyes sparked. She turned and walked away, only to return minutes later.

Her stern gaze softened, then she sat on the edge of his bed. "You have seen so much death. You've nearly been killed. How can you walk away from life so easily without a fight?"

"I don't have any fight left in me."

She waved her hand around the crowded ward. "I held a young boy a few hours ago who begged God to let him see the sun just one more time. Don't you want to see the sun? If not for yourself, then perhaps for him? He was one of your comrades. All he has now is the emptiness of death. You're alive, Lieutenant. You're alive! Don't let the war do to you in this hospital what it couldn't do to you on the battlefield!"

He wanted to say something; then she suddenly bolted upright from the bed. "There's something I have forgotten. Wait one moment."

She returned a few minutes later, saying, "This arrived for you this morning. A doctor coming from the front brought it to me. It's addressed to you."

In her hands she held a long parcel wrapped in a cloth, bound by twine.

She loosened the twine and carefully removed the cloth.

Two dented sabres, both blackened by time, each scratch on the hilt and scabbard a proud battle scar, lay on the bed.

"They do belong to you?"

His eyes glistened. "Yes. This one belonged to my father. The other to his best friend, my brother's father-in-law."

"Which one is yours?"

He pointed to the one she now held in her left hand.

With his only remaining hand, he gripped the metal scabbard, felt the weight of it.

He remembered the words of his father, telling him the sabre would remind him of who he was, where he came from, and the sacrifice made by his family in defending his nation.

He pressed the scabbard against his face, tears running onto the dented metal.

The nurse held an envelope. "There is a letter for you as well."

"Would you open it?"

She nodded and opened the envelope and unfolded the letter. "It is in French. Do you read in French?"

He shook his head and suddenly felt a deep sadness.

"Dear Lieutenant Sharps, As promised, here are your beloved sabres. I wish you a speedy recovery and safe journey to America. Sergeant Watts would have sent them, but he was killed at Monthois. France has lost a great soldier. We have lost a great friend. *Au revoir, mon ami.* François Girard, La Légion Étrangère."

Adrian wiped at his eyes, then stood shakily as the nurse placed her arm around his waist, and Adrian walked to the door, stepped onto a balcony, and stared into the sunlit sky.

48

✳ ✳ ✳

On February 15, 1919, First Lieutenant Adrian Sharps arrived in Willcox, Arizona, aboard the Colored-only passenger car of the Southern Pacific Railroad. He rose slowly from his seat, stretched out the soreness in his back, and took the sabre his father had given him and placed it between the handles of his valise.

His empty left sleeve was folded and pinned neatly just below the official symbol adopted by the 93rd Division: a round patch with a blue French helmet in the center. On the left breast of his tunic he wore the ribbons of the Distinguished Service Cross and the French Croix de Guerre with Palm; on his right sleeve he wore a narrow purple and white strip of cloth denoting that he had been wounded in combat.

He stepped down onto the platform and heard a familiar voice.

"Adrian!" Hannah's shout sounded like music.

He turned and saw her coming toward him, carrying a

bundle in her arms. She stopped a few feet from him, looked for a quick moment at the empty sleeve, then rushed to him, baby and all.

He hugged her with all his strength, then stepped back as he felt a movement between their bodies.

There was a shining in her eyes as she said softly, "You have to be more gentle or you might hurt your son."

He stared wide-eyed as she pulled away the blanket to reveal a tiny black face.

"His name is Adrian Augustus Sharps, Junior," she said proudly.

She held the baby out to him, and through a flood of tears, and memories good and terrible, he stood on the platform holding his child for the first time.

Selona was standing in the cemetery when the buggy arrived at the ranch. She had wanted it that way, insisting to Hannah that she meet Adrian alone.

When she saw him emerge tentatively from the buggy and she saw the empty sleeve pinned at the shoulder her heart fell as she thought of David, Augustus, and Joseph.

Then she straightened and became grateful that at least he was alive.

The sun was setting as she passed through the wrought-iron arch. She found herself running as she saw him running toward her. They embraced in the golden twilight of the day, saying nothing, their tears mixing as they held each other.

"Welcome home, baby," she whispered.

He hugged her and buried his face against her cheek and trembling shoulder, felt the softness of her buffalo fur wig and the strength of her small body.

Finally, he summoned the words: "It's good to be home, Momma."

Adrian's head rose and he looked past her to the cemetery, where three graves had been added to those of Sergeant Major Roscoe Brassard and Sergeant Darcy Gibbs.

One would be for his father, the other two for David and Joseph, whose remains now lay in the American battlefield cemetery at Mons, in the Meuse-Argonne.

At the buggy, Hannah stood holding the baby as Adrian and Selona approached. Adrian then saw Vina and Theresa, Benjamin and Jonathan trailing behind.

Vina and Theresa joined arms around Adrian as the boys hugged at his waist.

Nothing was said until Selona broke the silence. "You must be hungry after your trip. Let's go inside. I'll fix you a bite."

Adrian nodded, then reached for the valise. Both sabres were tied together between the handles. He took the sword that had belonged to Darcy Gibbs and handed it to Vina.

Vina stared at the sword as though a missing part of her life had been returned.

Selona's hands went out automatically, palms upturned, as she said, "May I carry the Sergeant Major's sabre?"

Adrian lay the sabre in her palms and watched her fingers close around the metal scabbard.

They walked into the house, where Selona went immediately to the mantel and raised the sabre onto the wooden pegs.

She stepped down and looked at the baby in Hannah's arms, her other two grandsons, then felt a chill thread along her spine as she said softly, "I pray to God that sabre will never again come down from that wall."

Then she went into the kitchen and began preparing supper.

EPILOGUE

1943: The War Eagle

On the morning of August 10, 1943, Selona Sharps, now age eighty-six, was pulled from a deep sleep by the sound of footsteps on the hardwood floor of her home at Sabre Ranch. She rose from the thick featherbed and, through squinting eyes, could see the outline of a tall man framed in the door.

She reached to her nightstand for her spectacles, then smiled as the image came into sharp focus.

"Good morning, Grandmother," said the young man, his voice a deep baritone.

She slid over slightly, then patted the bed, saying, "Good morning, baby. Now you come and sit with your Grams."

At twenty-four, Second Lieutenant Adrian Augustus Sharps, Jr., was tall with deep ebony skin, like his father and grandfather. He wore the uniform of the United States Army Air Corps; on his left breast the wings of an army aviator. He had attended college at the Tuskegee Institute, and while there become interested in aviation. He became a pilot, and when the war began he joined the 99th Pursuit Squadron, the first all-Negro fighter squadron in American history.

Selona's eyes brightened as two more people came into the room. The woman, Adrian's wife, Shania LeBaron Sharps, was the daughter of a Cherokee woman and a Tuskegee Institute professor. Shania was tall and lithe, with honey-colored skin, narrow facial features, and dark eyes. In her arms she held their son, Adrian Augustus Sharps III.

Augustus stood as Selona reached up and Shania gently placed the baby in her arms. Her ancient eyes joined those of the baby for a long moment, then she kissed him softly on the forehead. Momentarily she lifted the baby to Shania.

"I'm going to give him a bottle, honey," Shania said, then she left the room.

Selona looked quickly at Augustus. "Are you hungry?"

Augustus patted his stomach. "Momma fed us. If I eat another bite my uniform will start popping buttons."

She laughed, and her mind tumbled back over more than seven decades to another young soldier she had once fed.

"You look just like your granddaddy."

He sat on the edge of the bed and took her hands. "The Sergeant Major? Why, Grandmother, you know I'm better looking than he was."

She slapped playfully at his hands. "You hush now. He was the handsomest man God ever put on this earth." Then she paused for effect, and added, "Well, one of the best. You've done right well for yourself in the looks department."

He smiled. "I come from good stock."

Her eyes drifted toward the light bending through the window. "I expect you'll be leaving this morning."

He gathered her frail hand in his long fingers. "Yes. Pop is going to drive me and Shania and the baby to Willcox. I'll catch the train this afternoon."

"Seems the men in my life are always catching a train to go off to war." Her voice cracked. "Your daddy went off to war from that same train station. That old platform's done seen a lot of Sharps men go off to war. Even the same platform where they brought Darcy Gibbs's body when he was killed by old Geronimo's warriors."

Augustus nodded slowly. "At least Shania and the baby will be here to keep you all busy."

"There's some comfort in that." She sighed, then said, "I expect you'll be going over there and fighting them Germans."

"Yes, ma'am. I've been assigned to the Ninety-Ninth Fighter Pursuit Squadron."

"The whole world has done gone and got itself into another ruckus."

"That it has."

"You got to promise me one thing," she said.

"Anything for you."

"You come back safe and sound. Don't go getting crazy and try to be a hero. Do you understand?"

He nodded. "I understand."

She took a deep breath. "Now, you go on and get on over there and help stop this war."

He leaned and kissed her gently on the forehead, then held her in his arms, knowing it might be the last time he would see her alive.

He stood, bowed slightly, and said, "I'll see you again."

Then he walked out of the bedroom, not seeing the tears in her eyes. Nor did she see the tears in his.

All morning Hannah had found things to do to keep her mind off the coming sadness. Now fifty-one, she had nothing but gratitude to God for the good life He had given her. Adrian had come home from his war twenty-four years ago and she could remember few occasions since when she did not wake up looking forward to the day. Adrian, still the dashing Adrian she had married before the Great War, had

made a success in the real estate business and was still
Bonita's great war hero, and long ago she had taken over
responsibility for Selona's restaurant business and had her
own success and satisfaction. Yes, the passing years had
been good—even during what people had called the Great
Depression, when she had become a sort of local legend for
giving away more food than she sold.

But now she had to face the heart-tearing moment she
had hoped never to experience again after she had said
good-bye to Adrian back in 1917. Selona had had to do it
countless times when the Sergeant Major saddled up when
duty called; now it was Shania's turn and Hannah's heart
ached for her daughter-in-law.

So now she puttered in her kitchen as if keeping busy
would delay the moment. But through the window she
could see Adrian and Augustus walking toward the cemetery, and she knew what that meant: It was Sharps family
tradition to say farewell to the gallant men, and the gallant
woman Vina Gibbs, who lay at rest there.

She watched them talk a while, then start back toward
the house.

She knew what would come next.

Hannah put away the last of the washed breakfast dishes,
wiped her hands on her apron, and went into the sitting
room. Shania was sitting on a divan, feeding the baby, when
Augustus and Adrian entered.

Augustus's heavy military suitcase was packed and sitting
by the front door.

Augustus said nothing as Adrian walked to the mantel,
where he reached up and removed the dented, battered
sabre from the two wooden pegs.

"Augustus, your grandfather carried this for nearly forty
years in the defense of this country. It was given to me when
I went to war in France. Now it belongs to you. I know you
will carry it with honor."

Augustus turned his palms upward and received the

sabre, and as the metal touched his skin, he thought he could feel the presence of the Sergeant Major.

"I will, Pop."

Augustus placed the sabre on his suitcase. Adrian looked at Hannah and said, "I guess I'll load his gear into the car."

Hannah came to Augustus and put her arms around him. "You be careful. If you get hurt I'll break your arm!" Tears began to streak her face as she held her only child.

He hugged her, kissed her forehead, then turned and left quickly, followed by Shania, who carried the baby.

She watched him until the door closed, then went into the kitchen and sat at the table, listening to the doors slam, the engine start; then the car drove away.

From the bedroom Selona heard the familiar sound that echoed from her past on so many occasions.

She heard a mother weeping.

Afterword

★ ★ ★

The author wishes to thank Command Sergeant Major Leo B. Smith, U.S.A. (Retired), director and curator; Mr. Bryan H. Jackson, chairman of the board of trustees; and Ann Moyers, secretary-treasurer, all of the National Medal of Honor Museum, Chattanooga, Tennessee, for providing the following citation of Corporal Freddie Stowers, the only African-American soldier to receive the Medal of Honor for Valor during World War I.

Stowers was born on an unknown date in 1897 in Anderson County, South Carolina. He was killed in action on September 28, 1918, in the Champagne-Marne sector, France. The citation reads as follows:

By Direction of Congress, the MEDAL OF HONOR is awarded posthumously to Corporal Freddie Stowers, US Army, Company C, 371st Infantry Regiment, 93rd Division, for action in the Champagne-Marne Sector, France, 28 September 1918. Cpl. Stowers distinguished himself by conspicuous gallantry and intrepidity at the cost of his life above and beyond the call of duty while serving as a squad leader of Company C, on 28 September 1918. His Company was the lead Company during the attack on Hill 188, Champagne-Marne Sector, France, during World War I. A few minutes after the attack began, the enemy ceased firing and began climbing up onto the parapets of the trenches, holding up their arms as if wishing to surrender. The enemy's actions caused the American forces to cease fire and to come out into the open. As the Company started forward and when within about one hundred meters of the trench line, the enemy jumped back into their trenches and greeted Cpl. Stowers' Company with interlocking bands of machine-gun fire and mortar fire causing well over fifty percent casualties. Faced with incredible enemy resistance, Cpl. Stowers took charge, setting such a courageous example of personal bravery and leadership that he inspired his men to follow him in the attack. With extraordinary heroism and complete disregard of personal danger under devastating fire, he crawled forward, leading his squad toward an enemy machine-gun nest which was causing heavy casualties to his Company. After fierce fighting, the machine-gun position was destroyed and the enemy soldiers were killed. Displaying great courage and intrepidity, Cpl. Stowers continued to press the attack against a determined enemy. While crawling forward and urging his men to continue the attack on a second trench line, he was gravely wounded by machine-gun fire. Although Cpl. Stowers was mortally wounded, he pressed forward, urging on the members of his squad, until he died. Inspired by the heroism and display of bravery of Cpl. Stowers, his Company continued the attack against incredible odds, contributing to the capture of Hill 188 and causing heavy enemy casualties. Cpl. Stowers' conspicuous gallantry, extraordinary heroism, and supreme devotion were well above and beyond the call of duty, follow the finest traditions of military service, and reflect the utmost credit on him and the United States Army.

Corporal Freddie Stowers, by an act of the United States Congress, was posthumously awarded the Medal of Honor in 1993. He is buried at the American Battlefield, Mons Cemetery, Meuse-Argonne, France.